"I was genuinely gripped. and rare pathos. An entertair book...people will want to read."

> — Sarah Braunstein, author of *The Sweet Relief of Missing Children*

"*The Miraculous Flight of Owen Leach* kept me riveted from the book's stunning and dramatic opening scenes to its moving conclusion. Jennifer Dupree's smooth prose and wide-open heart makes this a notable debut novel."

> — Aaron Hamburger, author of *Faith for Beginners and The View from Stalin's Head*

"From its immediately compelling opening to its surprising and satisfying end, *The Miraculous Flight of Owen Leach* is a bold, funny and ultimately moving debut novel."

> — Elizabeth Searle, author of *Girl Held in Home and Tonya & Nancy: the Rock Opera*

"In its first pages, T*he Miraculous Flight of Owen Leach* plunges us into the lives of two very different women whose worlds unexpectedly collide when one acts and the other reacts. The engrossing story that follows unravels the strands of desperation and longing inside these complex characters and exposes the inevitable consequences of their decisions. With stirring and vivid prose, Jennifer Dupree probes complicated and unsettling questions about motherhood and family and forces us to reckon with our own established notions of both. A stunning debut from a writer whose voice will not soon be forgotten."

> — Melanie Brooks, author of *Writing Hard Stories: Celebrated Memoirists Who Shaped Art from Trauma*

The Miraculous Flight of Owen Leach

The Miraculous Flight of Owen Leach

Jennifer Dupree

Apprentice
House Press
Loyola University Maryland

First Edition

Casebound ISBN: 978-1-62720-392-0
Paperback ISBN: 978-1-62720-393-7
Ebook ISBN: 978-1-62720-394-4

Printed in the United States of America

Design by Leah Schofield
Edited by Charlotte Pratt
Promotion by Bri Rozzi
Author photo by Sarah Copperberg
Cover background by Bernard Hermant / Unsplash.com

Published by Apprentice House Press

Apprentice
House Press
Loyola University Maryland

Apprentice House Press
Loyola University Maryland
4501 N. Charles Street
Baltimore, MD 21210
410.617.5265
www.ApprenticeHouse.com
info@ApprenticeHouse.com

To my parents,
who raised me to believe
I could do anything I put my mind to.

1

The night Rose caught the baby, she and Hank were on their way to an anniversary dinner. They had reservations at the only decent restaurant in Parker, Maine—a place that faced the lake and dimmed the lights. While short on restaurants that didn't use paper napkins and plastic utensils, Parker was long on unpretentious charm: stores that stocked fishing bait as well as milk, porch swings that were used by people and stray cats, borrowed books returned in mail boxes. You'd never find any of that in the town Rose had grown up in Massachusetts, the town she and Hank had lived in for the first five years of their marriage.

As Hank parked, Melody from the post office drove by and tooted her horn and Rose waved. They weren't friends but they were friendly, and Rose found that comforting.

In the quiet parking lot, Rose flipped down the car's visor, ran her fingers through her dark curls, centered her part. She smoothed her dress over her tiny baby bump. It was early, still, but later than the three failed pregnancies that had followed Frederick, and Rose felt hope and fear in equal measure. "Do you think we should call home and check on Frederick?" He'd been fussy when they left, refusing to let go of the paper airplane Hank constructed for him. "I don't like the thought of him poking out an eye with the corner of that thing."

"It wasn't that sharp," Hank said. "You worry too much." And then, leaning across the console and pressing his lips to her shoulder, "You look great." He touched her belly, briefly.

She smiled at him. "Ditto." He was wearing his suit and the red-orange tie she'd bought him years ago, on a whim because it reminded her of a sunset they'd seen on their first picnic.

The dinner wouldn't last more than an hour, an hour and a half, tops. Even if they ordered an appetizer and dessert. Even if the service was slow. She would get some kind of pasta dish, Hank would order steak. They would talk but not much. She'd already told him her funny Frederick story of the day while she'd emptied her big purse into her smaller clutch and Hank helped Frederick eat squash and peas. That afternoon at the park, Frederick spotted a plane overhead. He held out his arms and swooped around until Rose thought his arms would fall off with exhaustion. He was so small and determined and perfect.

Hank laughed when she held out her arms and dipped her body, then he made a spoonful of squash swoop around and Frederick laughed and clapped.

She could repeat that story, and maybe tell him about the other mothers who'd smiled at Frederick. She could tell him about the dress she was hemming for a client, the car-themed quilt she'd just finished for their five-year-old nephew, the zucchini she bought at the farmers' market. Hank would tell her one or two anecdotes from work. They wouldn't talk about the tentative life growing inside her because talking about it would make the loss worse, if the loss came again.

Hank opened his door. "We're going to be late."

Rose tried not to think about her sweat pants, the couch, the weight and heat of Frederick's head in her lap.

She eased her legs out of the car, shifted her purse, and prepared herself to go. Then something caught her attention. Rose looked up and saw, across the street, a woman in the second-floor window of one of the houses. Over in this part of town there were a bunch of old colonials that had been converted into apartments. This one was white, with paint flaking off around the windows. In the front yard, a green plastic planter was half-full of purple and pink impatiens, but the other side was empty except for a fast-food cup with a straw. Herbs would be nice in those planters— basil, for sure, rosemary, maybe. Some thyme. Spread out the impatiens so they filled both planters, pick out the trash. Maybe a whiskey barrel full of vinca vine on the dirt part of the lawn would make the bareness less acute.

The woman in the window was backlit by lemon-yellow light and she was pacing back and forth with a screaming baby clutched in her arms. When the woman paused, the light looked like a halo, and Rose thought fleetingly of the Virgin Mary. She stopped, tipped her head up to the window. The window was open and the baby's cries were unrelenting. Rose felt an ache of sympathy for both the woman and the baby. She felt heaviness in her own arms, exhaustion in her back, and the desire to simultaneously run away and sit down.

"It's none of our business," Hank said, taking her elbow. The baby's face was red, the mother's hair frizzed. Rose could see her hurry and slow, hurry and slow. She thought about knocking on the ratty gray door and offering to hold the baby while the woman took a cool, unrushed shower. Hank started to walk away, tugging at her elbow and then letting go. "We aren't going to make the reservation."

So what if they didn't? They wouldn't starve. They could pick up Chinese food and bring it home and lay out a blanket on the living room floor. They could send the babysitter home and give Frederick an egg roll, cut into bits, or some fried rice mushed up with milk. They could lean against pillows and eat with chopsticks and watch their son watch them. Rose's feet cemented to the pavement. For a moment she watched Hank's receding back, the wisps of toffee-colored hair ticking over his shirt collar, the way his hands swung on either side of his legs. On the long-ago first morning after they'd made love, she'd watched him leave the apartment and thought of the hand-swinging as awkward but endearing. She hardly even noticed it anymore. "Wait up," she called.

And then, Rose saw the gap close between the woman and the window. She saw the hesitation in the woman's step. The woman lifted her arms like she was making an offering and Rose saw the baby suspended in air. Instinctively, Rose ran.

2

A ball of fire erupted inside Sophia's belly, right where the baby had been. She could feel heat licking her entire body. She paced. Back and forth, back and forth. Fast, slow, fast, slow. Heat from the inside she couldn't escape.

Screaming, screaming—he wouldn't stop. She went to the crib and stood over him, watching his pinched-up face turn the color of canned beets. It started as a cry, then moved into a wail, then to something ragged and sharp. An occasional hiccup, cough, breath, then the revving up again. Inconsolable. In a fit of inspiration, Sophia dangled the caterpillar toy she'd lifted from Reny's and he looked at it, briefly, and then screamed louder.

The crib was pushed up against the refrigerator because there was no other place for it and because the humming seemed to placate the baby, usually. Sophia threw the toy aside, braced her hands on the cool refrigerator, tipped her face down toward his. "I don't know what you want," she said.

She picked him up, even though her mother said picking him up every time he cried would only spoil him. But right now, her mother was at Bingo, in her green shirt-dress, and the screaming was boiling Sophia inside-out. Her mother was probably sipping on an iced coffee, chatting with the ladies on either side of her about lucky daubers and praying for B6. Sophia hated Bingo but right now she would have given anything to be there—in the air conditioning, with the soothing rattle of little balls in a cage.

With the baby flung over her shoulder, Sophia walked the length of the apartment, from the kitchen, out past the evergreen-colored couch, to the little metal table big enough for one chair, past the knee-high stack of canned peas and corn she'd bought on clearance. Back and forth, back and forth. Heat came from everywhere—her body, his body, she couldn't tell. She turned, repeated. Ten steps in either direction. On and on he screamed.

Her body that used to be her own. Enticing, inviting. Now, she ached like a beaten dog—her arms from holding him, her un-milked breasts, her back. Once, she'd let boys pinch and rub and suck at her and now the fabric of her t-shirt made her want to curl up into a ball and scream.

Yesterday, the fat landlord with the hefty belt and sweat-stained t-shirt told her he was selling the place and that the couple buying it was going to convert the house back to a single-family. "That means you and the kid gotta go," he said. Shrugging, like it didn't matter. Shrugging, like she had all kinds of options. Through the slit in his fat face he said, "Pretty girl like you, you'll be okay."

"Fuck you," she said, out-loud now, even though he wasn't there. She knew he wasn't there but she could smell the salty ham and pickles he must have had for lunch. "I'm not going to beg."

What had they told her in the hospital about crying? She'd changed the baby already but now she ran a finger along the inside of the diaper. Still dry. She rocked him and he wailed louder. She shifted him to her shoulder and he cried in her ear. The piercing felt intentional and she almost let go, just let him slide right out of her arms. Hateful little creature. She paced past the window, caught her ankle on the edge of the rinky table she kept her TV on, stumbled forward and nearly dropped him. She gripped him tighter to her chest.

The heat-fogged window winked at her. She pushed aside the cheap lime-green curtain and looked out there at the gray-blue dusk sky. Out there—a deep pool of quiet. Endless quiet.

She set the baby on the floor on a blanket, wiped her forehead on her sleeve. The baby's face was nearly purple. His eyes accused her of incompetence. She turned her back on him. His screaming filled the room, filled the air, filled her lungs so that she couldn't breathe.

At the counter, she mixed a bottle of formula and sang the only thing that would come to her: "Row, row, row your boat gently down the stream. Merrily, merrily, merrily, merrily life is but a dream." She sang and shook the bottle and thought about how her mother must have sung that song to her, or maybe it was one of her mother's boyfriends. Sophia sang it again, loud enough that she could only hear her own voice. Emptying out her lungs, she sang it again. Let the neighbors call the cops. Let them. She scream-sang until her throat felt raw.

The baby was gasping for air in between cries now. Sophia picked him up, cradled him in her arms. If she tripped, if he fell and hit his head. She'd be lost without him. She'd be found. "Okay," she said. "Okay." She'd fed him just before the crying began and she didn't think he was hungry now. But she didn't know. How could she know? How did anyone know? She pressed the bottle to his lips. He turned his head, wailed as if offended.

"Give me a break," Sophia whispered. "Please. Someone just give me a break."

Her mother did not keep her cell phone on when she was at Bingo. Sophia found the phone book propping open the bathroom door and looked up the Bingo hall. She dialed with an unsteady hand.

A sing-song hello, cheery voices in the background. "May I please speak to Vicky Leach?"

Silence. And then, laughing, "She says she isn't here right now."

On the other end of the line, the phone clicked against the cradle and Sophia threw the baby bottle against the wall. It hit her ancient TV, thumped to the floor.

It had to be a hundred degrees in her apartment. She went to the window that faced the back, yanked it open as hard as she could with one hand, not caring if she was letting in the stink of the dumpsters. It opened an inch. No air moved in. The baby wailed, kicked, sucked in a wet breath.

Sophia gave in to her own tears. "I know you hate me," she said. "I know and I don't even care anymore." Why couldn't he be quiet?

She crossed the apartment to open the window that faced the street. Across two lanes of traffic was the high school where she'd been a girl who was fun, who was not the useless mother of a miserable baby. Back then, she'd lied about cramps to get out of history tests, snuck sips of Jack Daniels from a shared thermos at lunch, blew kisses to the boys trying out for football. She thought she knew everything.

The window stuck a little and by the time she forced it open she was crying harder, sweating a river down her back, into her eyes. She could hardly see, could hear nothing except the screech of her mercilessly unhappy baby. Her breath felt tight, her shoulders and back ached like she'd been on the losing end of a fight.

For the life of her, she could not remember what she'd named him. She'd been calling him the name for three months now but it was erased from her memory—something with a long vowel sound, something that reminded her of something else. Emil? Avid? Ulysses?

She had him in her arms again and she was moving faster and faster, practically running, knowing that you shouldn't run with a baby because you could shake him and you should not shake him, ever. It was when she slowed that her foot stuttered on the rug. As she pitched forward, her arms loosened. It was not until the baby was released into the thick blue heat that she remembered: Owen.

3

Rose ran. Her breath was nothing but useless huffs of air. She held out her arms. The baby was in the air and she was certain her two measly arms would not be enough to catch him. There were a thousand places he could land and only two outstretched arms. She kept her eyes open, prepared to bear witness. He was in the air—a fallen angel. And then, he was in her arms, heavy and solid. She tottered on her heels, stepped back, to the side, crazy with trying to hold on, to not fall. Only when the baby was in her arms did she think about the tiny life inside her, blooming like blown glass. Becoming. Until now, she'd been so careful. "Oh, God," she said. She held the caught baby close to her chest, sank to her knees. "I've got him."

The baby felt like a bag of apples in her arms, loose and unwieldy until she steadied him on her shoulder and stood shakily. He was so still and pliable Rose thought he might have died during the fall. But then he gasped, a hot breath in her ear, and began wailing. She whispered a quick Hail Mary—for him, for herself, for her unborn baby.

Even red-faced and wiggling, he felt good in her arms. Solid, snug. Rose leaned down and kissed his pink cheek, tasting the salt from his tears. She hushed him and for a second, he looked at her and caught his breath.

People were accumulating around her. From the corner of her eye, she saw the glass door of the restaurant wink open, a man with a wineglass walk towards her. Car doors slammed shut, an ambulance wailed, there was a quiet roar of many voices at once. Rose rocked the baby. She was aware that the crowd was giving her space. She was aware that Hank was somewhere in the crowd. Soon the police came.

After they pried the baby from her, and told her she did a good job, and took her statement, and Hank's, the police said Rose and Hank could go. She put a hand to her stomach.

"Where's the mother?" Rose said. "Is that who threw him—the mother of the baby?" She felt ill with pity, astonishment, fear.

The police officer wrote something down. "I'm afraid I can't say."

Hank rubbed her back with his palm. "Do you need to see a doctor?" He looked from her face to her stomach to her face again.

"I don't know," she said. His worry was making everything worse. "I don't think so."

Hank headed in the direction of the car. Rose hung back, touched the tall police officer's arm. "What's going to happen now?" Her arms felt cool and empty. She wanted to know the baby was all right. She didn't want to just walk away as if nothing happened.

The officer, who smelled like black coffee, said. "Have to wait and see."

He was turning away from her, already moving on to check on a report of drunk and disorderly or domestic assault.

"But the baby," Rose said. "Will he be all right?" Rose touched her own stomach again. Her miscarriages after Frederick had been "spontaneous" which made Rose think of surprise parties thrown for ex-boyfriends.

The officer shrugged. "Have to wait and see."

Was that all he ever said? Rose could see Hank huffing back up the sidewalk.

"I thought you were right behind me," he said.

"I'm coming," she said. But she stood where she was for another moment, watching a woman she guessed was a social worker lean in toward the police officer and laugh. Rose did not know what could be funny right now.

Hank, suddenly, was beside her, his arm around her waist.

She said, "I want to wait."

He squeezed her. "What happens next isn't up to us. You have to think about you."

"He was no heavier than a pumpkin."

Hank began to walk and she let herself be pulled along beside him. "I don't know that you're supposed to be catching pumpkins." He gave a half-smile half-grimace over his shoulder.

In the car, Hank chose a CD by rummaging through the pile Rose kept in the glove compartment. He didn't look at the one he selected and it ended up being the peppy guy who sang about mud and alligators. It was Frederick's current favorite. Hank ejected the disc. "Sorry. Where's the classical?"

He slid the alligator CD back into the case. "Didn't we have a Bach in here?"

Rose stared out the window. Between the few street-lights—because who needed illumination in a sleepy town like Parker, Maine?—Rose could see the swept-clean side-walks, the window boxes planted with mums and a few hearty impatiens. The ice cream shack still had its sheen of summer-painted newness. There was a Sale! sign in the win-dow of the building that sold bathing suits and plastic water toys. Parker had not one lake but two. People semi-joked about how one was for tourists, the other for the locals.

Hank put in another CD. "You probably want to listen to something soothing."

She wanted to think. Had the baby made any noise when she was holding him? He was alive, wasn't he? And her own, new baby. And Frederick. She felt sick rise up in her throat. Rose said, "Let's just get home."

4

Suddenly, inside the apartment was very quiet. The baby was crying, and then he was not. Sophia stood by the open window, her hands on the sill, the damp air brushing her knuckles. The heat from the apartment was all around her, but her insides had turned to ice. *No baby no no no no no no.*

Someone from below gasped. "There she goes."

She should go out the window but her feet felt glued to the ground. If she went, she could save him. But maybe she could not save him. She had killed him. Her baby. She killed her baby. Sophia shrank back into her apartment. She looked down at her arms, at the crib where the baby had been.

People were in the street with their necks craned up. Sirens sliced through the voices, emergency lights flicked the air.

Sophia crawled deeper into her apartment. *No no no no no.* She felt her way along the wall, to the closet. He had been in her arms, and then he had not. She should get her coat and go get him. He had to be somewhere. He must be so afraid.

Up the stairs, the police officer's feet fell like stones. "Hurry," Sophia heard him say, and she imagined an army of toy soldiers.

Sophia put on her coat—the heavy one with the wood-like buttons, oval-shaped. She found a used tissue in her left pocket and withdrew it, looked at it as if it might do something to help her. The coat felt like sleep around her shoulders and she sank to the floor and closed her eyes.

In her mind the baby grew great butterfly wings that sprouted in the tender place where his shoulder blades were. By now, he would be up in a tree or, better, bedded down atop a cloud.

She was sitting on the floor with her arms hugged inside the military-green coat. The officer offered his hand.

Sophia looked up at his leafy eyes. The tissue she held was nearly disintegrated from the heat of her hand. She shifted it to her other hand, reached up and let herself be pulled to her feet. "Did you find the baby?"

"You don't need the coat," he said, sliding it off her shoulders.

The flashing strobes of the police cars and the ambulance were reflected in the windows. Sophia thought of a nightclub she'd been to in her sixth month of pregnancy. "Brain damage happens early," her friends said, gulping from pale pink drinks, bottles of beer, little bronzy shots. Sophia had sipped virtuously from glasses of seltzer with lime and danced until the baby slid against her bladder and she peed right there on the dance floor. She'd laughed and sworn that everything would be back to normal soon.

The officer had her arm, like a gentleman on a date.

Sophia said, "Just tell me he's all right. He's all right, isn't he?"

He gave her arm a gentle squeeze, lowered his voice to a whisper. "A woman caught him." And then, he called down the stairs to the unseen, "She's here."

In the back of the police cruiser, Sophia closed her eyes and inhaled the scent of wet socks, pine air freshener, French fries. They were taking her to the hospital "for observation." "I tripped," she said.

She asked about this woman who caught Owen, but no one knew anything. Sophia imagined her as a giant, as tall as the tree out front, as round as a car. She imagined man-icured hands the size of soup bowls, legs like an Olympic speed skater. Sophia imagined this giant-woman reaching up and plucking Owen from the window, as easy as picking the Christmas star off the tree. She imagined the beast-woman stealing him right out of her arms, cradling him to her own humungous body.

5

Hank slid to a stop at Parker's single traffic light. He leaned over and kissed Rose, softly, a little to the left of her mouth. "You're positive you don't want to go to the hospital?"

The dashboard clock read 8:11. Someone had said the baby's name was Owen. Was he with a social worker now? In the hospital?

Hank said, "We could drive around a bit if you want. Maybe go down to the water. We've got the babysitter until nine."

Rose felt a heaviness like a fist against the back of her neck. "After what just happened, how can you think of leaving Frederick for one second longer than we have to?"

"You don't think the babysitter is going to hurt Frederick, do you?"

"I just want to get home."

Rose pressed her hands to the spot where she'd caught the baby—below her breasts, above her stomach, that little ridge of scarred flesh from her most recent surgery. The trouble had not been getting pregnant but staying pregnant. She'd had three miscarriages after Frederick, the last one requiring a D&C. Her doctors advised against trying again and Hank said he was fine with their little family just the way it was. When she got pregnant this time, Rose's mother declared it a miracle.

If she and Hank hadn't been right at that spot just then, Owen's head would have been flattened against the sidewalk, as dead as the squirrels she swerved for but couldn't miss. She touched Hank's leg. "Think of all the things that had to happen for us to be there at that exact moment." Hank flipped the windshield wipers on and off. "God must have been with me," Rose said. Her breath snagged.

Hank took her hand. "You're lucky," he said.

"What if he'd landed on the sidewalk?" She could see his body, which had become Frederick's body, splayed open. She started to shake. "Do you think she meant to throw him out the window?"

Hank glanced at her. "Everything's going to be okay, Rosie."

There had been times with Frederick when she'd been on the edge—she could almost understand how you could be sane and then not sane in the span of a single breath. She closed her eyes and warned herself away from those thoughts. "It must have been an accident."

Hank said, "What you did was really amazing, Rose. I'm proud of you." He touched her arm, her thigh, her hair. "You're probably starving. Let's get you something good to eat."

The thought of food made her queasy. She took a breath and imagined clean white space. "I'm okay."

"We could stop and get Chinese."

"Let's just get something at home." Her entire body felt upset. "What if I'd dropped him? What if I'd been just a little closer to you? I would have missed him all together."

She tried to feel her baby move. She knew it was too early for that, but still she wanted it and wanted and wanted it.

"I have no idea how you knew what was going to happen. Some kind of women's intuition?" He shook his head. "If you'd said something, I would've run for him. It might have been easier for me to catch him."

He meant safer. "How could I have known?"

He said nothing and Rose asked him again, "How could I have known?"

Rose had kicked off her brand-new fire-red heels as soon as she'd gotten in the car and now, in the driveway, she left them on the floorboard and got out. Parker wasn't the kind of place with broken bottles washed up on lawns, at least not at this end of town. Kids could run around outside. The grass tickled through Rose's pantyhose.

"You forgot your shoes," Hank called after her.

"Leave them," she said.

But he carried them in and set them next to the door.

"Thanks," she said.

Rose told Hank to pay the shiny blonde babysitter and she went upstairs to check on Frederick. He was sleeping, his fat fist in his mouth, his black hair and the back of his blue pajamas dampish with sweat. She wanted to touch him but she didn't want to wake him and so she stood, her hand hovering over his back, the heat from his body rising up to her palm.

From here, she couldn't see the scar along his thumb.

A few months ago, Rose was on the phone with her sister in the kitchen when she heard Frederick banging on the living room window. Slap, slap, thud. His palm and then his fist against the glass. Slap, slap, thud. She'd left him on a blanket when she got up to get the phone. She just needed a minute. Slap, slap, thud.

That night, she told Hank she'd been right behind Frederick when the window broke. "I had my eyes on him the whole time," she lied.

"These things can happen so fast," Hank said, kissing the top of her head. "Nobody's perfect." He'd been sweet in a way that made Rose wonder if he enjoyed her failure.

In the end there was a lot of blood but only two stitches. Still, the black stitches against his baby-white fat, the brown particle-board over the window, the look on Hank's face when he told her it would be all right—all of it glared neon Bad Mother at Rose.

Now, she turned the volume down on the baby monitor and leaned in closer to her son. She thought of the baby flashing like the sun as he flew from the window, the heft of him landing in her arms. She thought of the baby in her womb, hanging on. She leaned down and picked up Frederick, even though she knew she should just let him sleep. Against her chest, he wiggled and whimpered, then settled down. She paced the room, kissing the soft fuzz of his curls, telling him over and over that everything was going to be all right.

6

Under the kitchen pendant light that had cost more than a week of Hank's salary, Rose's eyes were red and the skin beneath her left eye twitched off and on. Her blush was smudged on her cheeks, the severe part in her hair was muted, mussed, and she looked both soft and wild. Hank wetted a paper towel, squeezed it out, and handed it to her.

Hank could see that she was on the brink of tears, close to falling apart. He didn't want to make it worse, but still he needed to know what he'd failed to see. "How did you know what was going to happen?"

"It was just luck," Rose said.

It was, wasn't it? Miracles were like fairy tales. And yet, if anyone were to be on the receiving end of a miracle, it would be Rose. She'd probably been praying for a baby and this was God's idea of a joke.

Hank was glad the night didn't end up with the baby's head smashed open like a pumpkin on the street.

So many things could have not happened, or happened differently. Hank opened one kitchen cabinet after another, looking for something to eat but finding himself unable to settle on anything. "Did you hear that woman in the curlers? She was going on and on about it being a miracle, about how they needed to get ahold of someone from the paper and have them write up an article."

"People believe in miracles," Rose said.

"You sound like your mother." Hank shoved a handful of vanilla wafer-cookies into his mouth. Rose drank a glass of water. Neither of them bothered to pull out a stool and sit. Instead, he leaned his elbows on the counter, while she stood straight under the light which she had loved, and had to have, no matter how much it cost.

He didn't want to think about the possibility of a miracle. He just wanted this night to be over so they could both get some rest. Rose, especially, needed sleep.

"I wonder what will happen to that poor baby now," Rose said. She rubbed her face and then settled her hands across her stomach.

After she'd caught the baby, someone called the police and before Hank could get his story straight, a crowd gathered. People in dress clothes, un-tucked work clothes, housecoats—all of them murmuring, pointing in the direction of the catch. There were a couple of women he recognized as customers at the store, a guy he knew drove the milk delivery truck, an old man he'd seen at church. A lot of them focused their attention on the window, on the door of the apartment, waiting for the police to drag the woman out in handcuffs. "I hope it wasn't the mother," someone said. "It's always the mother," someone else said. The women Hank knew from the store strolled over to Rose to thank her, to congratulate her, to hug her. They were smiling and crying and blotting their eyes with balled-up tissues. "I called Channel Eight," the million-coupons lady said. "You should stay until they get here."

Rose glanced at Hank and he shook his head. The air smelled like car exhaust—temporarily like a real city—because people were arriving, and lingering. He wanted to be alone with Rose. He didn't want these people pawing at her, closing in on her, tugging her away from him. And, they needed to get her checked over.

One lady with hair like hay smiled at Hank and stuck out her hand. "You must be the husband," she said.

Their anniversary dinner that didn't happen was the first time in two years Rose had dressed up a little, worn perfume and high heels, agreed to go out without Frederick. Their last time out had been for Hank's blow-hard coworker Jeff's wedding. Back then, Rose had been hugely pregnant and too tired to dance, too worried to drink as much as a sip of champagne, too nauseated to eat her steak. Hank had danced, and eaten mouthfuls of both dinners, and watched Rose out of the corner of his eye.

For all the years before they had Frederick, he and Rose had done what they wanted, when they wanted. They went to the movies on weekdays, drank vodka tonics with lunch, had sex on the living room couch. Even her quilts—they took up the dining room table and he always complained about them—but these days he missed the time they spent with their heads bent, quiet and alone, talking about nothing or everything while he helped her pin the top to the bottom of the quilt, a layer of cotton in between. After Frederick, she made small wall-hanging quilts that didn't need to be spread out on the floor. "Too much trouble with Frederick crawling all over them," she'd said. "Maybe when he's older."

The doctors said they shouldn't try for any more kids, that it was dangerous for Rose to keep putting her body through the trauma of losing one baby after another. Hank didn't understand why she couldn't she just accept their family the way it was. Hank was an only child, and Frederick would be fine as an only child. Still, he was surprised when she refused to go the ER after catching the baby.

Now, his mouth aggressively full of cookies that tasted like sugared cardboard, Hank said, "Ordinary people do not perform miracles." He swallowed the cookies. He sounded reasonable. His argument was solid. And yet, there was the ping of doubt somewhere behind his ribcage. "Are you sure you feel alright?"

Rose said, "I'm just glad it happened the way it did. I hope he'll be okay."

Hank sighed, rubbed his eyes, felt cookie crumbs stick in his lashes. "I'm glad, too." He crossed the room, held out his arms to her, and felt soft with relief when she stepped into his embrace.

Against his chest, she murmured, "The whole thing is so sad. Do you think he'll end up in foster care?"

He rubbed a circle on her back, like he'd seen her do with Frederick, like he had done with Frederick, in imitation. "There might be an aunt or somebody he could go live with. A grandmother. A cousin." He felt her heartbeat—choppy, agitated. She wouldn't sleep tonight. "Are you sure you're okay?"

"I'm alright." Rose pulled away and tugged her fingers through her black-as-night curls. Once, he'd loved to stick his nose in those curls, inhale the scent of her shampoo, make love to her with his face half-buried. She'd done something with it recently, parted in down the center in a way he found severe and strange. He wouldn't ever tell her that. "So many people are trying to have children, and then other people..."

"I know."

Rose rinsed her glass and put it in the dishwasher, on the top shelf, neatly next to the other practically clean glasses.

"Let's go to bed." Remnants of vanilla wafer cookies lodged in Hank's gums, and with increasing frustration, he worked at them with his tongue, then his fingers.

He washed his hands, took a drink from the tap, then stuffed the bag of cookies back into the box and left them on the counter. Rose would put them away. He came around the counter, kissed her cheek, and told her to come to bed. She didn't follow him up the stairs. He waited ten minutes, twenty, before finally turning off the light and feigning sleep until it came.

7

Sophia woke with a blanket over her feet, her bare arms sticking out of a sheet wrapped across her chest. The first thing she thought was: toga party. She turned her head side to side to see if anyone was beside her and that was when the glare of the white walls reminded her of the baby screaming, her foot sticking to the rug, the whoosh of air, silence.

When the nurse came in, Sophia closed her eyes again. She was trying to think of pink-wrapped birthday presents, organ music, colored lights on pine Christmas trees. Her uncle used to tell her to think of happy things in order to ward off nightmares. The month after she turned eighteen, she got pregnant by a boy she barely knew who had sand-colored hair he wore in spikes and a tattoo of what he said was the Chinese symbol for peace on the inside of his wrist. When she started to show, her uncle stopped telling her anything.

The nurse said, "I brought you breakfast." Sophia tried to disappear into the blackness behind her eyelids. She remembered that she fed the baby his formula yesterday morning, and that he was fussy right off. He twisted his head, pursed his lips, spit up the little she'd managed to get into him. That was when the landlord with his jello-y belly showed up and told her she'd have to move out by the end of October. He said this while he waggled Owen's foot and Owen laughed until the landlord left. He started screaming again before the door was fully closed and he wouldn't stop even though Sophia took his foot and shook it and tickled it and rubbed it. "The baby is doing fine," the nurse said. Sophia felt the coolness of a spoon touch her lips. The smell of oatmeal made her want to gag and so she pressed her lips together more tightly and turned her head away from the spoon.

A woman lawyer came in and told Sophia that she would be facing charges of child endangerment, at the minimum. It could be worse, someone had said. A nurse, a social worker? Postpartum Depression, someone said. The baby is three months old, someone else said. There had been people in and out of the room from the time she was brought in until the time she closed her eyes and they all disappeared. What she took from it all was that what mattered was what she said and did now.

Finally, the nurse scuttled the oatmeal away.

A few hours later Sophia was sitting up in bed with her hair combed back, her face washed. The white-coat doctor pulled up a chair and reached for her pulse. Sophia said, "It was a terrible accident. I tripped over the rug. It was so stupid."

The doctor nodded, let go of her wrist. "The window was stuck."

"Have you ever wanted to hurt your baby before this?"

"Are people not allowed to have accidents?"

She'd hoped for the baby to be gone, and then he was gone. There was a woman she'd seen on a TV talk show who said she couldn't remember all kinds of things—stabbing her husband in the neck, stealing the neighbor's chainsaw, eating cake in the middle of the night. Sophia craved amnesia but she remembered despite herself. The way he felt sliding out of her hands. The suddenness of air between her palms. The beautiful silence, which was like Pepto sliding down her throat, over her heart, through her roiling stomach. In the moment he went out the window and finally stopped screaming, she felt like she'd done the exact right thing.

She couldn't tell the doctor that. He put his stethoscope against her back and told her to take a deep breath. Again. Sophia was glad to have a specific task.

She remembered the slip-slide-y way the baby tumbled from her hands—his shirt, blue cotton, lifting, briefly to reveal his peach-warm skin.

She told the doctor she was certain he was dead, because he was so quiet.

"And how did you feel about that?"

She felt like she could think, like she could breathe. The doctor was watching her with his cow-eyes so she looked down at her sheet-covered feet and said, "I felt awful."

The doctor nodded and told her to get some rest.

The day wore on. Sophia shuffled from one end of the hall to the other when she wasn't in therapy or being seen by the doctor and when the nurses weren't handing her pills in little cups followed by slightly larger cups of warmish water. Group therapy was at nine, individual therapy at three. Breakfast at seven, lunch at eleven thirty, dinner at five, snacks at ten and two.

She'd washed her face and brushed her teeth this morning and she had been issued deodorant but she had not been allowed a shower and her hair felt itchy and stiff. She was wearing paper slippers. This was what the nursing home patients must feel like. While Sophia sat behind the receptionist's desk at Merry Pines, the old people were herded past her on the way to the dining room or the living room for music, the activity room for crafts. She'd made small talk with the ones who were interested in conversation about how the Bingo game went or what flavor the pudding was but mostly she never thought about the monotony of their days. Until now. No wonder the women sometimes lifted up their shirts and scratched the undersides of their saggy breasts right there in the middle of the hallway. Sometimes it just didn't matter anymore.

Sophia shuffled up to the nurses' station. "What day is it?"

The nurse didn't look up from the chart she was writing in. "Sunday."

It was Saturday night when Owen went out the window. Not even a full day had gone by. "Time feels all stretched out in here," she said. The nurse flipped a page, wrote something. Sophia asked, "What time is it?" It was the kind of gray day that made six in the morning look the same as six at night.

The nurse glanced at her watch. "A little past one."

She'd been excused from group therapy this morning so she could see the medical doctor. Tomorrow, she'd have to sit through a bunch of strangers whining about their bad childhoods.

Last night, the psychiatrist told Sophia that her mother had temporary custody of Owen and that he was fine. The psychiatrist, in his plaid shirt and jeans, a thin yellow tie hanging nearly to his zipper. Always touching the gel spikes of his hair, gently, as if to make sure they were still upright. Today she would ask him what he meant by fine. Had they done an X-ray on Owen? There might be a fracture. Had they even taken him to the hospital?

None of this was anyone's fault but her own. If she hadn't wished him gone, if she hadn't been pacing with him, if she hadn't ever bought that stupid striped throw rug because it made her happy. If she hadn't let him go.

Sophia leaned a little more into the nurses' station. "Are you sure he doesn't have any broken bones? No fractures?" Her fingers ached to examine the ridges of his ears, the dent of his nose, the hard and soft of his fingers and feet.

"As far as I know."

Sophia stared at the nurse and the nurse blinked. She wanted to hear Owen cry again so that she would know she hadn't scared it out of him. The sound of his sucking breath, the end of a cry and the beginning of stillness, echoed through her head. "Do you know when I can see him?"

"You'll have to ask the doctor."

She had no right to want him, but she did.

From down the hall, a woman screamed. Sophia moved off in the opposite direction.

In what they called the day room, people had visitors. They wore jeans and rock concert t-shirts and hairspray and mascara and Sophia stood in the doorway and wished she could be sucked into one of them—any one of them, even the boy with the patch on the knee of his jeans and glasses so thick they magnified his eyes. Who wore patches anymore? People made intentional holes and left them, gaping, even in the cold. That boy probably lived in a house with two stories and a mother who made chocolate chip after-school cookies. He was sitting next to the woman Sophia guessed was his mother. Her hair was the same shade of watery tea his was and she swept a hand over her head the same way the boy did. They were sitting across from a male patient Sophia had seen around the halls. He was tall and had a beard that reached to the middle of his chest. As Sophia watched, he took the woman's hand, turned it palm-up, brought it to his lips, and licked it.

Sophia shuffled back to the nurses' station. "Can anyone have a visitor?"

"You'll have to ask the doctor."

"Can I make a phone call at least?"

The nurse handed her the cordless and then stood to put back one chart and get out another.

Vicky answered after four rings, just when Sophia was starting to think she wasn't home, or didn't want to be bothered. "They letting you out already?"

"Not yet. How's the baby?"

"Crying half the night, pooping the other half."

"But he's okay?" Sophia couldn't quit picturing his head squished in on the side, like a car that sideswiped a light pole. "Do you think he's crying because he's scared?"

"He's crying because he's a baby."

"Have you tried singing to him?"

"I don't sing."

"I want to see him."

The nurse passed her a box of tissues.

Vicky exhaled a smoker's exhale. "I took him to Bingo with me last night and he was fine. I think he liked everyone cooing over him."

Sophia pictured the ladies with their flowered dresses and pink lipstick leaning over Owen, letting him suck on their inky fingers. "There're too many germs there, Ma."

"It was a jackpot night." Vicky laughed. "Everyone's saying you were damn lucky that lady made a good catch."

The nurse tapped her watch.

Sophia wanted to give her the finger. What did she know about missing her kids? She probably went home to a husband and a roasted chicken and three kids with A's on their report cards. But Sophia tucked her fingers into her fist and reminded herself that these people could medicate her as they saw fit. "Give the baby a kiss for me," she said before hanging up and dutifully giving the phone back.

At two, Sophia headed down to the shrink's office. It was like being called to the principal's office, only worse now. Back then, she always knew the right thing to say, the right way to tip her head and make herself look innocent. She knew to say it wasn't her under the bleachers in the gym, or coming out of the boys' bathroom.

Dr. Fogg wore a different plaid shirt today but the same yellow tie, jeans, hands hovering over the gel in his gray hair. "Did you sleep well last night?"

"Not great." His office was windowless, like it had once been a closet and then the hospital higher-ups realized they needed another shrink and a place to put him. Two yard sale bookcases stood half-empty behind his metal desk which held almost nothing except one of those huge calendars— scribbled all over with notes and doodles—and two blue pens.

Dr. Fogg nodded longer than necessary, tented his hands. Sophia ran her palms over the weave of the chair she was sitting in. Back and forth, wondering if she got going fast enough she'd set herself on fire. Dr. Fogg just watched her, writing nothing down, asking nothing.

"When can I see Owen?"

"Do you want to see him?"

"They keep telling me he wasn't hurt."

"But you don't believe them?"

If he wanted her to seem paranoid, Sophia wasn't falling for it. "I need to see him."

He nodded, used the end of a pen to scratch above his ear. "What do you think has to happen for you to be able to see him?"

"It was an accident. The window was sticking and I pushed it up and I was holding him but not tight enough. He fell." No need to tell him about the running, about her desire to have him gone, about the rug she had purchased with the perhaps subconscious intention of tripping on it.

Dr. Fogg nodded but Sophia couldn't tell if he really believed her or not. The medical doctor, the nurses, the psychiatrist—Sophia was going to have to stick to one story no matter how many times she had to tell it.

"I want to be a good mother," she said. He nodded again. "I made a mistake."

The wall clock ticked and Sophia jumped. "Are you having a lot of anxiety, Sophia?"

Was she supposed to say yes? It seemed like it would be normal to have anxiety but if she came across as too unstable, they would keep Owen from her. Wouldn't they? "It's this place," Sophia said. "And being away from Owen."

"How do you feel about him being with your mother?"

"Do I have a choice?"

"You have a choice in how you feel about it."

It was high school all over again. The guidance counselor asking her why she seemed to think of her sexuality as "disposable." Sitting there, looking at Sophia with mopey eyes, waiting for her to say something when the truth was she had no idea how she felt.

"I try not to think too much about how I feel," she said now, laughing a little.

Dr. Fogg smiled. "Interesting."

What the hell was that supposed to mean?

"I'm not trying to be interesting." Sophia picked the remains of pink polish off her thumb.

"What are you trying to be?"

Again, the pinch of self-doubt. Sophia sat on her hands. "I don't know."

"You don't know?"

Sophia watched the clock's hand. How much longer was this going to take? She thought Dr. Fogg might be gay. She'd heard from Emily down the hall that he had a boyfriend who had once been a patient. Sophia wasn't sure she believed the part about the boyfriend but Dr. Fogg did have a certain gayness to him. The filed cleanliness of his nails, the slightly high pitch of his laugh, the way he tipped his head when he listened. If he wasn't gay, Sophia might be able to stroke his arm or say something suggestive, get him off this topic of what she wanted to be. But if she tried and failed either because of his gayness or professional boundaries, it would be a mark against her.

Dr. Fogg was looking at her. She said, "I want to be a good mother. That's what I want to be."

8

Rose awoke from a dream of a dark street, a darker sky, a flash of falling birds. In the grayed black of the bedroom, she opened her eyes, disoriented, believing she was still outside, still craning her neck upward. Her mouth was cottony and she ran her tongue in and out, seeking moisture. Her arms and legs ached and she stretched them across the clean yellow sheets, and tried to calm her breath. Beside her, Hank breathed with a fierceness that suggested dreams of his own. Later, when they were both dressed and caffeinated, they would tell each other their dreams. It was something they'd started the first night they were together, as if a dream was a gift, one frequent insomniac to another.

She felt restless, achy, disoriented. Rose leaned up on her elbows and listened for Frederick through the monitor. When she heard nothing, she got up and padded to his room.

In the rocking chair, she sat with her hands on her stomach and watched Frederick sleep. His blue-pajama body was curled into a comma, his tiny hands fisted next to his face. His breath was so light Rose had to lean in close to be sure it was there.

She wondered if Owen Leach slept so soundly. She spread her hands across her belly, trying to quiet her discomfort.

She remembered how the dream-birds fluttered, and that they fell. She knew they were hummingbirds, small and slight and barely there in real life. Her stomach pinched and she stood.

She and Hank had not talked about names for the new baby because that would imply too much hope.

Her stomach pinched again, harder. And then she felt wet between her legs and knew without looking that it was blood. She yelled for Hank, and Frederick woke with a terrified wail. She could do nothing except lie on the floor and cry.

Hank called her mother and asked her to come watch Frederick and her mother arrived in a cream-colored blouse and matching pants, pearl earrings, lipstick. It was one o'clock in the morning.

Hank drove too fast and Rose, her head almost touching her knees, told him it didn't matter anymore. "Don't say that," he said. "We don't know anything yet."

When she woke, she was in a bright white hospital room. On the orange chair beside her bed, Hank drooled in his sleep. He stirred, met her gaze, and said, "Hey." And then, "Let me get the nurse."

The way he lurched toward the call bell made her furious. "Tell me," she said.

But then the nurse was there, and she said "emergency hysterectomy." Rose closed her eyes until everyone shut up.

*****

Cloris said, "It just wasn't meant to be, Rosie."

Her sister's hand felt like a skeleton's. How could someone who barely ate create two healthy babies? Rose wanted to shove a pie down her throat.

Rose said, "I don't understand why this is happening to me."

"You have Frederick." Cloris sucked in a breath and nearly disappeared.

Rose said, "No one wants to have an only child. What will happen to Frederick when we're gone?"

When Cloris didn't answer, Rose said, "Remember when we were five and seven and we walked to the 7-11 for Slush Puppies and Ma didn't even know we were gone until we got back and we were covered in sticky blue?"

She thought of the weight of Owen Leach, the suddenness of him in her arms. Followed by the abrupt departure of her own baby. Own. Owen.

9

In the days that followed the baby-catching, neighbors, friends-of-friends, people from Church, even strangers came to the house in droves. Some of them clutched children, casseroles, flowers, rosaries. They wanted to know how she caught Owen Leach, how she knew, if she thought she could do it again. They wanted to touch her, and for her to touch them. Almost every one of them said catching Owen was a miracle. She walked and stood and sat painfully. She did not mention her lost baby and neither did Hank.

The woman who came to the house on Tuesday was wearing yellow pants and a white sweater that bagged around her hips. She had on gray sneakers that looked new, as if she'd considered taking up running but had not yet begun. With the sleeve of her sweater, she wiped at her red-rimmed eyes. "I saw a story about you in the Portland paper. Normally, I read it only for the movie reviews but when I picked it up and saw what you'd done to save that baby I got right in my car and drove down from Bangor. It was just the tiniest piece in the paper." She handed Rose the scrap of newspaper. "They should have given you a full write-up but I guess they don't care what happens in the sticks."

"It was in a few other papers, too," Rose said.

Frederick was banging a spoon on a pan. The beat-beat of the spoon matched Rose's heartbeat. Rose handed the little piece of newspaper back to the woman. "What can I do for you?"

"I think you're wonderful."

Rose stilled. Something about the woman's tone made Rose afraid. Rose shifted closer to Frederick, her weight on the balls of her feet so she could crouch over him, if necessary. The woman drew a breath, met Rose's gaze for a second, and then studied her shoes. "I understand you can't be everywhere at once," the woman said, raising her voice above the racket Frederick was making. She scratched at the hair around her long, low ponytail. "But it would have changed everything if you'd caught my baby for me."

Rose got up, swapped Frederick's pan for her plastic mixing bowl, put the pan in the sink. She picked Frederick up but he kicked and Rose's stomach ached. She put him down. She did not want to hear any more. "I'm sorry you came all this way," Rose said. She stood and moved between the woman and Frederick.

The woman tipped her head up and stared at the ceiling. "I was hearing voices at the time. I'm not any more so you don't have to worry." She added the second part quickly, plaintively, probably sensing Rose's growing discomfort. Still, she went on, "But I swear on my grandmother's grave that I heard a man tell me to throw Wendy off that bridge." She swallowed. "He told me she could swim."

Rose inched closer to Frederick. To the woman she said, "I can't help you." And then, "I need to put my son down for a nap."

The woman pulled out a chair, sat, and leaned across the table so that her sweater drooped low enough to reveal fleshy cleavage barely contained in a gray-white bra. Rose looked at Frederick, who showed no signs of needing a nap and who would probably scream if Rose tried to take him away from his spoon and bowl. The woman tapped her hand, cool fingertips on Rose's searing hot fist. Rose pulled her hand away, tucked it behind her back. The woman cleared her throat. "The thing is I still don't know if I did the right thing."

The woman's eyelids were swollen along the crease. The whites were pink, the light behind them dim. She was crazy. She'd killed her baby and, either before or after, she'd gone nuts.

The woman said, "Maybe you can tell me you didn't save my Wendy because she wasn't meant to be saved. Maybe she was supposed to die."

"My husband will be home any minute," Rose said. "He doesn't like company when he gets home from work." Rose wanted to shove her toward the door, but she didn't want to leave Frederick alone on the floor. This woman, in her new sneakers, might be quick as a mountain lion.

Rose could see the shallow breaths in the woman's chest, the tremble of expectation in her body. She should pity her. She could say something to give her some sliver of peace. Instead, she said, "All babies are meant to be saved." She felt self-righteous, her son on the newly mopped kitchen floor, her baby-saving all over the news. There were crazy people in the world, that was all.

Hank's keys jangled in the front door and then he was in, shuffling off his shoes, pulling off his jacket. The woman in yellow sucked in a breath. "Is someone here?"

"My husband's home from work. He's not going to like that you're here." Rose didn't want Hank thinking she wasn't a good mother because she let this nut job near her son. She stood up, went to the freezer like she had an idea for dinner, pulled out frozen chicken breasts. The woman reached up and scratched her ponytail, but didn't get up.

Hank wandered into the kitchen. His face was pale, black-blue half-moons beneath his eyes. Rose said, "You look exhausted."

"Long day." He held out his hand to the woman. "Hank Rankin."

The woman looked at Hank's hand but made no move to shake it.

"She's just leaving," Rose said. "I was about to start supper."

"I'm not overly hungry." He stepped over Frederick, his hands resting briefly on Frederick's head, and took down a glass from the cabinet, then the bottle of scotch. The woman watched him. "Maybe we can just have cheese and crackers," he said. Hank poured his drink, kissed Frederick on the head, Rose on the forehead, and left.

Rose heard his steps all the way to the bedroom, listened as he closed the door. She picked up Frederick and balanced him on her hip. He wacked her head with his spoon. The edge of it connected just below her eye. She caught his hand, let it go. The woman sat at the table, watching. Rose, calmer now that Hank was home, that she could yell for help if she needed to, said, "I should see about supper."

Finally, the woman left, wiping her nose on the sleeve of her white sweater. She blew Frederick a kiss over her shoulder.

Hank was sprawled on the bed still in his work clothes—the blue shirt and gray pants Rose had ironed last night, his tie with the squares on it skewered to the left. He was staring at the TV and the weather-girl rattling off a forecast for snow. He said, "She was weird."

"She wouldn't leave."

"We don't need this right now."

Rose put her hands on her stomach as if she might be able to feel a pulse through her skin. "She's gone now." She meant the crazy woman. Rose sat down on the edge of the log cabin quilt she'd made when she was pregnant with Frederick, all those pieces a puzzle she had the time and patience to manage, back then.

Hank rolled away from her. His stomach strained against his shirt and she wondered if he'd been gaining weight. She thought there was more fleshiness to him, maybe even love handles at his waist. He was thin when they met—like a nervous runner. Over the years he'd gained weight—probably from too many nights on the couch with a tumbler of scotch and reruns of M.A.S.H.—but she liked having a little more to hold onto.

Rose stretched out beside him, her body along the length of his, her hand on his belly. She felt his body relax into hers.

Hank said, "What did she want?"

"Her baby died. She threw her off a bridge and she drowned. She spent three years in prison."

Hank tensed. "That's awful. But what are you supposed to do about it?"

Rose could hear Frederick downstairs banging his spoon on the floor now. She should go check on him. Just yesterday she'd found him holding himself up on the garbage can.

There might have been glass from the dish she'd broken the other day. He could have cut himself, or tried to swallow something. Everything went in his mouth these days. She got up from the bed, smoothed it down. "How about if I get the grill going?"

"You didn't leave her alone with Frederick, did you?" Hank was still talking to the wall, his voice echoing, his body outlined in shadow.

"Of course I didn't. Frederick was practically under my feet the entire time she was here." She was not a bad mother. "I wouldn't have let her in if I'd known what she wanted."

"Maybe you just shouldn't let strangers in the house."

There was an absence of noise from the kitchen and Rose felt the silence like a stone in her stomach. Had Frederick poked the spoon into his eye?

On her way downstairs, Rose felt untethered by uncertainty. Maybe she shouldn't have let that woman in the house. She'd have to be more careful in the future. But right now, Frederick was fine. Fine, fine, fine.

She lifted Frederick off the floor, took his spoon and threw it in the sink. He smiled at her and relief made her grateful. She wanted her family to be a happy one. From the freezer, she grabbed a teething ring, handed it to Frederick, and carried him upstairs. She placed Frederick next to Hank, then sat on the edge of the bed. She leaned in, spread her arms to encompass both of them, and said, "I'm sorry. I'll be more careful from now on."

10

The phone rang early Sunday morning. "It's my day off," Hank said into the receiver at seven forty-five. If this was something about the deli order not coming in, Hank was going to fire Jimmy Graff on the spot. "This better be an emergency."

A pause, throat clearing. "This is Caroline Weatherby from Channel Eight. I'm sorry to bother you, Mr. Rankin…"

Shit shit shit. He'd probably sounded like a prick. "No bother. Sorry about that."

He could hear Caroline Weatherby smile into the phone. "Is your wife available?"

Rose was not in bed and he hadn't noticed her get up. From downstairs, he heard her signing to Frederick. Sweetly, peacefully. He didn't want to interrupt her. Hank said, "I can tell you whatever you need to know."

The reporter paused, and Hank filled the silence with a monologue of where they'd parked the car, how close they were when they saw the woman in the window, how Rose ran with her arms outstretched and how perfect it was when the baby landed. "He looked as surprised as she did," Hank said, laughing.

Caroline Weatherby thanked him and he promised he'd have Rose call when she was more rested.

Rose, with Frederick balanced on her hip, stood in the doorway. "Who was that?"

Hank got out of bed, crossed the room, took Frederick and tossed him in the air. Frederick squealed. To Rose, Hank said, "Caroline Weatherby from Channel Eight. I figured you were too tired to talk. Did you sleep at all last night?"

"Not much. Do you want pancakes?" The phone rang again. "I can get it."

"Let the answering machine pick up." He lifted Frederick's shirt and tickled him along his belly.

"I don't mind talking." But she didn't reach for the phone and Hank took that to mean she really was tired. Rose held out her arms for Frederick and Hank handed him over. "I need to change him," she said.

Hank reached behind his nightstand and unplugged the phone jack. He pulled on a pair of jeans. "I say we go for peace and quiet."

Rose yawned. "Maybe you can watch Frederick and I can get in a nap after breakfast." She touched her hair, and then let her hands linger over her stomach. What could he say except that he was sorry, too?

When he went outside to get the paper, he found a casserole dish pushed against the door. He uncovered it, sniffed it, and brought it in along with the paper. "Someone left us dinner, I think."

Rose was cutting a pancake into pieces. "I hope it hasn't been there since last night."

While Hank scraped the casserole into the trash, the doorbell rang. "This is ridiculous."

Rose shrugged. "It could be my mother."

"Your mother would call first." Hank went to the window. A woman Hank recognized from down the street stood on the porch with a bouquet of supermarket flowers.

Behind him, Rose said, "It's not every day someone saves a baby's life." She was laughing, but with an undercurrent of ache, of despair. They'd told no one except Rose's family about the miscarriage, but the casseroles and flowers were reminiscent of death even though they were meant, in this case, to be celebratory.

"You need to rest," he said.

While Rose went to the door and thanked the woman with a hug and kisses on both cheeks, Hank stood in the kitchen, wishing he'd thought to have flowers delivered. Something huge and extravagant featuring those big primary-colored daisies Rose loved so much.

When she came back, she trimmed the stems with her kitchen scissors and arranged them in the vase she kept under the sink. She held a rose out to Frederick. "Sniff," she said, and then leaned in close and showed him how.

"Supermarket flowers," Hank said. "They probably don't smell like much anymore." He rubbed a hand over his hair. "I say we get out of here for the day."

Rose moved a pink rose so that it leaned against a white daisy. "And do what?" She left the flowers, sat back down at the table, ran a piece of pancake through the puddle of syrup on her plate, then held the fork out to Frederick. He picked the pancake off the fork, shoved it in his mouth, grinned.

Hank grabbed a pancake off Rose's plate, folded it in half, and winked at Frederick as he chewed. "Mom's a good cook, huh?"

Rose said, "Don't make him talk with his mouth full."

Hank swallowed. "How about the zoo?"

Rose made a face. "That didn't end well the last time."

"Because you got him all worked up about the monkeys."

"He was afraid."

"You made him afraid."

Frederick, still chewing, said, "Not 'fraid."

Rose napkinned Frederick's mouth. "I don't think I have the energy for the zoo." She pushed back from the table, went to the sink and washed her hands. Her movements were slow, weary.

Hank expected her to offer another suggestion— take the kid to her mother's, maybe. Possibly the mall. Hank remembered Rose telling him that Frederick liked those little quarter rides they had out front of JC Penny. But Rose dried her hands on a paper towel and said, "I have a few dresses I need to finish hemming. I promised Margo I'd have them done this weekend. Why don't you take him?"

He could do that, couldn't he? It would be nice to let her rest. He said, "I don't want to leave you home alone with all these lunatics bringing you cheesy meals and tacky flowers."

She leaned over and kissed his cheek and he could smell maple syrup on her breath. "I'll be fine. I'll keep the door locked and I won't answer the phone. You guys will have fun."

He thought of their unborn baby, now gone. The surgery, the end of trying. If he'd been the one to catch Owen, she might not have lost the baby. "Sure," he said. "It'll be great."

He'd take Frederick to the zoo first and then maybe out for an ice cream. Spoil his supper but who didn't love a treat you weren't supposed to have? He retrieved Frederick's shoes from where they were lined up next to the door, wiggled the kid's feet into his mini Nikes and did the Velcro straps. "You ready for some daddy time?"

Frederick put a fist in his mouth and smiled.

Hank moved Frederick's hand, wet with spit. "Hey," he said, "You just ate."

"He's teething," Rose said. She went to the freezer and handed Hank an iced-up teething ring.

Frederick looked like he was about to start crying. Hank lifted his shirt and gave him a raspberry on his belly. Frederick laughed. Hank smiled. How hard was that? He set the teething ring on the counter. "Are you ready for some monkeys?"

Frederick threw his arms up. "Monkeys!"

"Those are my favorite, too, buddy." Hank made some oooh-ooh noises and scratched under his arms. Rose laughed and told them to get lost.

It was a two-hour drive down to the zoo, all highway. Hank peered in the rearview mirror. Frederick's eyes drooped. As a kid, Hank had always fallen asleep on long car rides. His mother told him she used to put him in the car on nights he couldn't sleep, drive down 495 until he conked out, then carry him in the house where he'd sleep until she woke him the next morning. Maybe Frederick would sleep on the way down and then be ready to face the monkeys with gusto. Hank turned on the Oldies station, kept the volume low, and tapped his hands on the wheel to "Hound Dog."

The zoo was the same zoo Hank had gone to with his mother, way back before his father died of a massive heart attack at forty-one and money got too tight for extras. Hank was ten the year his father died. He'd been back here only once since then, last year, when Frederick screamed bloody murder the second he laid eyes on the monkeys.

Hank's favorite had always been the monkeys because they were careless, not just carefree. Mischievous, intentional. He liked that they didn't just laze around like the bears, didn't stare dumbly like the goats. His mother, because she said they were filthy animals, always waited a few feet away while Hank pressed himself up against the cage. Unlike other kids, he didn't make noises or throw peanuts. He just stood there, watching, and he was rewarded, once, when one of the smaller monkeys trundled up to him and touched a finger to Hank's.

The zoo still had the same metal archway, the same welcome sign. The parking lot was all Massachusetts plates.

They might see someone Hank used to know and it would be nice to catch up, reminisce about his days managing various Loaf and Lemon stores. Hank would balance Frederick on his hip and whoever it was would say how cute he was, how much he looked like Hank, how nice it was that he'd named him after his father. Rose's baby-catching wouldn't have made the news down here. There were shootings and stabbings and bank robberies that would have usurped the happy news from Maine. Maybe he'd mention it. Maybe he'd even say he had known what was going to happen before Rose did, that she'd just been closer to the window.

"We're here, buddy," he said, nudging Frederick's feet to wake him up.

They'd moved to Maine because Rose thought it would be easier to conceive once they got away from the stress, took things slower. He'd taken a job for less pay at a rinky- dink local place with little opportunity to move up, wanting to make Rose happy. Some of the guys he'd played softball with in Massachusetts placed bets on how long it would be before he'd be wearing flannel and mud boots. After their last Christmas card—the one that showed the three of them in red plaid shirts—Jeff Dalton e-mailed Hank to say he'd won the pool.

There wasn't much Hank liked about living in Maine. It was just far enough north that it snowed more, and was colder. You had to drive twenty minutes or more to get to a big box store, an hour for a mall. Cell phone reception was spotty. People were indiscreet about the affairs they were having and haphazard with personal grooming, both of which seemed like laziness to Hank.

Pretty much the only thing he liked about Maine was that even though he made less money, it went a lot further. They'd bought a newly constructed three-bedroom on a half-acre in a community of like houses with bylaws that banned the keeping of broken-down cars on lawns. He made sure the Christmas card he and Rose sent out every year showed the front of the house with white lights on the shrubbery he'd planted. Most of the people who said they'd come up and visit never came, even when they were on their way up to the lakes or mountains. So there was no way, other than the card, to let them know how happy they were.

Frederick opened his eyes, looked around, and started to cry.

Hank lifted him out of the car seat. "We're at the zoo," he said. He bounced him against his shoulder. "What's the matter, buddy?" He'd forgotten the stupid teething ring on the counter. "Are your teeth bothering you?" They were at the pay window. Hank set Frederick on his feet on the ground and squatted so they were eye level. Hank scratched the top of his head and made his monkey ooh-oh noises again. Frederick blinked, then, without moving another inch, vomited pancake residue all over himself.

"Oh, man." Hank rummaged through the baby bag, found a clean diaper, and used that to mop up the vomit. "Are you sick or was that a one-timer?"

Frederick drew in a breath. Hank waited.

Hank had planned to be the kind of father he'd missed out on having. He'd figured on being home for dinner, tossing a ball in the backyard, building go-karts from scrap lumber on the weekends. Hank usually made it home for dinner, but Frederick was still too young for the rest of it and Hank often felt like they were still just getting acquainted. How did Rose make it look so easy to know what Frederick needed?

Hank didn't want to be the kind of father who didn't have a clue. He took a breath and tasted dirty peanuts. "Should we go in and see the animals or not?"

Frederick nodded.

"You're sure you aren't sick?" Frederick stared at him.

Hank gave in and rented a stroller, seeing how he also forgot to take the collapsible thing Rose was always folding and unfolding like some kind of magic trick. They'd gotten as far as the bear exhibit when it started to rain. Frederick pointed to the sky.

"I see it, buddy."

Like a pro, Hank pivoted the stroller and headed for the birds. The air inside the aviary was damp and smelled like rot. Birds flapped. Leaves rustled. Frederick batted his hands in front of his face and started to cry. Hank bent over the stroller. "It's okay," he said. Although the flapping made him nervous and the smell was making him worry about his own pancakes.

Frederick sucked in his lip.

Hank straightened. "They are kind of creepy." A mother with a ribbon-braided girl in each hand walked by and gave him a look. "I didn't mean you guys," Hank called after her. One of the girls looked at him over her shoulder but the three of them kept right on going to the other side of the exhibit. Frederick stuck out his tongue. Hank laughed.

In the relentless flapping, the humidity, Hank felt his legs soften with exhaustion. He wheeled Frederick over to a bench and sat down. In the oversized quilted baby bag, he rummaged around and found a banana, peeled it, and handed it to Frederick.

Frederick stared at the banana.

"Maybe that's too much. Here." He broke off a piece and touched it to Frederick's lips.

Frederick licked the banana and made a face.

Hank set the banana on the bench next to him and went back to the bag. "There's a yogurt. Do you want a yogurt?" He pulled the plastic spoon off the top, opened the container and offered Frederick a spoonful. "Here comes the plane! Zoom, zoom!"

Frederick watched the spoon and laughed. Hank dribbled some yogurt into his son's open mouth. Frederick swallowed, then promptly threw up again.

Hank ate the yogurt with one hand, container squeezed between his knees, and with the other hand he wiped Frederick's mouth with another clean diaper. "I guess you weren't hungry."

He handed Frederick the plastic water bottle. "Maybe this?"

Frederick batted it away.

"So. Not that," Hank said. He considered calling Rose, admitting he was in over his head. But she might have fallen asleep and he didn't want to take the chance he'd wake her.

Frederick gave a half-laugh, half-vomit. After Hank wiped him off with the last clean diaper, he found the container of wet-wipes at the bottom of the bag. Of course Rose had packed wet-wipes, which he hadn't even thought of until he had his hand on them. "Your mom's pretty great," he told Frederick. "I think it's time to get back home to her."

He'd wanted this to be a day Frederick could hold onto after Hank was six feet under. Hank could remember fishing off a bridge with his dad. He remembered the feel of the pole in his hand, the sun beating down on the back of his neck, the cars thumping across the bridge. The smile on his father's face when Hank threaded his own worm onto his line. But he'd been older than Frederick then, maybe five or six. Still, Hank's heart was fine, as far as he knew. Plenty of time for good days.

He wheeled Frederick out, right past the woman and her two little princesses. They stared at him as if he'd just landed from another planet. Hank waved. In his stroller, Frederick copied the gesture exactly.

On the way home, Frederick fell asleep. "We had a good time," Hank said out loud. Frederick didn't flutter an eyelash.

11

Nighttime was the worst. Nine o'clock was lights out and Sophia climbed obediently into bed, thinking about how a year ago, she'd be just sliding into her purple high heels and tucking a five-dollar bill into her bra in case she needed cab fare home. Nine o'clock had been the beginning, back then. After she had Owen, she went for a walk at nine o'clock, no matter what. She didn't tell the hospital shrink that—about the hundred steps she took, fifty away from him, fifty back towards him. It was bad to leave him alone but it wasn't the worst thing she could do. It wasn't as bad as bringing guys home to sleep over like her mother used to, making Sophia sleep on the living room floor on two blankets because she didn't want her on the couch, in case she wet during the night. A woman down the hall wailed. Sophia turned her face into her pillow. There were people who had been here for weeks, some for a month, some who had lost track of time, who didn't even know they were past summer now. There were people here who wanted to kill themselves, or other people. In the dark, Sophia didn't know where they were or what they had in their hands.

When Sophia fell asleep, she dreamt she was in the grocery store, hunting for Owen among the peaches, and then the corn. She couldn't find him even as she dug all the way to the bottom of the bins. And then, she remembered her grocery list and began to paw through her pockets, and the pockets of people near her. A man handed her one of the ripest peaches and she took a bite, thrilled at the juice dribbling down her chin. She loved the fuzz, the sweetness. Only vaguely did she know there was something else she was supposed to do.

She tossed off the sheet and the thin blanket. She was sweating. Yesterday in therapy fat Bev asked her if she thought Owen would be better off without her.

"It was an accident," she said. "I'm a good mother."

There was no guarantee that his brain hadn't rattled around in his skull, knocked against the hard edges, swollen here or bled there. She'd seen enough TV to know that it could be years before they saw signs that he wasn't going to be okay, after all. He might end up being one of those kids who wore an adult-sized diaper and sucked his fist. Because she'd needed to be free of him. And now she didn't. What the fuck was wrong with her? Nothing this place could fix, that much she was sure about.

She got out of bed. The screamer had stopped. Probably they'd given her a pill. Or a needle. Sophia padded down the hall. Despite her fear, she mostly liked this place at night— the dim lights, the hushed voices of the aides checking on the sleeping. No TVs, few buzzers, no ringing phones. But she couldn't stay here forever—she couldn't end up as the crazy woman who'd tossed her kid out a window and then lost her mind.

Up until now she'd been saying all the right things in therapy but what if she didn't? What if tomorrow she told them she wasn't sure she could be trusted? What if she told them that sometimes she hated Owen for always demanding food and dry diapers and walking and bouncing? And that she thought he.didn't love her enough to compensate for the friends she never saw, the dates she never went on, the selfish, lazy days she could no longer spend on the couch with beer and TV?

They would keep her here. Or send her to prison. They would give Owen to a stranger. Or her mother.

What if she said she needed him to grow up to love her? Sophia slid down against the cool wall at the end of the hallway. The back of her shirt rose up and so it was her blazing skin against the cold wall and it felt so good she closed her eyes.

Eventually, someone tapped her hand and helped her to her feet. Without opening her eyes, Sophia allowed herself to be led back to bed.

Monday bled into Tuesday and the only thing that changed was that the palm-licker had been taken away during the night.

"Did he get to go home?" Sophia asked the nurse, taking her pills from the little cup and swallowing them dry. She opened her mouth for inspection and the nurse peered in.

The nurse said, "I hear you're going home today."

"For real?"

The lawyer-lady who'd been in to see her had said as much but Sophia hadn't been sure if she could trust her or not. *You're still going to have to work to prove you're a fit mother*, she said. *Reunification is the goal.* Sophia hadn't asked what she'd have to do, exactly, because she had thought most of what she was being told was bullshit. What kind of system let you back into the world like nothing happened just because you could fake being ok? Normal people did not drop their kids out windows. Most people keep a better grip on their cell phones than she had kept on her kid. Sophia didn't believe in clean slates, start-overs, re-dos. But so far no one was saying she wasn't getting the kid back. She sat up. Maybe what the lawyer had said about getting Owen back by Christmas might come true.

Last year for Christmas, Sophia and Paul Demmons had snuck in between Joseph and a camel in the big plastic Nativity out front of Sacred Heart. They'd passed a bottle of peppermint schnapps back and forth, made out a little, and told each other how shitty things were that this was how they were spending Christmas. This year Sophia had planned to bring Owen to the nursing home on Christmas Eve, when they lit the big tree in the lobby and sang carols. She'd imagined him in one of those miniature Santa hats, the residents oohing over him.

"I definitely want him home for Christmas," Sophia said. The nurse was handing out pills to the next patient and she didn't even look up. Still, it felt good to say it out loud.

12

Rose figured it was another miracle-seeker when the door-bell rang on Tuesday morning. Her mother and Cloris had kept everyone at bay for almost five weeks, but Rose sent her family away and now, stomach still tender along the scar, she went to the door.

Greasy-hair pulled into a messy bun, a bloom of pimples along her chin, thin lips glossed peach-pink—Rose didn't recognize Sophia Leach at first. The night Rose caught the baby, Sophia had been just a shadow in the window. And then, later, on the news shows they'd shown pictures where she'd been made up with foundation and eyeliner and, in one live shot, the kind of mascara that ran down her cheeks when she cried.

Sophia Leach introduced herself with a limp handshake and sliding eyes. She smoothed her hair, her blouse, the legs of her pants. "I came here to thank you."

Sophia Leach, nineteen, wearing black pants made of the kind of shiny material a waitress might wear, a blue short-sleeved blouse with a ruffle down the front, black loafers with a white scuff on one side. Probably the best clothes she had and Rose could picture her, standing in her disastrous bed-room, peering into her open closet for something adult-like.

What was she supposed to say? Rose watched the girl's hands fold and then part, fold and part. She thought about the thank you cards her mother used to make her write—eggshell white paper with a heft to it, her black ballpoint pen, her practiced handwriting.

Rose wanted to tell her about her miscarriage, wanted to say something about the cost of what she'd done.

Sophia took out a picture of Owen and Rose gazed down at him. Sophia, biting her lip, said, "He's with my mother." She pressed a thumb into the soft flesh of her palm. "I can't have unsupervised visits with him yet."

According to the papers, child endangerment charges had been filed. First time offense, they said. No history of abusing the baby. No prior arrests. If he'd died, she would have certainly faced jail time. Eventually, if Sophia did all the right things, and said all the right things to the right people, she'd regain custody of her son, whether she was ready or not. This caused an ache in Rose's womb so profound she found it hard to draw a breath.

Rose turned back into the house and, without being invited, Sophia followed. In the living room, Sophia sat on the edge of the upright chair. "I just wanted to thank you," she said again.

They sat across from one another, the glass coffee table between them, a plastic fire truck among Frederick's finger prints. Rose wanted to scream.

Sophia said, "He's been all checked over." She paused, touched the ruffle of her blouse. "It was crazy—I tripped over the rug and the window was open...you know the rest." Rose did not believe her. Even though it was un-Christian of her to not give this girl the benefit of the doubt, Rose was sure she had thrown her baby out the window and it was only by the will of God he was still alive. Rose had wanted her baby, and this girl had not, but things had not worked out the way they should have. From upstairs, Frederick began to cry. Rose stood so quickly her head fuzzed. "I have to go get him," she said.

All night he'd woken himself and whimpered. In the quiet dark, Rose sat up with him, rocked him, laid him in his crib and rubbed his back. She'd wanted to carry him to bed with her but Hank didn't like that. He said it spoiled Frederick, and kept them all awake. Even though her body felt tender all over, she'd made a pallet of blankets on the floor in Frederick's room, nestled him in close to her body, and told him the story of the tortoise and the hare.

Now, Rose changed her son, tickled his belly until he laughed, then put him over her shoulder. Into Frederick's ear, still warm from sleep, she told him she would never throw him out a window, not ever. She thought of Owen Leach, stunned into silence, staring up at her with his new-blue eyes. When she came back down with Frederick, Sophia was asleep. Rose put Frederick on the floor with his fire truck and studied the near-child face of this girl who had only just escaped killing her baby. Rose thought of herself at nineteen—finishing her Freshman year at Boston College, frizzy-haired and only marginally smarter than she'd been as a high school senior, eager to please her parents with her high grades and ability to avoid trouble. She was crushingly lonely, although she made up stories for her every-other- night phone calls to her mother about trips to the mall with girls named Laurie and Kristen, dates with boys who took her to the Museum of Science and, once, a Red Sox game, nights spent at poetry readings with groups of coffee- drinking friends. The poetry readings were real but she went alone, and sat in the back and chewed her nails until they bled and then she sat on her hands and wished she was someone else.

Sophia woke. "I'm sorry," she said, rubbing her eyes in a way that made Rose think of Frederick. For a long moment, Sophia watched Frederick and Rose watched Sophia. And then, Sophia leaned forward and touched Frederick's hair with her broken fingernails. The gesture was tender and sweet and Rose wanted to cry. Sophia said, "It's a good thing kids don't remember every terrible thing, right?"

Rose thought of the broken window, Frederick's bloody thumb, her moment of inattention that could have been longer and more disastrous. "Kids are resilient," she said. She felt generous with her kindness, her restraint.

Sophia looked at her lap. "You don't believe it was an accident." Sophia swallowed hard. "It could have been an accident." And then, "I don't want him taken away for good."

Rose looked out the window. She would not tell this girl about her miscarried baby. Not to save her feelings, but because they were not friends and this was not the confessional.

There were times she'd left Frederick, wailing in his room, and gone into her own bedroom to scream into a pillow. And there was the time she'd cried in the shower while Hank watched football and Frederick played on the floor and she thought, while the water ran over her in scalding rivulets, that she didn't even care if some maniac broke into the house and killed them both. Or the time when she left the remnants of Frederick's spaghetti dinner on the kitchen floor, left him in his high chair, and went out into her car to pound her fists on the steering wheel until her skin stung.

She'd survived those moments and become a better mother. She'd read parenting books, gone to confession, learned to take deep breaths and count backwards from one hundred. She learned to ask for help from Hank and from her mother. She'd given anonymous donations to the Shriner's and Muscular Dystrophy Association, even when she and Hank could have spent the money on a vacation to Disney or new snow tires for Hank's car. She'd listened to her mother's advice on feeding Frederick, holding him and not holding him. Rose got up, stumbled to the bookcase, and handed Sophia her worn copy of *What to Expect the First Year.*

Sophia took it, and balanced it on her lap. She said, "I think I need more than a book."

Rose said, "Maybe you could bring the baby here some time." She said it before she had time to stop herself. But, as soon as the words were out of her mouth, her arms began to ache with longing.

Sophia fingered the pages of the book. "My lawyer says reunification is the goal."

Rose felt Sophia's luck like a stab wound just below her rib cage. She had to stop herself from doubling over.

"I want him back." Sophia rubbed her palms on her thighs and the motion plus the material made a kind of swishing noise. She said, "I have to go for treatment every day."

"That's not bad." She wanted to be compassionate, but God wasn't helping her.

Sophia took a breath and Rose could see she was trembling all over. "I was so tired. I hadn't slept in days. My mother wouldn't watch him, even for a few hours. She said I got myself into this mess."

If Sophia got Owen back, what would be the guarantee that she wouldn't throw him out another window? Or down a flight of stairs? She could smother him with a pillow or put him in an oven. Rose felt a wave of anxiety course through her body and she steadied her breath against it.

Rose bent over, pulled the fire truck out of Frederick's mouth. He screamed. She wiped the truck on her shirt and handed it back to him as if it was what she meant to do all along. "I think I'm going to put him down for a nap." Inanely, stupidly.

Sophia looked at her, looked at Frederick. Let her say something about the fact he'd just woken up from a nap as if she knew anything about motherhood.

Rose walked Sophia to the door, watched her step over the cracks in the sidewalk as she made her way to her car. As if luck had anything to do with anything.

That night, Rose managed to grill a steak. Ignoring her own pain, she massaged Hank's shoulders while he ate the apple pie she'd picked up for dessert. She should have made the pie from scratch but she'd never made a successful crust without making several failed ones first and she was too exhausted to deal with failure today. She kissed Hank's neck above the collar of the rust-colored shirt she'd ironed for him. "How was work?"

He sighed, leaned back into her kisses. "It was fine. Uneventful."

With her hands on his shoulders, she waited for him to ask how she was feeling. Finally, he reached up and patted her hands. She said, "Mine was uneventful, too."

13

Caroline Weatherby from Channel Eight leaned in and asked Sophia, "What do you think will be different if you get your son back?" She said this in such a falsely chipper voice that it made Sophia think of girlfriends in the sixth grade, on the living room floor in sleeping bags, squealing over secrets and promising not to tell.

When Caroline had called and asked Sophia to do the interview, she'd said it would be a chance to tell her side of the story and Sophia had agreed because she'd been sure she could come across as sweet and sane. But now, in the overly hot room, she was less than sure.

Caroline Weatherby had come to the door all glossed up like Sophia would be if she was still going out for the night. "We've been trying to reach you for weeks," she said, all Colgate smile.

"I'm in treatment," Sophia said, not at all sure this was the right thing to say. She felt the tickle of hysteria at the back of her throat. She was sitting on her mother's couch, in her mother's living room-slash-dining room because it looked more like a home than the trailer she'd just moved into, which, aside from her couch, a coffee table she'd picked up off the side of the road, and her double mattress, was empty.

She'd had no way to pay the rent on her apartment—
she'd blown through her vacation time from work in four
days and because she had to go to therapy every day, she
wouldn't be able to go back to work for a few weeks, anyway. Sophia's uncle had a trailer that was unrented at the
moment, thanks to the druggies who'd been arrested and
hauled away, and he was willing to let her crash there as long
as she cleaned it. Which she was working on but the place
was still pretty gross. When she agreed to the interview with
the Channel Eight chick, she hadn't thought about the cigarette burns on her mother's couch or the stain on the carpet
from where some friend of her mother's had thrown up last
New Year's Eve.

The camera guy was wearing jeans and sneakers and
looked about Sophia's age but she couldn't place him from
high school. He fussed with the lights, aimed the camera,
took it down and moved a few steps to the right. Without
ever making eye contact with Sophia, he said, "We're good
to go when you are, Caroline."

Sophia smiled, automatic, nervous. But then she thought
maybe she shouldn't look too happy so she tried for a more
neutral expression. She wished she had Owen with her so
she'd have something to do with her hands—wipe his mouth,
fix a strap of his overalls, waggle his feet. But, while she was
still waiting for her court date, she wasn't allowed unsupervised visits with him and Vicky hadn't wanted any part of
watching what she said was sure to be a shit show. She'd
taken Owen to the lake for the afternoon. The lake. All of a
sudden she was some kind of picnic-making grandmother.
Sophia had tried to make a case for having him on camera so she could fuss over him and maybe they'd show it on

the news and maybe everyone wouldn't think she was such a terrible mother, at least not all the time. But Vicky hadn't bought it. So here she was, prim and upright, trying to look like the picture of sane dedication, minus the kid she was supposed to be dedicated to.

Caroline Weatherby smiled. She was probably one of those women who got their nails done professionally and shopped at Macy's instead of Kmart like the rest of the world. She certainly looked it, with her navy suit and pink blouse and high heels that must have cost more than Sophia made in a month.

Sophia was wearing a puffy-short-sleeved polyester flower-patterned dress that came to her crossed ankles. It was something she'd picked up at the Goodwill a few years ago, when the nursing home was having a staff/resident tea party and she needed something decent to wear. The old ladies had loved the pink and yellow flowers and this morning when she put it on, she was positive she'd give the mother vibe. But now she was sweating and the sweat against the armpit seams was itching like crazy. She was tempted to ask Caroline if it was okay to go change but what could she wear that was Vicky's that wouldn't make her look like she occasionally worked the street corners? She shifted around, re-crossed her ankles, tried to focus on Caroline Weatherby's questions.

"You must miss him."

"Of course I do."

"Can you talk a little bit about what led up to the incident?"

To get ready for the interview, Sophia had scrubbed under her fingernails, filed, taken off the purple, and applied clear polish. Her hair was in a bun; her makeup was minimal. She didn't want Caroline Weatherby saying she was dirty, or trampy. She wanted to look neat, put together, sane. And now, the first question right off was basically asking her if she'd always been crazy or if it was just for that one minute. "Good question," Sophia said. She licked her lips.

What led up to the incident was a whole bunch of things, starting with the boy who was Owen's father. He was tall, and blond, and home on leave. Sophia was at a bar in the Old Port with her girlfriends, well into a second pitcher of beer. He was quieter than the other guys, and that made her lean in close, give him her full attention. They drank for a while, skipped out on dancing, and walked three blocks to a motel with orange shag carpeting and a disco light over the check-in desk. Sophia liked that he hadn't asked her to do it in her car or down on a bench by the bay. She'd liked him, and in the morning when he kissed her goodbye, she'd made the mistake of asking him to call her sometime. She wrote her number on his palm and let him walk her back to her car. By the time she realized she was pregnant, she'd figured out that he wasn't going to call. In her mind she called him Owen, Sr.

She wasn't stupid enough to say any of that to Caroline Weatherby. "I tripped over a rug," she said. It was both the truth and a softened truth, like telling an old lady she looks beautiful when what you mean is that she has mostly put her lipstick on straight.

Caroline Weatherby sat there all cool and calm and Sophia started to really regret that she'd agreed to this interview. She could see now that she wasn't going to look good at all. She was going to come across, in her awful dress and teacher hair, as nervous and sweaty and probably a little insane.

"You tripped. And he just tumbled out of your arms?"

Earlier that day, she'd changed him, put him over her shoulder, patted his back. All day he screamed. When she put him down, when she picked him up. Her apartment was small and hot. She carried him down the stairs, him in one arm, the stroller in another. On the second to last step, she lost her footing and slipped and before she righted herself, before she knew the baby was okay, she had the briefest flash of his head smashed open on the sidewalk. *A terrible accident*, everyone would say. She propped herself against the steps, the baby intact but wailing against her chest, and she thought how, without him, there would be silence. And then, Sophia stood, gained stable footing and, with her heart thumping shamefully, headed off to the park with him.

"It was terrible," she said to Caroline Weatherby.

"Do you think people are judging you too harshly for what happened?"

"Probably. Definitely." She was about to tell Caroline about the doll's head she'd found in her yard but she didn't want to give other weirdos any ideas.

Caroline Weatherby smiled her perfect smile. "What's happened to make you think people are judging you?"

"Nothing, really." What the hell was with people who looked at you like you might as well just say it because they could figure you out anyway?

When she started telling people about the baby she was going to have, her girlfriends asked her why she didn't just take care of it. Sophia told them it was too late, by the time she figured it out. "I thought it was something bad I ate," she'd said, laughing. But really it was because Owen, Sr.

hadn't come across as such a bad guy and having his kid seemed like it might be the beginning of something.

"I love my son," she said now, hoping she sounded sincere, hoping Caroline Weatherby would say something in her story about how Sophia seemed young and sad yet hopeful. She did love Owen, especially when he was asleep, with his little fist up near his mouth. She loved the way he watched her while she fed him a bottle, like she was necessary and fascinating, and she especially loved when he tucked his head into her shoulder on those brief, rare moments when he exhausted himself. But those times didn't happen often enough. In the three-and-a-half months since she'd brought him home from the hospital, she could think of maybe four or five times that he'd been quiet enough for her to hear his heartbeat.

Caroline Weatherby smiled.

Sweat puddled at the small of Sophia's back and above her lip and she thought probably her hair had frizzed out of its bun. She might look like a madwoman. Sophia said, "People do things in the heat of the moment that they regret later. Don't they?"

Caroline smiled wider. Patient, sweet, the kind of smile Sophia gave the nursing home residents when they stopped by her desk to ask if she knew when the bus was coming. Sophia desperately wanted Caroline to acknowledge the truth in what she'd said, to agree with her even just a little, to lead them through the awkwardness of the moment. In the deepening silence, Sophia went on, even though she knew she shouldn't, "I love my son but it's so hard, sometimes. Being alone with him all the time." With her fingertips she blotted her eyelids, the crevice above her lip. Sophia had tried every suggestion she could find to make Owen stop wailing:

she rocked him, ignored him, walked him, sang to him, murmured, whispered, bounced, fed, changed, bathed, and dried him. Yet still, in three months, she doubted she'd gotten more than an hour of uninterrupted sleep. "Do you have kids?"

Caroline touched a manicured hand to her heart. "I have two."

Relief rolled in on top of the heat and for a moment Sophia could breathe. "Then you must know what I mean about the way sometimes no matter what you do they just scream and scream and you're at the..." She stopped, because the look on Caroline Weatherby's face said she thought Sophia was crazy. She took a breath and finished because Caroline was waiting and it was too late, anyway. "...end of things."

Sophia felt herself sliding out of her body, out of the hot room. Caroline would say that she shouldn't have her baby back. She would say that Sophia should be in prison or a mental hospital, the baby placed in foster care with some stranger who would, undoubtedly, be more stable than Sophia or her mother.

Caroline Weatherby leaned over from the straight-backed chair they'd dragged across the room. She put a hand on the couch next to Sophia. "It's hard to be a single mother."

Sophia felt immense relief that maybe she understood, after all. She smiled. She could have told Caroline Weatherby about how just a few hours before she lost Owen out the window, she had called her mother. "Please help me, Ma. He's been crying for hours. I can't get him to stop."

Sophia heard the click of the stove as her mother lit her cigarette against the gas burner. "I tried to tell you how hard it was going to be but you said you'd handle it."

Her mother sounded like ice and Sophia was sweating, and her back ached, and she felt like a crazy old woman with a kid who might have come from Mars for all they had in common. "I can't even remember what it was I wanted before I had him."

"Uh-huh. Tell me about it." Vicky said.

Her mother had probably been just about to slip into her flip-flops and head out to meet up with her old-crow buddies at Bingo. In her sweltering apartment, with her head boiling, Sophia pressed the phone between her shoulder and ear and tried frantically to recall what she'd imagined for her life.

She'd wanted to be a bank teller. Wear her hair in a ballerina bun or neat braid down her back. A steel-colored suit, never pants, always the skirt and jacket. Expensive black heels, a red blouse, one single silver bracelet. She'd start out as a teller but she'd be the one people waited in line for because she didn't make mistakes counting their money out to them and she always had cherry or grape lollipops for the kids. She'd work her way up to be the lady behind the desk who did loans for cars and mortgages. She'd get her nails done every week and people would notice it when she pointed to where they should sign.

"Can't you just take him for tonight?" She'd asked her mother.

Vicky exhaled and Sophia imagined the blue plume of smoke. "I can't, sweetheart. I've got Bingo."

Sophia could have told Caroline Weatherby how things would have been different if she'd had even a little bit of help. She said, "I'm just so grateful that my baby is okay."

14

Portland was only an hour south of Parker, but the air felt warmer, greener. Here, in late September, people still walked around in t-shirts. Rose, overdressed in her light wool coat, slowed her pace so that she wouldn't arrive sweating at the psychic's.

Margo recommended Psychic Lucy. "Why not give it a whirl?" Margo said. "It'll be better than wondering about it forever."

Wondering if catching Owen Leach was what made her lose the baby, Margo meant. Wondering if she had sacrificed her own baby to save another. "I don't believe in voodoo," Rose said.

Margo raised her bushy eyebrows. "Unless it's Joan of Arc hearing voices?"

"Good point."

If Rose had told her mother the truth of her errand, Camilla would have gone to church and lit a candle for her. So, Rose said Margo was backed up with work and that she needed Rose to take in a dress for one of the bridesmaids for this weekend's wedding. It couldn't wait, Rose said.

"It's too soon for work," Camilla said.

"The doctor said I'm okay."

"Doctors don't know everything."

Rose walked up and down one side of the brick street, then the other. There were cigarette butts and torn off fake fingernails in purple and black and pink littering the sidewalk. Shops with bread and dresses and shoes and jewelry had their doors open, catching the last warm days. Rose could have gone in and asked one of the baggy-shirted women with messy hair and black-rimmed glasses for directions, but she didn't want them to think she was one of those women—sad and disoriented—who sought out the help of a psychic. A reader, Margo had called her. She taps into the spirits around you for information that can guide you. Rose thought it was probably a con but what else could she do? The refrain of "what ifs" was killing her.

Cars and tractor-trailer trucks slid past her, navigating narrow turns, spewing exhaust, squealing their brakes for pedestrians in crosswalks. The volume of traffic—the actual noise and the way they looked like they'd all smash into each other at any moment—gave Rose fluttering anxiety.

She stepped carefully over the brick sidewalks, nearly turning her ankle twice, before she realized Lucy's "office" was on the second floor of a gray-shingled two-story. To mark it, there was only a red plastic sign the size and shape of a small child's hand in the window, and, beneath it, a hand-written sign with the days and times open. Surely someone serious about her psychic ability would be bolder with her advertising. Or maybe she was so good she didn't really need to advertise at all. Rose stood on the sidewalk, debating, until a man walked by with a dog and the dog, likely sensing Rose's distress, squatted beside her.

Rose darted toward the door which led to a dim interior set of stairs. She smelled stewed beef and incense. On the red door with an outline of a hand drawn in black, Rose knocked.

"Enter!"

The room she stepped into was a living room done in red and purple—a low couch, velvet curtains, a panel of beads shading the window. There was a smell of nutmeg, vanilla, and cat pee. To the left was a buzzing, industrial-lit kitchen with shabby beige cabinets, an open drawer, and a cat's litter box over the sink. Rose held her breath and walked deeper into the red-bulbed room. A woman with a mountain of blond hair sat at a round table in front of a blooming lemon tree and dealt out cards. Rose hesitated by the velvet couch. She could turn and leave right now. She'd seen enough that she could make up something to tell Margo.

Lucy said. "Sit down."

Rose pulled out the wooden chair opposite Lucy. A cat leapt to the floor. Rose peered closer at the cards. She was expecting swords and wizards but these were ordinary cards. Lucy smiled. "Solitaire," she said. Her skirt jingled. The mass of dull blond hair nearly swallowed her small, slightly feline face. Lucy gestured toward the table. "Do you want tea?"

Rose shook her head. She would have liked tea but the predictable kind, and who knew what kind of tea a psychic drank. She wasn't even sure if she meant tea for drinking or tea for reading.

Lucy reached behind her, plucked a cup of tea off a shelf, and settled back into her chair. The steam from her tea made her appear fogged over. "Tell me why you're here."

Rose laughed. "Shouldn't you already know?"

Lucy raised her penciled eyebrows. "You're nervous."

Rose shrugged. How much was she supposed to tell the psychic? It wasn't like a psychologist or even the acupuncturist she'd gone to once, where you told them about your love of chocolate cake and your inability to quiet your mind.

Lucy set her cup back into its saucer. "I'll start by telling you what I feel." She closed her eyes. "I feel a woman, maybe in her late sixties. She's showing me a bird."

Rose felt her mouth go very dry. She wished she'd accepted some tea but it seemed too late to ask for it now. She didn't know if she was supposed to say something here— some affirmation or denial of her hummingbird dream. But she didn't want to say too much. Also, maybe Lucy wasn't referring to Rose's dream because Rose was not anywhere near sixty.

When she'd called to make the appointment, Rose had given Lucy her first name only. But Lucy could have filled in the rest. And now, she might recognize Rose from the newspaper. They'd run a picture of her from when she'd taken first place in the Fryeburg Fair for one of her quilts. Still, Lucy might know about Owen, but how would she know about the dream bird? Rose moved her hands away from her stomach.

"Has your grandmother passed? Your mother's mother?"

Again, it could be a guess. "Yes."

Lucy nodded. "Now she's showing me a baby in her arms. She's rocking it, cradling it."

Of course, she'd probably read about Rose catching Owen, but she could also mean Frederick, or the baby she'd lost. Rose asked, "How old is the baby you see?"

Lucy tipped her head like she was listening to something far off. Then she nodded. "She's drawing something in the air. A circle? An O? Does that mean anything to you?"

A cat wandered into the room, threaded itself between Rose's legs. Beneath the table, Rose crossed her legs. She might have kicked the cat. It gave a short mewl, jumped up on the table and lapped from Lucy's teacup.

Lucy scratched the cat along its body. "She says you've been upset, in pain. She says you have to be careful."

"It's too late for careful," Rose said before she could stop herself. It must be the red of the room that made her feel confessional.

Rose felt her heart rate slow, her breath become almost non-existent. It was crazy to believe this woman was actually talking to Rose's grandmother. Rose didn't believe in communicating with the dead. She'd expected Lucy to tell her something about why she lost the baby and maybe something about the future. Not with a crystal ball, not exactly. But not this listening-to-the-dead stuff either.

"She's shaking her head at me—she thinks you don't believe me." Lucy paused, put a hand to her temple. "She's showing me a porch. There's a set of stairs that aren't painted. She's pointing to her foot. Was there a splinter?"

It could be a guess. Kids get splinters. The one she got in her foot when she was seven or eight stuck out a good couple of inches. Rose said, "I don't see the point in going over things I already know." When she woke from the humming-bird dream, she had a suspicion it meant Owen Leach was meant to be her baby. She was here for confirmation.

From the kitchen, a cat scraped litter onto the floor. Maybe Lucy wasn't as old as Rose first thought. Maybe she was trying to make herself look like she'd had experience she hadn't, what with her crochet shawl and her heavy eyeliner. The blush painted thick and high on her cheekbones. Probably she wasn't much older than Sophia Leach. Probably she didn't know much about anything and this was just a waste of time.

Rose took her purse from the floor, brushed it free of cat hair, and hugged it to her stomach. "I thought you were going to tell me something useful."

Lucy said. "She says she's very proud of you." Lucy blinked, refocused. "She faded."

Rose stood, arranged her purse over her shoulder. "That's it?" she asked.

Lucy smiled. "I hope it was helpful."

How long had she been in business? Rose should have asked Margo. Margo was too nice to other small-business owners. If that's what you could call being a psychic. Rose paid the twenty dollars, kissed Lucy on her offered cheek even though it was slick with makeup and smelled like candy and cat food. She walked out past the kitchen, caught the eye of the annoyed cat, and made her way quickly onto the sidewalk.

The whole psychic experience had been worse than a Chinese-food fortune. Rose looked around as she hurried to her car. Had anyone seen her? That's all she needed— someone reporting back to Hank that his wife was soliciting the opinion of a woman who let her cat pee in or on the kitchen sink. He'd say the strain was getting to her, that she should see a counselor, that she should stay in bed and have her mother help with Frederick more often.

Rose could not remember where she'd parked her car. She walked quickly, up and down the streets, one looking as familiar as the next. The weather had taken a turn and now her lips felt iced, her fingers through her pockets chilled. She felt the creep of panic that she wouldn't find the car, ever. She could ask someone for help. People around here were like that—you could ask them where you left your car, describe it as a blue minivan and they'd schlep around even if they'd left their jacket at work. Not like in Boston. Which was one of the things she liked about Maine. The small-town safety of it. But right now, she didn't want to ask anyone. She was sick of people acting like they knew her because they knew about her. In Boston no one would care about a caught baby by now. They'd have moved on to rapes and robberies and the shady dealings of politicians.

Rose thought about going back to Lucy and asking her to think hard and tell her where she'd left the car. The thought made her giddy. Hysterical laugh-bubbles tickled her throat. One escaped, and then another. And then she was flat-out laughing, holding herself up against the filthy wall of the post office, a piece of chewed gum wedged beneath her palm.

Finally, she righted herself, scraped off most of the gum on her hand with the tissue Lucy had given her, then tucked the tissue back into her purse. She found her car parked unevenly between two spaces. She'd passed it once before, maybe twice.

15

Into her faux leather purse, Sophia put the picture of the baby when he was in his new denim overalls with a tiny plaid shirt underneath. Then she took the picture out and looked at it again. The three lamps and dim overhead light in the trailer barely illuminated Owen's outline. She moved to the window so she could see better. He was hers and no one was going to take him away from her.

People Sophia hardly even knew were coming up to her and telling her she had no right to be a mother after what she'd done. How they didn't believe it was an accident. Yesterday, in Rite Aid while she was getting her prescription refilled, some death-by-perfume woman barged right up to her and said how it seemed like it "would be best for everyone involved" if she gave the baby up.

Sophia wanted to rip her eyes out with her teeth. Instead, she'd said, "You can't just take someone's baby away from her."

The woman swatted at a mosquito that was buzzing around the store then smiled at Sophia as if she were an idiot.

But she wasn't an idiot. As soon as Sophia got home, she'd called the lawyer who'd been in to see her at the hospital.

Attorney Andrea said it couldn't happen just like that, not if Sophia was doing everything she was supposed to. "Just stay on track," Andrea said.

There had already been a hearing where the younger-than-expected judge ruled that Vicky got custody of Owen until Sophia got her shit together. Andrea said there would be meetings to check in, see how treatment was going, make sure Owen was stable where he was. That last part was what worried Sophia the most. Her mother wasn't exactly the queen of stability.

Andrea said. "How's your treatment going?"

"Swell. Couldn't be better. Talking about why why why for hours at a time with a break for slimy cold cut sandwiches in between is my idea of a good time."

"Glad to hear it," Andrea said. And then, "People probably think you'll willingly relinquish custody."

"Well, I won't."

"Okay."

"It doesn't feel okay." Owen was still young enough that if she did everything right from now on, he'd love her in the madly devoted way she'd always imagined: burnt-toast breakfast-in-bed on Mothers' Day, drawings of flowers from school, watching the Price is Right with her when she got old or lonely. A million moments where they'd be perfectly happy with just each other.

Andrea said, "Owen is still legally your child."

They said their polite goodbyes and then Sophia sat at the single barstool at her ratty kitchen counter, feeling like trash. Tomorrow at group she'd probably have to say what was going on, and how it made her feel lousy that everyone seemed to think she was a shit mother who didn't deserve another chance. Loony-bin Lisa, who had set her apartment on fire when she passed out with a cigarette in her hand, would say some bullshit about God never giving us more than we can handle. Gas-bag Gus would never shut up about the law not being on your side. And Feeling-Fine Fisher, who claimed he'd never been sober a day in his life until now, would sing some tune about rainbows being overdue. Sophia would have to take one of those deep cleansing breaths they were always going on about.

She needed to pull it together. Being gainfully employed would at least be one thing in her favor.

Merry Pines was decked out for fall: garlands of orange and yellow, plastic leaves in the lobby, a pile of stacked un-carved pumpkins by the front door, and an arrangement of dyed-to-match carnations on the receptionist's desk. At the first chirped hello, Sophia resented the gray-bunned hag sitting in her spot. But she put on her friendly face. "I'm here to see Gail Sparks."

"Do you have an appointment?"

"You can tell her Sophia Leach is here." It was just past five on a Friday night and Sophia hoped Gail hadn't already left to get home to her goat-milking and needlepoint.

Sophia had loved her job as the evening receptionist at Merry Pines. She liked answering the phones in her fake-professional voice. She liked the old ladies with their pearl necklaces clanking against the bars of their walkers. She liked the old men who said she was a "looker."

When she got big with the baby, she bought a cheapo ring and put it on her left hand, told the folks that her husband was off protecting our country. They seemed to like her even more after that—always stopping by to see how she was feeling, if she'd heard from Owen, Sr. recently and if he was safe. The old ladies liked to give her advice about not eating spicy food or taking baths. The old men winked and said her husband was a lucky man. Even though she was sometimes so bored she resorted to making paper snowflakes to keep herself busy, she still liked her job. They'd even thrown her a baby shower, complete with a yellow-frosted sheet cake with a cartoon sugar-duck and a word balloon that proclaimed: "Welcome, Baby!" They'd said they'd find a way to work around the baby, maybe even let him come in with her, at least until he started to crawl. But they'd obviously changed their minds after Owen went out the window. The day Sophia got home from the mental hospital Gail called to tell her to take some time off "until you feel better."

Sophia wasn't about to let gray-bun get too comfortable in her chair. Gray-bun picked up the phone and turned herself slightly away from Sophia, as if that meant she couldn't hear and couldn't still read her sickly pale lips as she said "That girl who used to work here says she's here to see you."

"I work here," Sophia said. "I've just been sick."

Gray-bun smiled at Sophia but it was tight at the edges, dim in her eyes.

Gail came out of her office and Sophia threw her arms open and ran toward her. "When do you want me back?"

Gail loosened herself from Sophia's embrace, smiled. "Why don't we go into my office?"

Of course, she didn't want to hurt gray-bun's feelings by hiring Sophia back then and there. Gail was sweet like that. She'd been nice enough about it when she told Sophia to take some time off until she was feeling better, even though

Sophia had said she was feeling fine and that she needed to work. It was best for everyone, Gail said, for the time being.

Gail closed the door behind them.

Sophia said, "I've missed you guys so much!"

"The residents have missed you, too."

"Have they? I knew they would."

Gail arranged some papers into a pile, then took the top ones off and stuck them on the bottom and patted the whole pile into place again. Her desk, aside from this single pile of papers, was immaculate. One flower-pot-turned-pen holder, one glass dish for silver paper clips, and one framed picture of her cheese award-winning goat.

Sophia smiled at the goat. "How's Daisy?"

"The thing is, Sophia, we can't really take you back right now." She looked up when she said it, at least.

Maybe Sophia didn't understand. Maybe they were going to ask her to come back and do something different. Maybe Gail was going to say they'd noticed how good she was with the residents, and how they thought she should be a CNA. It wasn't impossible to think they were going to offer to pay for the schooling. "What are you talking about?"

Gail waved her arm at the receptionist's desk. Her big silver-and-tourmaline ring glittered. "We've hired Judy, for one thing."

"As a temp, right?"

Gail shook her head.

"You said I should take some time." Sophia swallowed back tears, laid the picture of Owen on Gail's desk. "This is one my mother took the other day. Don't you love that shirt?"

"I can't believe how big he's getting."

"He's amazing."

"I'm sorry, Sophia."

"But, why?"

Gail sighed. "It would be better for you to go somewhere you can start fresh."

Sophia felt hot with panic. "Like where? Where am I supposed to go? Who's hiring? There's like, three places to work in town and no one's going to take a chance with me. You guys know me. You know I'm decent at my job."

At first, Gail looked like she might say okay, they'd give her another chance. But then she got up, walked around Sophia, and opened her office door. "The bottom line," she said, "Is that we don't really have any hours for you."

Sophia wasn't about to just sit there, and she wasn't about to beg. She grabbed Owen's picture off the desk and tucked it under her shirt. "Fine," she said. "I'll find something." On the way out, she stuffed one of those fist-sized pumpkins into her purse. She didn't bother to check to see if gray-bun saw her do it.

16

Frederick ran a red truck along the vine design of the living room rug. Rose picked up a blue truck, lowered herself to the floor so she could sit with him, and made vrooming noises. When he crashed his truck into hers, she fell over onto her back and he gleefully ran the truck up over stomach. She stayed still even though she didn't want him near her stomach, didn't want anyone near her stomach.

Camilla used her key to let herself in. "You shouldn't be on the floor, Rosie. Who knows what it's doing to your insides." She sat on the couch and Frederick hopped up next to her and put his head on her pillowy lap. "Give grandma a kiss." Frederick puckered his lips and kissed the air. "I don't think you're ready to be running around. You have to take care of yourself."

Rose pulled herself to her feet, stood holding on to the arm of the couch while the world righted itself, then pretended to need something from her purse. She didn't want to look at her mother, didn't want her mother to see that she was exhausted. It hurt to breathe, hurt to stand in the shower, hurt to grocery shop or cook dinner or do anything other than stretch out in bed with Frederick tucked in against her belly. When she got home from Psychic Lucy's, she'd left Hank in charge of Frederick and slept for twelve hours.

"I'm just doing one errand," she said.

Camilla pulled out her copy of *Jesus for Babies* and settled Frederick into her lap. "Did you have a plan for dinner?"

Rose said, "I have chicken defrosting in the fridge."

"I can make parmesan."

"You don't have to do that, Ma." Rose's plan had been to roast the chicken breasts with some olive oil and a few carrots because that was all she had in the fridge and she couldn't deal with grocery shopping today. The thought of her mother's lightly breaded and pan-fried chicken covered in sauce and cheese made her weak.

"Let me help you, honey."

If she'd still been seeing a therapist, the therapist would have told her to accept the help. "Sure, Ma. Knock yourself out."

*****

It was easy to find out where Sophia's mother lived. Vicky Leach lived in a trailer down a dirt road that housed two other trailers and a ton of pine trees. Her trailer had a fresh coat of white paint and a navy-blue door. Rose knocked twice before moving over to the window. She could see the kitchen from the sink to the refrigerator—no dishes piled up but there were no curtains, either. A white refrigerator with rainbow-colored Alphabet magnets that held up no drawings and no school pictures, a coffee maker with an inch of coffee in the bottom, a lime-green plastic pitcher holding utensils, three brown-spotted bananas.

Rose wondered if the reporter from Channel Eight had been after Vicky, too. If Caroline Weatherby wanted to talk to Vicky Leach, it would not be for the same reasons as she wanted to talk to Rose, or even Sophia. But maybe Vicky Leach wasn't the kind of woman who had the good sense to know when she was being held up as an example of lousy motherhood.

"Is there a reason you're standing on my stoop?"

Rose jumped back. Vicky Leach, with Owen in a stroller, had come up the walk behind her and scared her half to death. "I'm glad to see you!" Rose said, and it came out shrill and false. "I'm Rose. Rankin." She held out her hand, which Vicky took and shook limply. Should she add that she was the one who'd caught Owen? Surely Vicky recognized her name and yet she made no exclamation of thanks. Not even a flicker of a smile.

Rose could hardly stop looking at Owen long enough to meet Vicky's unamused eyes. "I thought Sophia might be here," she said. "I wanted to see how she was doing." A lie, but one that sounded like the truth.

Vicky pushed past her to open the trailer door. Unlocked, like most people around here left things and then wondered at the audacity of thieves. "It's good to meet you." Vicky unhooked Owen from his stroller. Her hair was a mass of brown that had been pushed up and sprayed into place. Once Vicky had the baby settled against her shoulder, Rose leaned her face close to Owen's. His eyes were wide and blue and clear. His skin perfect, smooth, not even a bruise she could see. "Hi," she said. "Hi, sweet boy." She touched his baby fuzz cheek even though it meant her hand was just above

Vicky's shoulder, her face close enough to smell Vicky's cigarette breath.

"I'd ask you in but I just got home from work and I need to get the kid fed and all." Vicky's legs were overly tanned and thick in a pair of short-shorts. She must go to a tanning booth because there was nowhere near enough sun in Maine in the fall for that kind of tan. Rose averted her eyes.

"You walk to work? It must be at least a mile to town." Although she hadn't ever been in, Rose knew the hair salon where Vicky worked. It had a reputation for big hair whether you liked it or not.

With the baby still against her shoulder, Vicky lifted the stroller up over the lip of the door jamb.

Rose held the door with her foot. "I could help you out sometime, if you needed it. I wouldn't mind giving you a lift. It's getting chilly out. I'd hate for the baby to catch cold." She clamped her mouth to stop the babble. Vicky couldn't be that cold or else she'd have on long pants.

Vicky shrugged. "Shouldn't be too much longer for the car to get fixed." She went in and switched on the kitchen light. Rose followed.

"Well, if it doesn't, I really don't mind." Rose sat down at the square kitchen table and folded her hands neatly in front of her. The table wasn't sticky, so that was something. The floor was old linoleum with a pattern of yellow and brown flowers. Rose couldn't tell if it was clean or not. The wallpaper was a shade of butter yellow that might have once looked nice with the floor but was now brittle and peeling at the seams. The stove was the color of a dirty lime. From the kitchen, Rose could see down the brown-carpeted hall into a bedroom that had a pink bedspread and matching curtains, a white plastic lawn chair piled with stuffed animals. She would have had to twist around in her chair to see the living room behind her. She recognized the edge of the tan carpet from the TV interview.

Rose pointed to the chair. "Are those Owen's toys?"

"Nah. Sophia still hasn't taken all her shit." Then, stiff-backed, she said, "Do you want a cup of coffee?"

"I couldn't have you go through the trouble." Rose guessed she and Vicky Leach were about the same age, which meant Vicky had Sophia when she was in her early twenties. For Sophia, having Owen at nineteen meant pregnant at eighteen, still in high school, still with an affinity for boy band posters and teddy bears. Rose was thirty-nine when she had Frederick, forty-one when she lost this last baby.

"I was just about to make some." Vicky dumped the remnants of the old coffee into the sink, measured out some grounds, poured in the water. She heated Owen's bottle while the coffee dripped into the pot. Tested it on her wrist.

Rose couldn't stop looking at Owen, at the perfectness of him.

Vicky shrugged. "Did you see that awful interview Sophia gave that girl from Channel Eight?"

Rose grimaced. "You probably warned her it was a bad idea." Vicky shrugged and settled Owen into his car seat on the floor.

"I could hold him," Rose said, but Vicky seemed not to hear.

She lit a cigarette against the stove. "How old is your kid?"

Rose waved a cloud of smoke away from Owen. She didn't want to insult the woman in her own home, but didn't everyone these days know about the dangers of second-hand smoke? "Frederick. He's two."

"Hellacious age." Vicky poured coffee into mugs she took out of the drainer, the cigarette hovering just above. She poured cream into a small red-tinted glass pitcher and set it in front of Rose.

"You didn't have to go through any trouble," Rose said. The milk appeared pink through the pitcher. "Two is kind of a fun age. He's curious about everything."

"I'm sure Freddy's a doll."

"Mostly we call him Frederick." Rose wanted to say something about the baby she'd lost. But if she told Vicky she'd been pregnant when she caught Owen, Vicky would know exactly what she wanted.

Vicky held her coffee with one hand, the bottle in Owen's mouth with the other. "Speaking of curious—how did you know to be right there when the baby fell out the window?"

She wasn't going to argue with Vicky Leach even though she could feel the words like pins on her tongue. At least she knew where Sophia got it from. Rose sipped her coffee which was surprisingly not burnt-tasting or watery. It seemed risky to say anything about a miracle—even half-joking—because she didn't see a crucifix or dried palms or anything that indicated Vicky believed in anything other than cigarettes and coffee. "It was lucky." Her stomach folded in on itself. Rose reached across the table and held Owen's sock-clad foot in her hand. He laughed and she laughed back.

And then, into the silence that followed, Rose said, "Is Sophia at therapy today?"

Vicky blew a perfect smoke ring. "And she'll come home full of indignation like she doesn't belong there with the crazy people."

"You think she does?"

"No idea." Vicky added three packets of pink sweetener to her coffee and gave the cup a small shake. "She needs to do something, though, if she's gonna get the kiddo back."

Rose said, "Sophia's practically a kid herself. Maybe she's just too young to be a mother." She felt like her words were spilled out among the sugar packets.

"Old enough to get herself pregnant."

Rose stirred a packet of sugar into her coffee. She smiled her best smile. "People make mistakes."

Vicky snorted. "That's the understatement of the century."

Rose sorted the little sugar packets into piles—all pink, all yellow, all green. She said, "I had this dream with falling hummingbirds." She'd meant to say something about feeling like the dream had meaning, but Vicky yawned and Rose stopped talking.

Lazily, Vicky wiped a dribble of formula from Owen's chin.

Rose finished off the last drips of her coffee. "Well, if you ever need a sitter..." She said it breezily, like it didn't matter. "...or anything." Vicky smiled back and, even though she didn't say anything, Rose left the trailer feeling like things had not gone as well as she'd hoped.

17

She said, "I'll be fine with him." Even though Vicky never asked. Sophia picked up Owen, cradled him against her shoulder, shushed him.

Technically, she still wasn't allowed to be alone with him but Vicky had a standing poker game on Tuesdays and Bingo on Wednesdays and Saturdays. Vicky's reasoning was that she was already doing enough and she wasn't about to shell out extra cash for a babysitter. And social worker Amy wasn't likely to make a night-time surprise visit.

It took twenty steps to cross from one end of Sophia's mother's trailer to the other. Owen screamed in her ear. At least here there weren't neighbors banging on the walls.

"Please, baby. Please."

She pictured Rose Rankin on the night she let Owen go out the window. Sophia had looked down, right after, even though she felt sick at the idea that she'd probably see her baby's head oozing all over the sidewalk. Instead, there was a woman with wild black hair severely parted in the center, two stories below Sophia's apartment window, and she was holding the baby. Or, a baby. Sophia wasn't sure. She felt queasy with relief, then fear. Rose's head, neck and shoulders were bent over the baby like she was protecting him from whatever might be next.

Owen was crying now like he had that night, on and on, unstoppable. Sophia sweated through her Def Leppard t-shirt. With one hand, she pushed her hair behind her ears. In treatment, they told her it was normal for babies to cry, normal to feel frustrated. It might even be normal to have feelings of violence, they said. What isn't normal is acting on those feelings. "I tripped," she told the group, and then she said it again to Dr. Lynch.

Sophia didn't mind one-one-one therapy as much as she minded group therapy, which felt more like the high school lunchroom than anything else. Pock-marked Paulette, lipsticked Leena, fat Bev. Half of them chewing on their cuticles until they drew blood. Crying and wiping at their noses and spilling their guts about all the dumb shit they'd done, ever. How they were avoiding their triggers these days. Sophia mostly listened unless she had to talk. With Dr. Lynch at least it was private. But she wished he'd give her more than just general ideas—she needed specifics. Go for help when you feel you need it, Dr. Lynch said. What help? Who could help her?

She picked up a magazine and fanned the air around Owen's head. He caught his breath, hiccupped against her shoulder. "You like that?" Sophia felt a wave of competency. Until he started up crying again. She set him on the couch. Leaned over him until her mouth was almost on his mouth. She pursed her lips and blew air over him. He stared at her, momentarily silent. She thought about how other people—people like Rose Rankin—seemed to know what they were supposed to do.

Hungry or tired or wet, the nurse in the delivery room had said. That's pretty much it for babies. She'd been all smiles, all sweet to Sophia, like they thought she'd be okay, even though she was young. And Sophia had left the maternity ward feeling really good, like she might not totally suck at something for once in her life.

Sophia's cheeks hurt and she felt like she might pass out from blowing air on Owen's face but he'd barely even moved since she started and the quiet was so perfect she didn't want it to end.

It would be nice to have a husband. Even a live-in boyfriend would be okay. Someone to fetch the newspaper on Sunday mornings, make sure she had gas in her car, set up the TV trays in the living room for dinner. Where was she supposed to meet someone like that, especially now? Having a baby was one thing. Most guys didn't care if you had a baby already because they wanted more. They figured the one was just a starter. But, throwing the kid out the window, getting locked up in a place for crazies, having a bunch of media people say you're unfit—no one wanted to take on that kind of damaged goods.

Her cheeks ached. She stopped blowing and almost immediately Owen scrunched up his face and drew in a breath. Sophia put her hands over her ears. How was she supposed to avoid her triggers if she could never get him to stop crying? How was she supposed to give this kid what he needed? She carried Owen to his crib and sat on the floor beneath him, her head in her hands, her breath hollowed out. His crying started and stopped, started and stopped. She willed her body to stay still. He screamed. She got up, leaned into the crib, picked him up and held him roughly against her shoulder. "What do you want from me? You want me to blow air on you until I pass out?"

The trailer was as hot as an oven and Owen was crying so hard the front of his yellow sleeper was soaked through. It had turned a deeper shade of sunny that should have been happy. She set him on the couch, knelt down beside him, and unsnapped the sleeper. Owen stilled.

Sophia smiled. "Is this what you want?" She worked his arms through the sleeves then edged the sleeper out from under him. She found a dry spot on the sleeper and wiped his damp skin with it. "There. That's better, isn't it?"

They looked at each other for a minute before Owen took a breath and started to cry again. Sophia picked him up and carried him to the window. It wasn't like she couldn't be trusted. Like any open window meant he'd fall again. She unlocked it, pulled it open two inches, took a breath of the cold air. Maybe he was just too hot. Owen flailed. In that second, he nearly pitched himself out of her arms. Sophia pulled him to her chest. "Jesus, kid." There was a screen, anyway. And the trailer was only a single story. Still, she walked away from the window.

In her mother's bedroom, Sophia put in the truck video Owen usually liked, climbed onto the bed and propped him against her so he could see the TV. When Sophia was a little girl, Vicky let her sleep on the big bed when she was between boyfriends. It was Sophia's favorite time—her mother solidly there beside her, snoring lightly, the rhythm of her breath something Sophia could count on.

The video calmed Owen only long enough for a logging truck to trundle through a tunnel. After thirty more minutes of his screaming, Sophia tried to call her mother at the

Bingo place. No one answered. She tried her mother's cell—straight to voice mail.

Sophia put him in the center of the bed, left the video going so the sound of honking trucks followed her, and went to get a frozen teething ring. Probably he could roll off the bed. Or roll over and suffocate. Although she didn't think he was rolling over yet but who knew? He might have and Vicky just didn't bother to mention it. She didn't even know if he was really teething.

She got the teething ring, a bottle (even though she'd already tried that), and the diaper bag. How was she supposed to know what he wanted? Maybe there was something really wrong with him. Or wrong with her and he could sense it and that's what set him off all the time. In Sophia's freshman year of high school, they'd had a sex-ed class where they handed out condoms and told them not to get pregnant. They told them babies were a lot of work, that they had their entire futures ahead of them, that babies change everything. They had not told them a single useful thing to do if you ended up actually having a baby.

Sophia lay on the bed and put Owen on her stomach, on his back so he could still see the TV. He paused for breath when a tractor flew down the TV highway but, otherwise he just kept at it, crying so hard his whole body shook.

Maybe she should have jumped out the window after him. She imagined her body hurtling through air, the wham of concrete against her bones. If she'd done that—even if she'd lived—people wouldn't hate her so much. But she was alive. She could feel the cookie crumbs from Vicky's midnight snacks against her bare ankles.

When she couldn't stand it anymore, Sophia got up, wrapped Owen in a blanket, carried him out into the damp-chill air, and loaded him into his car seat. Outside, in the cold, she pressed her forehead into the steering wheel while Owen screamed. If he wasn't fussy because he was too hot, or hungry, or needing to be changed, she just didn't know what his problem was. He didn't seem to have a fever and his lungs certainly sounded clear.

Rose Rankin would know what to do. Sophia could picture herself handing Owen over to Rose, car seat and all, and getting the hell out of there. "Keep him," she wanted to scream. Except that Rose might.

She started the car and drove. She'd heard other babies loved the motion of the car but Owen just wailed more fiercely. "What do you want from me, Owen? What do you want?" His face, round and blank like the boy who had fathered him, was blotched red at the cheeks and forehead, pale as dead fish around his eyes and mouth. Sophia had seen a guy have a stroke at the nursing home, once. He'd gone all pale and sweating, slumped over, drooled a puddle onto the front of his shirt. She didn't think babies had strokes but really, she hardly knew anything. Maybe she should take him to the hospital. She put in a tape of songs about purple monsters and a green moose. She tried smiling over her shoulder, grabbing his foot and giving it a playful shake. He paused, mid-scream, and she swore the look he gave her was pity. Screw him, then. She ejected the tape, turned the radio to a classic rock station, and sang at the top of her lungs to the Doobie Brothers.

Owen screamed and she drove and sang until her lungs burned. Out of the crappy part of town, down toward the lake, a turn onto a pretty, tree-lined road where people from away bought houses big enough for three families. Parker, Maine. Where all the transplants came to roost. The from-aways closed their eyes when they drove past the trailer trash on Sophia's side of town.

It was stupid to come here but here she was. There were no cars in the driveway at Rose's. Sophia turned down the radio and let the car idle. Owen stopped screaming. His face was red and wet down his cheeks. Snot puddled under his nose. She climbed over the seat and wiped his face with his bib. "I'm sorry," she said. Her heart hurt. And then she sat, her head pressed against the edge of his car seat, and waited for him to start crying again.

Forty-five minutes later she woke up, her forehead sore from where she'd had it resting. Sophia shifted herself, lifted her head. Owen was sweetly asleep. She saw movement and looked up to find Rose's husband looking in. His car was parked behind hers. She waved and he waved back. She got out of the car, closed the door softly behind her, held her breath. Hank closed the gap between them. He asked, "Are you okay?"

She waved a hand toward the backseat. "He was being impossible. I thought Rose might be able to help. I'm Sophia." She could have sworn she saw Hank flinch. Probably he knew who she was and he'd warned his wife not to get involved with Sophia and her problems. He opened his mouth to say something but then closed it again. Sophia's legs felt like rubber. She wanted to lean against Hank's sturdy frame.

He said, "This isn't really a good time." Hank peered into the backseat. His shoulder brushed Sophia's. She thought for the second time in one day how nice it would be to have a husband. He'd take the baby in his arms and walk him into the house and settle him down in his crib. "He looks conked out."

Sophia laughed. "He wore himself out, I guess."

"Your mom's not with you?"

Sophia felt a flutter in her belly. Did everyone in the world know she wasn't supposed to have Owen by herself? Stupid small town. "She's at Bingo. I was supposed to stay put at her place but he was stressing me out with his crying. Although you wouldn't know it to look at him now."

Hank looked at her with what she thought might be sympathy. "I took Frederick to the zoo a couple of weeks ago and he screamed like crazy when I brought him to the aviary."

"Oh no."

"And now he's been toddling around, flapping his wings and squawking. It's driving Rose nuts."

Sophia laughed. "That's kind of funny, really."

Hank smiled. "Only if it isn't your kid." They smiled at each other for a minute and Sophia thought Hank might invite her in for coffee but he shoved his hands in his pockets and said, "Rose is sleeping."

Sophia nodded. "I don't want to wake the baby, anyway." He didn't move away and Sophia liked the feeling of his nearness. She decided to take a chance. "Listen, I don't know if you can help me..." Hank waited.

Maybe he didn't like her so much. Most people these days weren't exactly lining up to join her fan club. But what was there to lose? Not her pride. "I need a job. The nursing home filled my position while I was in the hospital."

"I'm sorry to hear that."

Sophia shrugged. "Not your fault. But I know you're a manager or something at FoodTown."

"I'm just the deli guy."

"The deli manager though, right?"

"I don't hire people."

"You could put in a word for me, maybe." When did she get this pathetic? Begging for a job at Lame-Town. "I have to show the social worker I can hold down a job. It's one of the things they say they need to see from me. Otherwise, I might not get custody of Owen. Plus, I'm getting pretty short of cash." She laughed. Hank smiled halfway.

A sharp breeze blew across the driveway. Hank said, "You're going to freeze to death standing out here. I'll move my car so you can get going." He shrugged. "I'll see what I can do about the job."

Sophia took a step forward and landed her lips on Hank's cheek, just above a spot where he must have nicked himself shaving. She let her lips linger for a second or two, pulled back and smiled. "You're a doll, Hank Rankin."

He laughed. "I'm not making any promises."

He got in his car, backed out, and waved as she backed past him. She blew him a kiss, even though she knew she shouldn't.

18

Rose heard the car back out of the driveway, and she got
to the window in time to see Sophia's high ponytail. When
Hank came in, she was standing at the top of the stairs. "Who
was that?"

He looked like he might lie. But then he smoothed down
his hair and said, "Sophia Leach."

"Why?" *She was coming to give me the baby*, Rose thought. *She
can't keep him.* Rose tried to keep her face as plain as if it were
the UPS driver.

Hank sighed. "I thought you were asleep."

"I was. Is everything okay? Is Owen okay?"

"He's fine, Rosie."

"Then why was she here?"

Hank was a little out of breath by the time he got to the
top step and Rose nearly asked him if he'd made the doctor's
appointment they'd talked about, but he said, "She was having trouble getting him to stop crying and she thought you
could help."

"Why didn't you ask her to come in? Why didn't you
wake me?"

"They were both asleep when I pulled in the driveway.
She's managing, honey."

"You don't know that." Rose tugged on her loafers. They were too tight with the thick wool socks she had on, but she couldn't think straight to change either her socks or her shoes. She grabbed her keys from the hook. "I'll just go check on them. Maybe I'll bring her some ice cream."

"Ice cream?"

"Everyone likes ice cream."

"I know you're trying to help, but do you really think this is the best idea?"

"Frederick's still napping," she said. She was gone before he could say anything else.

Vicky had told Rose where Sophia lived, although not directly. She'd told her the street and the kind of trailer and it took Rose only one pass to spot Sophia's car. She didn't hesitate. What was there to hesitate about? She was going in, mother to mother, to offer help.

Sophia answered the door with Owen in her arms. Her bottom lip was bleeding.

"What happened?" Rose said, gesturing with her finger to her own lip.

Sophia stuck out her tongue to taste the blood. In her arms, Owen thrashed his head and wailed.

Rose handed Sophia the bag containing two quarts of ice cream—one mint chocolate chip, one cherry vanilla— and then scooped Owen from her.

"Hank said you came by," Rose said. Probably, she shouldn't have just taken Owen, but Sophia peered into the bag as if nothing unusual had happened.

"Ice cream," she said.

"I was sleeping. I told him he should have woken me."

Sophia stepped into the trailer and Rose followed. The trailer was small but neat. Owen's crib sat in the doorway between the hall and kitchen. Stuffed animals lined one arm of the tan couch. On the coffee table, rattles and pacifiers sat in a pink basket that might have been from the Easter Bunny not that long ago.

Owen quieted. "Change of scenery," Rose said. And then, when he started to cry again, she laughed. "Or not. Let me watch him for a few minutes. Do you want to go take a shower or something?"

Sophia reached over and grasped Owen's foot. She didn't waggle it or tickle it, but held it like it might anchor her. "Where's your son?"

"Home with Hank." Owen took a deep breath and Rose felt the echo of it in her own body. "I really couldn't do it alone. I don't know how you're managing."

Sophia laughed. "I'm not, obviously." And then she released Owen's foot. "I'd love a shower, if you're serious. My mother has Owen most of the time but she had Bingo today and I haven't had five minutes to myself."

Rose smiled. "Take your time."

Sophia untied her hair. "Did your son cry this much?"

She wanted to know if there was something wrong with Owen, or something wrong with her mothering. Rose bounced him against her hip, then moved him to her shoulder. "Some babies are just colicky," she said. Or maybe he was unhappy. Maybe he knew he wasn't wanted.

"I'll be quick," Sophia said.

"Take your time." For the moment, Owen had stopped crying and was snugged into the space between Rose's neck and chin.

They stood in the hallway while Rose made circles on Owen's back. She felt magical until he started to wail again. She walked him to the kitchen so she'd be as far away from Sophia as possible, so that she might not hear, so that she might not hurry. Rose paced around the small square kitchen table, the two white chairs, the tied-on cushions in a cheery striped fabric. She held him and bounced him and shushed him and still he cried. "I know," Rose said. "Your life has been hard." She could walk right out the door, strap Owen into Frederick's car seat, take him home. Would Sophia even come looking for him? Or would she blow-dry her hair and slide on some lip gloss and go out to a bar?

Rose stepped one inch closer to the door, and then another. She listened to the sound of water still running. She opened the front door.

And then Sophia stood next to her, toweling off her hair, a pale blue robe wrapped around her steaming body. "I can't thank you enough." She reached for Owen, cradled him against her shoulder. "You probably have the worst headache now." Sophia smiled and kissed Owen's head.

"I'm fine," Rose said. "I'm happy to help anytime."

19

Two days later, Hank was filling the front case when he saw Sophia Leach come down the soup aisle. Hair piled on top of her head, black skirt, black blazer, white blouse, black heels two inches high. She looked like a teenager playing dress-up and Hank found her getup both charming and sad. It wasn't impossible that she had been playing dress-up just a few years ago. She was looking directly at him, smiling. "Hey," he said. "Can I help you find something?"

She licked her glaze of lipstick. "I hope so." She laughed. "How about a job?"

Hank smiled back even though his face felt like stone. He hadn't taken their conversation in his driveway seriously. She'd been asleep, and then sleepy, the side of her face red from the edge of Owen's car seat. He'd been pretty sure she wouldn't follow up on the job thing. "I did say I'd try. But I haven't had a chance yet."

She was close enough to him now that he could smell the cookie-sweet of her perfume. She asked, "Is there someone I could talk to now?"

There were two ladies peering at the sliced ham. Hank could tell by the way they were tipping their heads that they were listening, and trying to figure things out. Sophia's face had been in the papers and on TV and even though the media had mostly moved on, people in Parker were still talking about her.

Hank gave a little wave to the ladies. "Something I can help you folks with?"

They smiled, glanced at Sophia. "Were you all set, hon?"

She smiled. "I'm just waiting for a job interview."

They smiled again, bigger. "Isn't that nice? Good for you."

Did they know who she was? Or did they just think she was just a trying-too-hard teenager? Hank waved over the Graff kid working behind the counter. "I think these ladies want some ham," he said. He put a hand lightly on Sophia's back, felt the slipperiness of the blazer fabric. He had a feeling she'd bought her outfit just for today. "How about coming back tomorrow?" He hardly knew her, didn't want to get involved with her. Still, it was nice to feel needed.

Sophia leaned into him, just a little, enough so he felt the pressure of her body against his hand. "You're a doll," she said.

He walked her up front and watched her clip-clop out to her car. Hank stood there for a minute, straightening the display of free newspapers. He didn't want to be the one stuck hiring her. But she was pathetic, really. Just a kid. No one else was going to give her a job any time soon and, in the grand scheme of things, what the fuck difference did any of it make?

He went down to Jay's office, knocked once, then closed the door behind him. "Sophia Leach is looking for a job," he said.

Jay was standing by the window, a putter in his hand, bent over like he was about to put one in the hole. There was no ball in sight. "Am I supposed to know who that is?"

"She's been in the news lately. But I don't think most people will recognize her." He was proud of himself for guessing Jay's argument before he gave it, but then Jay was looking at him like he was an idiot.

Probably, he should have said *No, you wouldn't know her. She's a neighbor of ours. A friend of my wife.* Jay was staring at him with raised eyebrows. Hank shrugged. "She's a cute girl and I don't think she'll be any trouble." Jay liked to hire good-looking girls for bagging groceries.

Jay rolled his shoulders. "What'd she do?"

Hank felt his body heat into a flush. He hoped his face wasn't red. "She's the one who lost her baby out the window."

"The baby your wife caught."

"Right."

"And now you're all cozy friends?"

"She just needs a break."

"Tell her to look somewhere else."

Self-righteous prick. "You think people are going to think it's a big deal?"

"We don't need any negative publicity."

"I thought maybe it would be good for us. Show we care about someone trying to right a wrong and all that." He thought of the shiny fabric of Sophia's cheap suit, the hope in her eyes. Jay was probably right about the publicity.

"Maybe that's how you do things in the big city, but not here. Small town, Hank, my friend. People don't just let things go."

"Tell me about it." Hank wasn't from the city, just a town. Bigger than Parker but not by much. At least in terms of population. In Massachusetts, he'd never known people to dislike you because you skipped the church potluck supper when the Patriots were playing.

Jay squinted at him. "You sleeping with this chick or something?"

Hank laughed. "No. Why?"

"You seem awfully invested in us giving her a job."

Hank would have liked to throttle Jay with the putter but he took a deep breath and shoved his hands in his pockets. What did it matter if Sophia Leach got a job or not? He should be home taking care of his wife instead of advocating for a job for someone he didn't really give a fuck about.

"I'll tell you what, Hank. If you think it's the right thing to do, then do it. But if something goes wrong, I'm holding you personally responsible." Jay swung his club. "I'd say I birdied the hole, what do you think?"

*****

When Hank got home, Rose was giving Frederick a bath. Hank stood outside the closed bathroom door. He could feel the steam, could hear the splash of Frederick's hands and feet, the low murmur of Rose's voice. His heart turned over with love for both of them. He pressed his mouth to the crack. "Are you supposed to be doing that?"

"I'm sick of not doing things," she said.

"Where's your mom?"

"I sent her home. But, there's lasagna in the fridge for dinner."

He and Rose had met at a support group for insomniacs. Rose, puffy-eyed, her hair pushed back in a clip, her face shiny. He'd asked her if she wanted some tea and she shook her head and went back to picking at the skin around her nails. There was no one else even close to his age to talk to, except two guys in the corner he thought might be gang members. So, he sat down next to her, asked her when was the last time she slept. She'd shown him a picture of a blue and red quilt spread out on a dining room table. "I sew when I can't sleep," she said. "I have more blankets than one human being will ever need."

He'd told her he was always cold and she laughed and gave him the picture.

Now, he cracked the bathroom door and poked his head in. "Need a hand?"

"We're almost done," Rose said. "You can come in."

She was leaning into the tub, her sleeves wet up to her elbows, her curls frizzed in the way she hated but Hank found mussed and sexy. Hank sat on the closed toilet lid and watched her rinse Frederick's hair with a measuring cup. Frederick struck his fists against the water and squealed with joy. Rose looked tired, but less so than she had the past few days. The doctors said it could take a few weeks or a few months for her to recover physically. Mentally, emotionally— they really couldn't say. They suggested counseling and Rose said she'd think about it, but Hank knew she wouldn't.

"We should get him in swimming lessons," Hank said. She wouldn't talk about the miscarriage, wouldn't talk about what she needed from him. He felt like he'd been moved to his own planet and he didn't know how to get back.

Rose nodded. "He'll be doing this on his own before we know it."

Hank leaned over, pushed damp hair off Rose's cheek. When she didn't flinch or pull away, he slid off the toilet, knelt behind her, wrapped his arms around her, felt himself get aroused. "Do you remember the day we met?"

She shifted slightly away from him. "Of course I do."

He wished she would at least let him hold her. "Can I help you put him to bed?"

She shrugged. "I'm okay."

They'd gone out for breakfast after that first insomniacs meeting. Hank's mother's dementia had taken her somewhere else, in a way that felt sudden and terrifying to Hank. He told Rose that was why he wasn't sleeping, because he couldn't stop thinking of all the things he needed to remember for his mother. Rose had listened with such complete understanding that he couldn't help but love her.

The first morning after they had sex at Rose's apartment, Hank slept until noon, anchored between Rose's air-dried sheets and the blue and red quilt, and woke to the smell of coffee and pancakes. He liked that she didn't overcomplicate things. She'd never been to Europe, didn't do yoga, had no desire to have them join a couples' book club. She had real cream, real sugar, and actual maple syrup. The pancakes weren't banana, or chocolate chip, or multigrain. He ate five pancakes, drank three cups of coffee-flavored coffee, and told her it was the best meal he'd ever eaten. She'd blushed and wiped crumbs from the counter.

Now, in the steam-softened bathroom, Rose reached for a towel.

Hank handed her one. "Let me put him to bed."

She wrapped the towel around Frederick and hugged him to her chest. "I'm all right," she said.

"The doctor said you shouldn't be lifting—"

"I do it all day." And with that she lifted Frederick out of the tub and carried him through the door. Frederick tucked his head against her shoulder.

"Why won't you let me help you?" He couldn't keep the edge of frustration out of his voice.

Her eyes filled with tears. "I just need to keep going," she said.

He closed the gap between them, put his arms around her so that towel-clad Frederick was wedged between them. "It's my loss, too."

She lowered her voice to a near-whisper. "It didn't really matter to you if we had another baby or not."

He wanted to reel back, pull away. But he forced himself to stay still, to not get angry. It was true that he'd been happy with Frederick, but that didn't mean he didn't care they'd lost a baby. "It matters."

She stared at him for a long moment before nodding. "If you say so." And then she staggered out the door, the weight of Frederick too much for her. Hank should have insisted on taking him, but what was he supposed to do? Yank him out of her arms? He sat on the edge of the tub, listening to her footsteps on the stairs, feeling useless.

20

Rose's car was a four-year old minivan they'd bought used and with the hope they'd have at least one more baby after Frederick.

She was almost to Hannaford when the car shimmied, and then it shook, and then it bucked like a horse trying to rid itself of a rider. Rose pulled in along the muddy side of the road and listened to the tick of the cooling engine. In the back, Frederick laughed.

"I'm glad someone's having a good day," Rose said, turning around to get a better look at him. He clapped, which was something new he'd started.

Rose pulled the release, got out, went around to the front of the car, and lifted the hood. Trying to fix her car was probably another thing she shouldn't be doing.

She stood with her arms braced against the car, breathing, waiting. Years ago, back when they were first dating, Hank had shown her how to change her oil. He'd stood next to her, gazing into her old Jeep, and shown her what was what. He'd gone on to show her how to change a flat tire. Later that same day he showed her how to open a bottle of champagne. She was so happy back then.

They'd learned to be parents together. On the nights Frederick cried all night, they took turns walking him up and down the hall so the other could sleep for two hours at a time. The first time they put him in a car seat and stumbled over how to do the straps, Rose stayed in the car with Frederick while Hank went in and Googled a how-to video. The first time he got a rash, the time he ate a piece of notebook paper, his fear of Santa Claus.

Rose put her hands on the still-warm engine and closed her eyes. What if catching Owen Leach really had been a miracle? What if she had miraculous hands? What if, just by touching the car, she could fix it? She stood perfectly still, willing the power of her hands to flow into the car. She could still hear Frederick clapping.

Nothing happened. She should have known it wouldn't work—in the hospital, she'd put her hands on her womb, but it didn't save her baby.

If anyone saw her with her hands on her car, thinking she was Jesus raising Lazarus from the dead—if anyone told Hank—she'd never hear the end of what a fool she'd made of herself and him by extension. She needed to get herself together.

She heard a car crunch by on gravelly road and she opened her eyes. She'd tell whoever it was that she was fine, that she had triple A, that she'd already called for help.

The driver rolled down the passenger-side window. "You need help?"

Rose shook her head.

"Hey!" He was out of his car now, a big man, taller than she was by a foot, wide across the shoulders, wearing the kind of plaid jacket it seemed everyone around here wore. "You're Rose, aren't you? I seen you in the papers."

Her heart rolled but she shook his beefy outstretched hand. Was he going to be like the woman in the white pants—someone who thought she could perform a miracle on an as-needed basis? Because she obviously couldn't, and she didn't feel like talking about it. "I was just about to call triple A," she said. She wondered about the last time she'd charged her cell phone.

The man with the plaid jacket leaned in toward the engine. "It looks like your belt slipped off. Want me to try and fix it for you?"

Rose shook her head. He might know what he was doing, but he might not. There were plenty of not-working cars on lawns around Parker. This guy might just be a tinkerer. She said, "We pay enough for roadside assistance." As soon as she said it, she regretted it. She and Hank had lived in Maine for years but still she sometimes forgot how much people around here hated talking about money. "Thank you, though."

He tapped his hand to his head in a way Rose thought was meant as a kind of salute. She smiled back. "Really. Thank you," she said to his back as he headed to his car.

Inside her car, she found she had enough juice in her cell to call for help. The woman with the honey voice said someone would be by within the hour. Rose brought Frederick up front with her, reclined her seat all the way back, and together they watched as a few sugary snowflakes landed on the windshield.

"Wow," Frederick said.

Rose laughed. "Yeah, baby. Wow. It's too early for snow." She hadn't even decided what to dress him as for Halloween. "Do you want to be a monkey?"

Frederick shook his head. "You could carry a banana."

He shrugged. "'kay."

She might not be a miracle-worker-on-demand but she was a good mother, a dependable wife. Even though it was chilly in the car, she was glad for the next hour to be with Frederick, without laundry to do or a meal to make. Her feet had dampened through her weather-inappropriate loafers and she could feel the cold starting to numb her toes. She checked Frederick's hands. "Are you warm enough?"

He gripped her fingers and she brought his hands to her mouth, kissed them all over. He giggled, tried to pull away. She mimed eating his fingers and he laughed harder. "You are a silly boy," she said. He sighed and leaned back into her. His fingers were cool but not cold. Rose pulled out the blanket from the backseat and spread it over them, just in case. She took in a breath, then another, felt her chest expand, felt her muscles relax.

*****

She had the tow truck driver leave her off at the garage because it was only a short walk from there to FoodTown.

There was a line of people at the deli counter but Rose didn't see Hank. "Is he out back?"

The kid with the bad skin shrugged as he weighed some-one's Provolone. "He's in with Jay doing an interview."

"Every time I come in, he's off doing something." Rose tried to say this like it didn't matter but she needed a ride home. There were no cabs, no buses, no public transportation of any kind in Parker. Unless you counted hitchhiking.

The kid shrugged again. He was the Graff's boy, as tall as his father with his mother's terrible sallow skin, bloomed all over with pink pimples. "They're interviewing that lady who threw the baby." The kid blushed so that his skin pinked all over.

"Sophia?"

The Graff kid nodded.

Why hadn't Hank told her she was coming in? Rose asked for a half pound of turkey breast and waited while the kid weighed it, wrapped it. She kissed Frederick's head. "I guess Daddy's busy," she said.

The kid was watching her. "Do you want me to tell him you're here?"

Rose shook her head. She felt foolish, intrusive, like one of those wives who brings coffee and donuts just to check up on her husband and the cute secretary. At the checkout, she paid for her deli meat, then went outside and called her mother. Rose was grateful when Camilla said she'd be right over, grateful that she'd soon be nestled in her white Honda.

When Camilla arrived, she seemed frazzled. "Were you in the middle of something, Ma?" Probably polishing the silver or dusting the silk flower arrangements she kept above her kitchen cabinets.

"I'm always happy to help you, honey. You could have called me for a ride."

Rose rested her head against the seat. "It's cold in here."

Camilla cranked up the heat and Rose relaxed into the warm breeze. "Are you feeling okay?"

"Fine."

"You don't look fine."

"Thanks, Ma." Rose rummaged through Frederick's diaper bag. She'd forgotten diapers and she could smell him from here. They'd be home soon. She cracked her window an inch.

Camilla said, "I thought you said you were cold." Rose rolled up her window. "I was."

"You can leave it open. I'm fine with the air. I'm just worried about you. Are you having hot flashes?"

"Not that I know of."

Her mother sniffed the air. In a sing-song voice, she called out, "Someone did a poop-ie."

Frederick laughed. "I'll change him when we get home," Rose said.

"Of course you will, honey."

After a pause, Camilla said, "Your sister really would have been a great help to you if you'd let her stay."

"She has enough to worry about." Cloris, with her near-mansion-sized house, two near-perfect kids, a husband who insisted on three square meals a day. Cloris with her running and her calorie-counting and the book she'd sent Rose: *Your Only Child Gets Social!*

When Rose got home, she called Margo. "Why do you think Hank didn't tell me he was interviewing Sophia Leach?"

Margo barked a laugh. "You think she's gonna throw customers out the window?" Rose could hear the whir of Margo's sewing machine.

Rose laughed. "I'd pay to see that."

"How are you, Rosie? I came by the other day with a casserole, but Hank said you were sleeping."

"I'm okay."

"Really?"

"I'm okay enough. I'll be back to work soon."

"Whenever you're ready. I've got dresses piled to my eyeballs."

The idea of sitting in Margo's trailer with a dress on her lap, stitching a hem and talking about the weather or Thanksgiving pies, or whatever, sounded like heaven. "Soon," Rose said. "I promise."

21

Sophia's friends never really came by anymore. But on Thursday night she squinted out the window to see Dene getting out of her rusty pickup. Sophia threw open the door. "What the fuck are you doing here?"

Dene laughed, held up a six pack of beer in one hand, a bottle of Captain's in the other. "Isn't it your birthday?"

Tears filled Sophia's eyes. Vicky hadn't remembered, or hadn't bothered to acknowledge it if she had. Sophia had gone down to the store and bought herself one of those miniature chocolate cakes, put a candle on it, sang to herself, and then ate the whole damn thing while feeling like an absolute loser. But now she grinned at Dene. "Get your ass in here before someone sees you!"

Dene came in and they hugged and she started to pull off her rubber boots when Sophia said, "Maybe we shouldn't drink all this here." She was thinking of the pimply social worker and her note-taking. Beer cans, the smell of old rum, ashes from their cigarettes.

Dene squinted. "Mark's at my place, sleeping off last night. He'll be in the worst mood if we wake him."

"We could go to the park," Sophia said.

"It's thirty degrees out."

"Right."

"Your mother's?"

"She's got the baby."

Dene frowned like she'd completely forgotten about the existence of Owen.

Sophia dug around in her purse. She was feeling exactly the way she'd felt skipping school or stealing from the drug store. The lift-off of elation, the prickle of fear and not-fear, knowing you were smarter than everyone else who was playing it straight. She held up the key she was looking for. "Gail forgot to ask for my key back when she canned me."

Dene made a face like she'd swallowed a bug. "You want to go drinking at the old folks' place?"

"They have a big activity room."

"Where they play Bingo?"

"There's a couch, too. And a door that closes and locks."

"Don't they have night janitors and stuff?"

"Not this late. And the nurses won't come down that way unless they're looking for someone." Sophia hoped that was true. If she got caught, she'd have to plead temporary insanity.

Dene shrugged. "Lead the way, birthday girl."

*****

The bottle of rum was more than halfway gone when Sophia started telling Dene how last year, she'd hung snowflakes in here. "I used fishing line and paperclips that I stuck into the drop ceiling. It looked so pretty." Sophia waved her arms in the air.

Dene said, "Great way to make all the old folks confused." She stood and spun, arms outstretched. "Look, Mabel, it's snowing—indoors!"

They leaned into each other, laughing. Dene snorted. "Shh," Sophia said. "We don't need miss-pole-up-her-ass-charge-nurse to come down here and find us." She sighed. "I miss working here." Dene passed her back the bottle of rum and she drank until she felt a flood in her stomach. "I miss how much everyone liked me."

"Or pretended to like you."

"That's not nice."

Dene shrugged. "Life isn't nice."

"Tell me about it." Sophia put her head back on the couch where countless white-haired heads had been. She thought about wrinkled faces, lives gone past their expiration date. Managing to make it to eighty and feeling pretty good about the scale of regrets in your life. She said, "I think I'm always going to have to pay for what I did to Owen."

"We're too young to have kids," Dene said. "Remember how Rebecca Lawrence got knocked up in junior year?"

"Whatever happened to her?"

Dene shrugged. "I thought she gave the kid away but then she dropped out anyway. Who knows? Probably she couldn't handle the guilt or whatever."

"Exactly," Sophia said.

Dene popped the top on a can of beer. "She should have just had an abortion. I mean, why go through all that?" She looked at Sophia. "Sorry. I didn't mean that."

Sophia shook her head. "I'm glad I had Owen."

"Seriously?"

Sophia felt the prickle of tears but she'd be damned if she started blubbering away in the Merry Pines Activity Room on her twentieth birthday. She wiped her hand across her face. "He's awesome. He's so sweet. And he's perfect and small and good. And someday he'll grow up and maybe he'll be the kind of son who won't put me in one of these places. Maybe he'll build me a little room above the garage and his wife will bring me a covered plate of pot roast on Sundays." Dene drank from the rum bottle and smiled at Sophia.

"Or, maybe he'll dangle you out the window."

"Geez, Dene."

Dene shrugged. "Sorry."

When they were playing beer-pong, Dene dared her to call Hank. They were sitting on the floor, and Dene had pulled out Sophia's phone. "You already have him programmed in!"

"Only because I work for him now."

Dene laughed. "I'll bet."

Sophia snatched her phone back. No way was she going to call Hank.

But then, she was throwing up in the bushes in front of Merry Pines and Dene was running down the street, hooting. At some point, she staggered to her trailer and called Hank. Why had she called Hank? Because she didn't want to be alone, and he was the nicest and most responsible person she knew at the moment. She'd called her mother but Vicky hadn't answered. Naturally.

Now, Sophia closed her eyes and let Hank tuck her hair behind her ears. "Why are you even here?" She'd called him, but why would he come?

"You sounded awful."

"I *feel* awful."

Hank pressed a glass of cool water to her lips and she sipped it, then felt an instant wave of sickness. Sophia closed her eyes.

"You should get it out of you if you need to be sick," he said.

His voice was so calm and soothing Sophia leaned into him and felt better. "But I don't want to."

"You'll feel better if you get it up." If she ever had a husband, she'd want someone nice like Hank.

"I'm not sick, you know. I mean, in the head. I've been 'assessed' in treatment. Borderline Personality Disorder, they say. Such bullshit."

"You don't have to listen to everything they say."

She smiled. "You believe I tripped. And, it's my birthday," she said. What if someone had seen her, throwing up in the bushes or staggering home? Someone might have called the social worker who might be getting in her tiny bright blue car and fastening her seatbelt right now.

"Happy birthday," he said.

She let him lead her to the bathroom and hold the hair off her face. He rubbed her back, handed her a damp washcloth when she was finished emptying her stomach. She thought of her vomit in the bushes at Merry Pines and wondered if they'd trace it back to her, press charges for vandalism. "Is it supposed to rain?"

"Get some sleep," Hank said. He led her back to the couch and Sophia closed her eyes and let the room twirl.

She tucked the couch pillow in next to her stomach. She'd loved being pregnant—the fullness of her body, the sensation of being a home for another living thing. If the baby was a girl, she was going to name her Simplicity. Some of her friends, when she played tug-of-war with their parents' dogs, said *You're going to make a great mother.* And she'd put her hands on her stomach and beamed at them.

She'd fucked it up pretty much from the beginning. First, she hadn't even guessed she was pregnant until three months in when she started to gain weight around her middle and she still hadn't gotten a period. But even then, she kept going out with her friends, dancing and drinking. By her fifth month she looked either pregnant or like she had a huge tumor and she finally went to a doctor.

She rolled onto her back and put her hands on her belly. If she could do it over again, she would start thinking about the baby seriously right from the beginning. She'd eat spinach and drink water and take vitamins if she could steal the right ones from CVS. She'd buy or borrow a baby name book and highlight in yellow all the possibilities.

She fell into a drunken sleep and dreamt she was an old woman in a butter-colored nightgown, gargling in the bathroom when Owen walked up behind her. In the mirror he was as tall as she was, but with the same infant face he had now. He pushed his knee into her back until she walked to the window. She laughed, thinking he was teasing her. She wasn't afraid until she realized the window was open. And then he pushed her forward, grabbed her feet, and shook her until her nightgown floated over her head and her entire world turned yellow.

22

The Monday Mass was just ending when Rose got to the church. She made the sign of the cross as Father Rob gave the final blessing and then she tucked herself into a pew while he stood in the open doorway and wished each of the old ladies a wonderful day. They all loved him, taking his smooth fingers in their wrinkled hands, laughing when he kissed them on their cheeks, touching their newly permed hair and asking him to dinner one of these nights. They took their time, and Rose felt a growing anxiety. The church was cold and she crossed her arms and shivered.

Finally, Father Rob finished his goodbyes and slid into the pew beside her. He was young, not more than thirty, without even the hint of gray around his temples. "Where's the little one this morning?"

Rose smiled. Father Rob loved Frederick and Frederick, for some reason, was usually on his best behavior in the church playroom. "With my mother."

"You've had quite a couple of months, I hear."

Rose nodded. She'd been avoiding church mostly because she couldn't stand everyone's curiosity and/or sympathy. Now, even though she'd rehearsed what she wanted to say, she felt the words caught up in her stomach. She thought of fish in a net and this made her close her eyes with nausea.

Father Rob touched the back of her hand. "Are you all right, Rose?"

"Just a little tired, Father."

They sat in silence, listening to the tick of the building settling back into itself. Finally, Rose took a breath. "I came to ask you if you think what I did was a miracle." *Say yes. Say yes say yes say yes.* She hadn't seen Father Rob since the Saturday afternoon she and Hank had attended Mass before their anniversary dinner. Before she caught Owen Leach. But she knew Father read the paper, watched the news, heard the gossip from his parishioners.

He looked at her, steady and serious, for what seemed like a very long time. "Is that what you think?"

Hot irritation crept across Rose's skin. She wasn't in the mood to play therapy games. "For years and years, we tried to have Frederick." She stopped. She'd planned to mention the dead babies, the emergency hysterectomy, but she found she couldn't. She was too on the verge of the kind of grief it was hard to come back from.

Father Rob smiled. "And now you have him."

Rose swallowed and nodded. "But we want more." It was wrong to lie to a priest. What she should have said was that she wanted more. Hank would go along with what she wanted. It wasn't a full untruth.

"You know that God will provide as He sees fit."

That was what she'd been told in Sunday school and from her parents, her aunts, the parishioners her mother invited over for coffee after Mass. "But maybe He isn't going to go the traditional route. Especially since..." She made a gesture toward her stomach and left it at that. Other women seemed to find it cathartic to talk about their operations but Rose found it humiliating. She took a breath to steady herself. "I think He sent Owen to me. People have been saying it was a miracle."

Father Rob frowned and she hated him. "Miracles are very complicated, Rose. It can take years—decades—to prove a miracle."

Rose stood, her hands gripping the top of the pew in front of them, the cut-through bits of her cuticle on display for anyone who wanted to see what a mess she was. "I'm not asking to be sainted. What else could it be but a miracle? That baby could have landed anywhere. But I caught him."

"It's powerful evidence, for sure."

He was placating her. Like she was one of the third graders asking why God wanted all the animals in pairs. "I don't need it to be documented by the Church. I don't need accolades. I just want you to talk to Hank. Tell him it was meant to be." She was breathless. Hank would hate the priest's intrusion but he might be convinced by it anyway. "Tell him you believe I need to save this baby."

"You already saved him."

"I caught him. And now I can't just let him go back to a woman who threw him out a window." An image of Sophia weighing apples at the FoodTown checkout floated into Rose's mind and she had to grit her teeth against it. Rose folded her arms across her stomach. "The baby's mother is not a good woman, Father."

The priest looked at her with alarm and pity. "That isn't for us to judge, Rose."

"Of course it is. We judge all the time. We take children away from unfit mothers because it's the right thing to do. The holy thing to do." The more she talked, the more certain she became. She could see that Father Rob was about to say something she wasn't going to like.

She took the long way out of the pew so that she wouldn't have to climb over his cassock. She needed him to talk to Hank, not tell her to show mercy to sinners or judge not lest she be judged.

He stood, tried to follow her, but she was fast, and he was hindered by his billowy white vestments. "I'd like to talk about this more," he said.

Over her shoulder, she thanked him, said she'd be in touch, that she'd make sure Hank came to Mass with her this week, maybe they could talk then? And then, she hurried across the parking lot to her car, feeling Father Rob's sinless eyes on her back.

23

Sophia sat in front of the TV and blew up red and purple balloons. Her favorite colors because they reminded her of royalty. No one told her most people got their balloons filled with helium. Sophia only found out about it when she called Vicky to complain about her aching cheeks and near-exploding head and Vicky laughed at her. Also, no one told her that if she blew them up too early the balloons would all be limp by the time of the party, which was how come she ended up throwing most of them away.

Sophia bought a sheet cake with blue waves and a guy on a surfboard because it was on the day-old case and it's not like Owen would remember or care. In the center of the cake, she'd had them write "Happy 6 Months!" She'd bought a big 6 candle to go with it and she'd stolen the packages of balloons, along with red paper napkins, purple paper plates, and some heavy-duty yellow plastic forks from the Hannaford because she wasn't going to steal from FoodTown when she'd just started working there. Hannaford had been out of the red and purple forks and she didn't want ordinary white. Although, looking down at the table now, white might have looked clean and would have probably been a better choice than yellow which reminded her of bad teeth.

Vicky was sprawled on the couch in a sparkly black sweatshirt and black shorts with her nylon-covered veiny legs flopped over the end. Owen was propped up against the couch, slapping at Vicky's dangling feet.

"Not sure why you couldn't wait until he was a year old to have a shindig," Vicky said.

"You never even had a regular birthday party for me," Sophia said.

Sophia had managed to get Owen a present—a pop-up book she'd slid under her shirt while the guy at the bookstore was helping another customer. She'd smiled and thanked him for his time, said she'd be back the next day when she'd made up her mind. He was so distracted by the other customer that he'd barely even nodded at her.

She'd borrowed the coffee pot from her mother's hair salon. From the kitchen she called out, "How much of the coffee powder am I supposed to put in here?"

Vicky didn't move from her spot on the couch. "Read the directions on the can. I think it's a tablespoon per eight ounces. Suddenly you're Suzy Homemaker?"

There were ten people total coming—her, Hank, Rose, Frederick, Owen, Sophia's best-friend Dene, the twins Erin and Angel, and Angel's boyfriend Buzz. Plus Vicky in case the social worker stopped by. The rest of her friends said they weren't into kids' birthday parties. They'd suggested playing a drunken version of Pin-the-Tail-on-the-Donkey. Sophia didn't think that would make the impression she was going for.

"I think this is a dumb idea," Vicky said. "If I didn't say that already."

"It's a brilliant idea." Wasn't this the kind of thing people did? You love your kid so you celebrate him by having people over as proof that you aren't a complete fuck-up.

Sophia borrowed the boom box and easy-listening CDs from the salon, too. She came out of the kitchen and pressed play. "Bridge over Troubled Water" started right up. Vicky rolled onto her side and lit a cigarette. "That about sums it up," she said.

Sophia scooped Owen onto her hip and stuck her tongue out at her mother. She'd dressed him in his jean-looking pants and a knit blue and green striped sweater she'd found at the Goodwill. She was wearing jeans and a same-shade blue sweater because she liked how it made her and Owen look like they belonged together.

The day she'd given birth, her friends who said they'd drive her—Erin and Angel, the twins with the dolphin tattoos on their butt cheeks—were out drinking with some guys they'd met the night before. Vicky was playing Bingo. When her water broke, Sophia called a cab. The driver—from Somalia, young, skin the color of burnt toast, heavily-accented—was nice enough to stay with her while they got her into a wheelchair. She'd glanced over her shoulder and he waved. She never even paid him.

The nurses and doctors helped her into a bed and all she could feel was hurt—all over, in ways no one had ever told her. "Is there someone we can call for you?" A red-headed nurse, a thick-middled doctor, an old-lady nurse all asked her. Vicky was probably still waiting for B6 so she could win the coverall. She wasn't coming. The nurses nodded with sympathy while Sophia brought Owen into the world all by herself.

And then, after they cut the cord, after they washed him up and whisked him away—where were they taking him? — they'd let that stupid social worker in. One of those old maids with the hippy skirts and socks under sandals. Smiling, sitting on the edge of Sophia's bed without asking if she minded. Smelling like fruited gum and moth balls. And then she said, "Single motherhood can be very difficult."

Sophia had told her to go fuck herself.

And now she'd nearly killed him by dropping him out the window. This little person who would someday be someone who would understand her, love her, tell her not to date guys who weren't good enough for her.

She'd make it up to him, starting right now. She kissed his little head, tucked him on the couch next to Vicky, and went into the kitchen to cut carrot sticks into skinny pieces. When the sour cream was mixed with the powdery ranch mix and the coffee was dripping down into the pot the way it was supposed to, Rose and Hank showed up with a box covered in shiny silver paper with neon yellow happy faces all over it. Hank shook Sophia's hand, formally, politely, like they were here for a bank meeting about a loan or something. He talked to her sometimes at work, but mostly just about the weather or how her car was running. He'd never mentioned the night she puked up her guts. Sophia took in his styled hair and his filed nails and thought that everything about him seemed safe.

The face-box gave Sophia the creeps, but Owen loved it, putting his mouth up against the smiles and making kissing noises. Frederick went right over to the balloons and starting squeezing the half-life out of them. Sophia wished her friends would hurry up and get here. She should have told them the party was at one instead of two.

After some small talk about the leaves turning and how it seems sooner ever year, Rose said "He's really doing well, isn't he?"

Sophia looked away, pretended she had a thread loose on her sweater so that she wouldn't start bawling her eyes out. Finally, she said, "The doctors say he's doing everything he should be doing at this point."

Rose smiled. "You must be relieved."

Did Rose think she *wouldn't* be relieved? That she'd want her son to have lasting damage? What kind of sicko would want that? Sophia bent and kissed his perfect little head. The kind who throws him out a window in the first place, obviously.

No one was eating the carrot sticks or dip. The music was too loud for conversation and when Sophia got up to turn it down, she let her hand brush against Hank. He was sitting on the reclining chair and when her fingers touched his thigh, he bolted upright like he'd been electrocuted. She wanted to tell him to relax, that she wasn't going to climb onto his lap or anything. She smiled at the room. Rose smiled back.

Hank was wearing a green plaid shirt that matched Rose's button-down sweater, another announcement of who belonged with who. Rose perched on the very edge of the couch now that Vicky was finally sitting up. But Vicky was smoking another cigarette and Rose had her face turned away. Owen sat on the floor, patting his face-covered box while Frederick opened and closed the pop-up book that was supposed to be Owen's. Owen had hardly even looked at it and Sophia didn't have anything else. Maybe tomorrow she'd try to get downtown to lift a stuffed animal. She wanted him to have something to keep, so that when he was thirty or forty, she could pull it down off a shelf and say, "You were only six months old when I gave you this but you played with it for years." Maybe she'd pass it on to Owen's kids someday. Her grandkids. It was crazy to think of but it made her shivery with pleasure.

Sophia knelt on the floor in front of Owen. "You're supposed to open this," she said. She peeled back a corner of the paper. "See?" Owen swatted her hand. Sophia kissed his fingers as though this was all just fun. Fun, fun, fun. She took his hand and pushed off more of the paper. Owen scrunched up his face. Sophia felt a trickle of sweat run between her breasts and she wished she'd thought to turn down the trailer's heat. She said, "No, baby, no crying."

"He's fine," Rose said. "He really likes the box."

"But the box isn't the point." Sophia looked at Hank to see if he'd back her up but he was staring at the blank TV. "Do you want me to see if there's a game on?" Sophia asked.

He smiled. "That would be great."

Rose frowned and for a second Sophia wasn't sure if she should switch on the game or not. What the hell, men always liked her better than other women anyway. Sophia flicked on the TV and tossed the remote to Hank. "I bought stuff to make sandwiches," she said. She wasn't sure if she should wait for everyone else but she'd definitely hit a dead-end with conversation.

"Can I help you with something?" Rose was already half-standing.

Sophia shook her head. She didn't want Rose to see what a mess she'd made in the kitchen, especially compared to the hospital-clean of Rose's house.

Rose sat back down and let Owen grab her finger. "He's got quite a grip."

"Especially when he's got a hold of your hair," Vicky said.

Rose grinned up at her like she was both brilliant and hilarious. "That's always the worst."

Mother-to-mother, that's what it was. Sophia felt like she might be sick. In the kitchen she laid out the bread on a platter, the ham and turkey on another dish. She should have bought cheese. The good deli kind with the slices so thin you could see right through them.

She found a package of American cheese singles in the fridge and set those out with the cold cuts. Mustard, mayo, relish, ketchup. She tried to call Angel but it went straight to voicemail. Sophia opened the top of the ketchup and scraped off the dried-on bits. At the last minute, she decided to mix the mayo with some jarred bacon bits—fancy it up a little.

Rose popped her wildly curly head into the kitchen. "Sure you don't need a hand?"

Sophia had an image of Rose literally lopping off a hand. The blood, the stump. "I'm all set," Sophia said.

It took two trips to get everything on the coffee table. "Help yourselves," she said. No one except Frederick moved. He lurched over, grabbed a plastic-wrapped slice of cheese, and shoved the entire thing in his mouth. Rose pulled it out, unwrapped it, and handed it back to him. "Small bites," she said.

"I should have taken the plastic off." Sophia started unwrapping the slices, tucking the wrappers in the back pocket of her jeans.

Rose shrugged. "Kids are fast."

Never in her life did she imagine herself trying so hard to be domestic. Trying and failing. Sophia could feel Hank watching her and she wanted to turn around and smile at him but she didn't dare. He was probably thinking that Rose would never serve plastic-wrapped cheese. Or maybe he was wondering what kind of idiot he'd hired. Rose seemed like the type who would have made a real lunch, even for a kid's party. A big ham with the pineapple and cherries stuck all over it or those chicken breasts that turned out to be filled with ham and cheese when you cut them open. Side dishes like creamed spinach and roasted cauliflower. A homemade cake for dessert. Probably she'd rent one of those bouncy houses. Even though Owen was way too little for that.

Rose picked up a slice of cheese, tore it in half and ate it. "I forget how good regular American cheese can be."

Sophia felt relief like a bottle of beer through her veins. "It's good, right?" She heard a car and felt hope like a fountain in her heart that it was her friends, but the car only slowed and kept going.

Rose nodded. "Hank, do you want me to make you a sandwich?"

He shook his head. "I ate a huge breakfast."

Sophia said, "How about some coffee? We should at least have a piece of cake."

To Rose, Vicky said, "Do you color your hair?"

In the kitchen, Sophia leaned against the counter and wished for them all to go away. Her friends had clearly bailed on her. Once she was alone, she could feed Owen a smushed up piece of cake and sing to him and swear to him they were going to be okay. Until then, she had to fake it. She had to at least pretend she could do this. That she could not and would not be merely the crazy person who threw her baby out a window.

She took the plastic cover off the cake and carried it out to the living room, holding it in front of Rose, then Hank, then Vicky so they could see how pretty it was.

"It's a cake," Vicky said.

Sophia set it on the coffee table. "Thanks, Ma."

"It's very nice," Rose said. "You did a great job picking it out. Does Owen like the water?"

"I guess. I mean, I don't know. He's never seen the ocean. Not yet, anyway. But who doesn't love the beach?" Sophia wanted to smash surfer dude and his board right into Rose's pleasant face.

She cut pieces and handed them around. Everyone took a piece and started right in eating which made Sophia happier than it should have. Rose even let Frederick have a small corner piece. And then she dabbed frosting on her pinky and held it to Owen's lips. His little tongue darted out and in. And then he smiled.

Sophia wanted to cry. Why hadn't she thought of the frosting-on-the-pinky thing?

Sophia carried the cake knife into the kitchen. Because you couldn't leave knives hanging around little boys. They might hack themselves or each other into little pieces. And then she might throw them out the window. Whole or in pieces. You couldn't trust Sophia Leach. She ran the knife under the hottest water she could get, watching the bright blue frosting slide off and melt into her drain. She tried to fight back the tears but they came anyway, hot down her cheeks, probably ruining her double-coat of mascara. Her whole body ached with the effort of trying too hard to make this party fun. Carefully, she dried the knife with a paper towel, then put it in the way back of the drawer. She was going to have to remember to get those baby safety locks. She dried her face on a paper towel and thought about how she was going to have to be better at a lot of things.

24

Margo said, "Do you really think she'll just give up her baby?"

They had no sewing jobs this week so they were at Margo's trailer, making cupcakes decorated to look like monsters to give out for Halloween. Last week, Rose and Margo had finished embroidering the new uniforms for the Parker Girls' Soccer team and this week everyone in town was talking about what was obvious as soon as the girls put them on. Right across their budding chests, in blue letters on white cotton: PGS. Mothers had been calling Margo to say kids oinked at the girls at school. "We should have spelled out Soccer," Rose said. Frederick was playing on the kitchen floor with a spoon. He threw it against the cabinet and wailed.

Margo shrugged. "You're changing the subject."

She was going to have to redo the shirts for free, even though Rose thought that wasn't fair. "They were ordered that way. The town should pay for at least half." Rose bent down, picked up the spoon, handed it back to Frederick.

"My reputation is my business," Margo said. "But I think they're going to split the difference." Margo licked frosting off her fingers. "I thought we were talking about Owen."

Frederick threw the spoon again and, when Rose ignored him, he screamed. Rose picked it up and handed it to him again. "This is the last time." She stirred the flour and baking soda into the butter and sugar. "Sophia isn't going to be able to get her act together. And Hank and I have always wanted more kids." The more she said it, the more she believed it.

Frederick threw the spoon. Rose knelt in front of him, her face inches from his. "I told you not to do that." She held the spoon aloft. Frederick wailed.

"How about a cookie?" Margo got a Fig Newton out of her cabinet and handed Frederick two.

Annoyed, Rose pried the cookies out of Frederick's hands. "No way."

Frederick wailed. She should just let him cry. She should not give in to the demands of a two-year-old. She handed him back the broken cookies. Gleefully, he stuffed them both in his mouth. She watched him chew, prayed he wouldn't choke, went through the steps for the Heimlich just in case.

Margo lined the muffin tins with orange cupcake wrappers. "So, you have an idea for getting Sophia on board with you adopting Owen?"

Rose was a better mother than Sophia. Unbidden, she heard the slap-thud of Frederick's palm against the window that day, the shatter of glass, his high, panicked cry followed by hers.

"She's getting there," Rose said. Another lie. Lies piling up like sequins on a dress, turning one thing into another, obscuring, obfuscating. Sophia still thought she could get her act together, but it was only a matter of time before she realized it was hopeless.

Rose ran her thumb along the edge of the bowl and licked the chocolate batter off it. The cupcakes were going to be fantastic—shaggy green frosting, chocolate candy eyes, red licorice sliced for a mouth, black licorice antennae. They'd bag them up individually because around Parker you could give out homemade goodies without people thinking you'd shoved a razor blade in there somewhere.

Frederick finished his Newtons and started to yell: "More, more, more, more."

"New word?" Margo asked.

Rose bit down on her back molars so hard she felt the left one crack. "I guess so."

Sophia planned to buy Owen a store-bought outfit for Halloween, but she hadn't even decided which one. When Rose suggested a bumblebee or peapod, Sophia shrugged and said she'd see.

Would Vicky even bother to take Owen out Trick-or-Treating? Rose had finished most of Frederick's monkey costume last night and it was perfect. "I think I'm going to let him carry a real banana," she said. Maybe she should make Owen a costume, too. The peapod one wouldn't take much other than green felt and a few stitches.

"Sounds messy." Margo scooped batter into the cupcake liners. "Sophia's mother has custody of the kid, right?" She slid the first batch into the oven.

Rose started on the frosting. Butter, confectioners' sugar, vanilla, milk, three drops of green food coloring, then four. It needed to be dark green. "The system is so screwed up. Sophia says she worries her mother is worse with the baby than she ever was."

Margo laughed. "That's pretty bad."

Rose grimaced. "According to Sophia, the baby cramps Vicky's lifestyle. But I guess there's no other family. I don't think she's abusing him or anything. I think she just doesn't care about him."

"Then why agree to take him at all?"

Margo's questions made her want to smash a cupcake against the wall. She gripped her cupcake a little tighter and said, "She gets money for being a foster parent, doesn't she?" Frederick was still scream-chanting. Rose wet a clean washcloth, twisted it, and handed it to him. "He's teething," she said to Margo. Frederick threw the washcloth and it slapped against Rose's leg.

Margo laughed. "Guess he didn't want that." And then, "I don't know, Rosie. It seems like there would be easier ways to get money if that's the only reason."

Rose bit back what she wanted to say about encouraging Frederick's bad behavior by laughing at him. Instead, she said, "Maybe because of all the media attention. She didn't want to look bad. I don't know. It doesn't matter why." Rose filled the piping bag with frosting while Margo sliced the red licorice in half—unhesitating, confident. That was the way Margo was with things. She measured a hem and then took to it with the scissors. She stitched in a zipper with the most precise running stitch Rose had ever seen. Rose could use a little of that sureness now.

Margo finished the red licorice and moved on to the black. "I just don't want to see you get hurt. Is Hank okay with all this?"

"Not totally." He'd already said no to adoption in general a thousand times because you never know what kind of problems a kid not genetically yours might have. He'd also unequivocally said no to adopting Owen specifically, because all of the not-knowing still applied, plus the addition

of Owen being media-worthy. Rose said, "I think I can convince him."

"If you adopt the kid, it's going to get the media going
all over again."

That peroxide Caroline Weatherby from Channel Eight,
the guy with the Science-teacher glasses from the Portland
paper—they'd finally moved on to a story about a hunter,
a miss-loaded gun, a hand blown off. It was possible—if no
other story got in the way—that the reporters would be back
like unfed dogs if they heard the Rankins wanted to adopt
Owen. "It won't last forever."

Rose thought of the oinking over Margo's shirts and
she hated that this small town maintained such a vise grip
on anything that gave them a little excitement. She said,
"People give up custody of their kids all the time. I just have
to get Sophia to see that it's the right thing to do—probably she thinks he'd just end up being shuttled from foster
home to foster home. She just doesn't see it yet—how good it
would be for him to live with us. Two parents, a brother. Plus,
we could arrange it so that she could see him all the time."
Rose paused to peer into the oven. The cupcakes were rising
beautifully.

"It sounds like you've got your argument laid out." Margo
pulled the first batch of cupcakes out of the oven, tested the
top with her finger. Satisfied, she lifted them out of the tin
and placed them on a wire rack for cooling. "Just be careful,
Rosie." She wiped her hands on her sweatshirt.

Even though she knew better, she didn't feel like waiting,
and so she pulled her hand away from Margo, picked up a
cup cake, and piped lines of green frosting to look like fur. It

was pretty but too hot and the frosting started to melt into a mess.

"We can put them in the freezer," Margo said. "Patience is a virtue," Rose said.

25

The day after the baby-catching, Hank had been out front, straightening the cases when FoodTown's owner, Jay Jackson, came by, trailing his second-in-command, Gary-the meat-manager. They stood in front of him, fat hands in the pockets of their Chinos, and congratulated him on Rose's quick thinking. They clapped him on the back, told him to keep smiling, told him they believed all publicity to be good publicity.

Jay had made like he was swinging for par. "Keep those cases sparkling," he said.

Not once had he asked Hank to golf with him.

In those first few days after Rose and her miracle, a few customers asked Hank what he saw, what it was like, if the baby cried. Hank broke it down, millisecond by millisecond, making his role of observer seem more important than it was. A week later, no one was really asking anymore. The Parker News hadn't even bothered to send in a reporter to try to get a cursory statement from Hank.

But now, two months later, people had moved on. He wanted their family to move on, too. He didn't want to hear how she'd gone to Father Rob to get him on her side. He didn't want to hear—again—that he didn't understand her grief, that he could never understand what it was like for her to lose not just this baby, but the chance to ever have another baby. He didn't want to talk about adopting Owen.

When he got to the store, Hank sent the Graff kid out front while he made himself busy with the schedule and the ordering out back. He told him to come get him if anyone asked for him, but only if they insisted.

He'd been out back for half the day when Jimmy Graff came out, rubbing at a patch of acne on his chin. "Mrs. Innis really wants to talk to you, Mr. Rankin."

Hank liked Joan Innis. White-haired, prissy in her pastel outfits and pearly earrings. She reminded him of money and his mother. Hank hadn't seen her since the baby-catching and he guessed she'd make a big to-do about it. Maybe she'd even insist he and Rose speak to her niece who did something over at Channel Thirteen. It wasn't too late for that. Hank tucked in the ends of his shirt. "Tell Mrs. Innis I'll be right out."

"She said to tell you it's something you need to hear right away."

Jimmy was turning redder than a cooked lobster and Hank felt bad for him. He pushed back from his chair, let it do a little spin-roll, and stood. "Lead the way."

Mrs. Innis was decked out in pink today, right up to the little pink button-earrings. She was fidgeting with the lacy edge of her blouse and just looking at her was making Hank nervous. She said, "Really, I just wanted to congratulate you."

Hank was smiling. Probably the paper was going to name Rose Woman of the Year or something equally meaningless and wonderful.

Mrs. Innis took Hank's hand and gave it a squeeze. "I heard it from Marjorie. You know she works down at the courthouse?"

Hank nodded even though he had no idea. Marjorie who? He'd never been in the courthouse. What did the courthouse have to do with anything?

Mrs. Innis, smiling now, but tight around the eyes. "Everyone I've talked to thinks it's wonderful. I don't see why no one thought of it before."

Hank put one hand on the deli case. The coolness was reassuring. "I'm not sure I follow."

Tug, tug at the blouse. "I was sure you knew." A sad smile, as if she didn't want to be the one to tell him he was the last to know. "Your wife picked up the papers this afternoon. So that you two can take custody of that poor baby Owen Leach."

The pinkness blurred. Hank tried to smile but his lips stuck to his gums. Mrs. Innis stepped back, into the canned goods aisle. She was asking if he was all right. Hank nodded, or thought he nodded. His head felt as light as a balloon. Rose wouldn't make a big decision without him. Would she? She was so sure of everything since she became the baby-catcher. Even before. Giving birth to Frederick had done something to her. She had all the answers. She was a food source. Hank's job was done as soon as he'd deposited his sperm. Rose hadn't said it but he felt it, felt that all he was good for now was bringing home his measly paycheck. Still, Rose wouldn't have just gone for custody of Owen Leach without even talking to him. There must be some misunderstanding. This was what he finally said to Mrs. Innis who stood like a cut-out display with her hand draped across the canned soups.

He made it through the rest of the day by telling Jimmy Graff he wasn't to be disturbed unless the building was on fire or the health inspector showed up.

When Hank got home, Rose was outside at the grill. Hank smelled steak, which was his favorite, which was probably not a coincidence. Letting the screen door slam shut behind him, he yanked an overpriced trying-to-be-Mainers-but-it-turns-out-most-Mainers-can't-afford-LLBean-furniture deck chair away from the railing and huffed down into it, then stood again. He wasn't about to give her the advantage of hovering above him. He said, "I heard some interesting news from a customer this afternoon."

Rose turned and he saw the sag around her eyes, the worry in her mouth.

Maybe he didn't need to be this mad. She was probably planning to tell him as soon as he got home. Maybe she'd been planning to tell him this morning and then they got sidetracked when Frederick stuck a Cheerio up his nose.

Hank tried to relax his shoulders, roll out the kink in his neck. But why had she done it without talking to him? Why had she done it at all? Hadn't he been clear that he didn't want to adopt Owen Leach? He lowered his voice. "She said you picked up some papers so you can get custody of Owen."

"So *we* can get custody. I was going to tell you tonight."

The anger returned like a beating down his back. "I don't understand why you didn't tell me before you did it, Rose. This is the kind of thing married people talk about. At great length. Before they do it."

She turned back to the grill. Her shoulders hunched forward. Shame? Guilt? Prepping herself for the fight? Hank couldn't be sure without seeing her face. She said, "I only picked up the papers so we could have the information in front of us while we talked about it. I would never make a decision like that without you."

Hank went into the kitchen, got himself two beers, walked back out to the porch with one in each hand. "And so that everyone in town knows what the plan is, thinks it's a fantastic idea, and I'll be the asshole if I say no. Because it isn't private anymore, is it?"

She looked at him over her shoulder, briefly, and Hank thought he saw hard determination in her eyes. "I wasn't thinking about it that way."

"You weren't thinking about it at all." He had to calm down. He had to say again—straight out—that he didn't want to adopt Owen or any other baby for that matter. It would have been one thing if they could have had another baby the regular way. But they couldn't, because Rose couldn't, and he didn't want to be the asshole throwing that in her face.

Rose put the steaks on a plate, and carried them into the house. Hank wasn't about to sit outside in the cold like an idiot so he followed her. She set a plate of food in front of him and he picked it up, carried it into the living room, switched on the news. He half expected a report on Rose and her good news—some honey-haired reporter outside the courthouse, waving duplicate paperwork. Rose sat at the dining room table. He could hear the occasional scrape of her fork against the plate. She could at least come in to apologize.

He brought his empty plate into the kitchen, then stood in the doorway of the dining room. She had her sewing machine set up at the end of the table, quilt pieces laid out in piles. When had she started a new quilt? Her plate still held her steak, uncut, and she'd pushed it into the center of the table. She was staring out the window. Hank said, "I don't want to do this."

She looked up, met his eyes. "Don't want to fight or don't want to adopt Owen?"

"Both." Just like he hadn't wanted to move to Maine. At first, Rose said it was just until they got pregnant, and then she thought maybe it was a better place to raise kids, and then her mother followed them up here and Hank resigned himself to the fact that Rose had always intended to stay. He said, "I like our family the way it is."

"You used to say you wanted another baby, too."

Hank swallowed. "I did. But, not like this." Hank set down his plate, touched the back of Rose's hair. "I don't want a baby that's been on the national news." Owen Leach, Miracle Baby. He didn't want Frederick to grow up the shadow of another kid's spotlight.

"It wasn't his fault he was on the news."

"And it isn't mine." He was trying to be the kind of husband she wanted him to be. Part of him wanted to give in, give her whatever she wanted. She'd lost so much. But he did not want Owen Leach. Not a kid that was going to inherently love Rose more than he would love Hank. He leaned in and kissed the ridge of her ear. "I'm tired of fighting," he said.

Rose said, "I didn't mean to go behind your back."

"So, we're done with this?"

She wiped her mouth on her napkin, leaving a peachy lipstick smear. "I don't want to be a single mother."

She laughed but there were tears in her eyes and Hank kissed her again. "Let's just be happy with the way things are."

"Okay," she said.

She didn't mean it, he could tell. Another time, another day, he'd have to say again that he didn't want to adopt Owen, especially, or any other baby. He'd say it with more clarity, less equivocation.

But what if Rose wanted Owen more than she wanted to be married to Hank? If he laid it all out, would she walk away? There was no court in the world who wouldn't give her custody of Frederick, and probably Owen.

He thought of the thinness of Sophia's back as he rubbed it through her shirt the night she was bent over her toilet. He was glad he'd never told Rose about the drunken phone call and his semi-heroic response.

He said, "I love you, Rose."

26

Sophia was feeling good because she'd been getting more hours at FoodTown and it was nice to have a little money of her own. If she could save up, maybe she'd buy Owen one of those bouncy swings.

She was singing "Thriller" because it had just been on the radio—gearing up for Halloween—when she got out of her car and found a severed doll's head on her lawn. Complete with ketchupy blood all around the neck. She kicked it with her toe. "Fuck you all," she said, but not loud enough that anyone would call the police. "Anger Management," they said in treatment. Keep it in check, they said. Three deep breaths. She should close her eyes, according to protocol, but she didn't dare. Some sicko could still be in her bushes. From anger to paranoia—that was probably symptomatic of something.

Even though she thought she'd come across as sympathetic in the TV interview, Sophia wasn't totally surprised by the dirty looks and the under-breath comments when she was at the bank or grocery store. She was used to people calling her cell—which was a number they must have gotten from her supposed friends or maybe even Vicky—saying she should be tried and fried. Sometimes they had a baby cry into the phone in the middle of the night. But the dolls freaked her out more than any of the other stuff because they took so much effort.

She went into the house and got one of the black trash bags she'd been using for leaves. Even though it was too big for the job, it was nice and heavy and thick. She gripped the doll's head with her hand protected by the bag, then flipped it inside out. For good measure, she swung the bagged head along beside her in case anyone was watching. Let them get the point that she didn't care.

Sophia carried the bagged doll head to the car and tossed it in the trunk. If the nosey neighbors were watching they'd probably think it was Owen, and that she'd really gone and done it this time. They'd probably call the police, who wouldn't have anything better to do than show up at her house and ask her about it. And then if she got defensive, she'd be in even more trouble. If she showed them the doll head, they'd say she deserved it. She put her head against her car. The cold against her forehead and up under her thin sweater felt punishing but good.

Eventually, she took a breath. Owen was not dead. He was with her mother. Probably downing a bottle of formula right now. He was fine. A severed doll's head was not some precursor of bad things for her son. She took another breath. That was one of the things they told her to do in therapy—breathe. She wanted to make a joke of it—all of these fucked up people who just need to learn to breathe and everything would be fine—but she didn't dare. They were pretty serious in treatment.

One of the other things they had her do was map out the possibilities. She thought how she could call over to Vicky's right now and Vicky would say everything was fine. Vicky might hold the phone up so Sophia could hear Owen coo or whatever. She might even say Sophia could come over for a little bit, just to hang out with them. But Sophia wasn't supposed to have unstructured visits and, even though they did it plenty when it suited Vicky, Sophia knew the more they broke the rules, the more likely they were to get caught.

Instead, she went inside the trailer and called Rose. It was probably a dumb idea but maybe she'd invite her over for tea, some company. She really wanted to call Hank but that would be pushing her luck. Rose was only being nice because she thought she could get Sophia to hand over Owen. Did she really think Sophia didn't know? That someone in this rinky-dink town wouldn't have told her that Rose had sauntered down to the courthouse and picked up custody paperwork? Or did Rose think she didn't care? Whatever. Sophia figured she'd just be nice right back until Rose realized she was a good enough mother and gave up the whole stupid idea. Until then, it's not like Sophia had a contact list full of role model mothers she could call.

When Hank answered the phone, Sophia thought of the way he smiled at her when he told her she had the job. Wide open, like he was seriously happy to have her around. And the way he held her hair off her face the night she was sick, like he really cared. "Thanks for helping me with that lady yesterday. I can't believe she wanted to return half a ham."

"My pleasure," he said.

"Really?"

Hank laughed and Sophia laughed and she felt good.

Because she didn't want the call to end already, Sophia told him her car was making a funny noise. "I don't know if you're busy, but could you come over and look at it?"

There was a pause and Sophia was positive he'd say no. But then, she could swear she heard him smile when he said sure, he'd be over in a bit. Sophia didn't let herself think about it for any longer than it took her to slide on some lip gloss. She was lonely, that was all.

She bagged up her trash. She didn't want Hank to see the Twinkie wrappers, the empty cans of Coors. Mostly she didn't want to take a chance he'd see the popped-through bubble wrap from the little blue pills she was supposed to be taking. She didn't want him to know she was supposed to be taking the pills and she didn't want to start blabbering about how she'd been flushing them down the toilet. Especially seeing how she worked for him now.

The psychologists or psychiatrists or whoever else they were supposed to be told her she needed the pills. Even though she kept telling them she'd tripped. They insisted there was more to it, some secret part of her that wanted Owen gone. She couldn't deny that, not really, but she did anyway.

At first, she just took the pills. It wasn't like she had any real objection to pharmaceuticals and she thought they might make her feel some kind of high. They weren't bad— they made her feel a little more relaxed, a little less edgy. But then she stared gaining weight. All around her stomach and hips, a thick pad of flab that made her pants dig into her at the button. Within two weeks of taking the pills, she had a roll of pizza-dough skin puffed out above her pants and that was the end of that.

Sophia gave her place a hard look around to get the feel of how Hank would see it. The carpet was the color of microwaved oatmeal and it was worn to shiny in front of the couch. Sophia had tacked up a pink beach towel over the window to serve as a curtain and now she pulled it down and used it to wipe down the top of the TV, the legs of the coffee table. The place wasn't the Ritz but it wasn't a total dump, either.

She'd gotten in the habit of taking out her trash every day because you never knew when the pimple-faced social worker would drop by. Amy, her name was, and it suited her Minnie Mouse personality just fine. Amy, who could probably afford better clothes and a good hair cut but was most likely saving sensibly for her thirty-years-from-now retirement. Amy liked to sit there with her imitation-leather purse on her lap, taking up more than her half of the couch Sophia had just sprayed down with disinfectant, all important with her clipboard and papers on top of her purse, and tell Sophia there was still "an excellent chance" she could regain custody of Owen. Sophia wasn't as stupid as Amy and Dr. Lynch thought she was. They were telling her what they thought she needed to hear in order to keep her talking, keep her taking their stupid pills. No one seemed to be working that hard to get Owen back to living with her. She needed to show them that she could do it. If she failed at being a mother at twenty, what kind of loser would that make her for the rest of her life?

Sophia checked the front lawn one more time, just in case there were any more doll heads.

She checked around the bushes, under her car. She didn't want Hank walking into a stuffed baby hanging from a tree limb or a pile of rotten pumpkins with their insides torn open.

Keeping up appearances had become habit, so it wasn't like she was doing it to impress Hank. She was relieved to find no baby dolls stuck in her mailbox, no signs on her lawn telling her to go jump out a window.

Hank showed up less than a half hour later, wearing jeans that bagged too low on the crotch and a sweatshirt already stained with grease. She smiled. "Don't you look handsome in your not-work clothes." She was only half-kidding.

Even with the extra weight, Sophia thought she was still pretty enough to get a guy. Not that she needed someone else's husband. But sometimes those were the best kind—occupied elsewhere most of the time but around when you needed them. She was glad she'd washed her hair and brushed it out until it was soft and shiny. She was lonely, that was all.

There had been nothing wrong with her car when she called. She'd thought about doing something to it, maybe throwing some sand in her gas tank. If she did that, she might be able to elicit some sympathy—make out like someone was harassing her. But she didn't have the money for a completely new car if she killed it. Besides, the neighbors all kept a pretty close eye on her these days. Probably they were taking bets on who would be the one to call the police and the paper if and when Sophia did something dangerous and stupid. Probably they'd be pretty interested in Hank's arrival. If anyone asked, she'd tell them he was an uncle. Not that someone wouldn't recognize him from the papers or from FoodTown. She was sick of caring about what other people thought.

Hank followed her out to the driveway. "What kind of a noise was it making?"

Sophia leaned in so that her shoulder was against his. She'd sprayed on her best perfume—the Chanel No. 5 she'd swiped from JC Penney back in high school. She only wore it on special occasions. When she dabbed it on her wrists an hour ago, she tried not to let herself think about what she was trying to accomplish here. Now, looking into the engine of her perfectly-fine car, she said, "It was like grrr grrr." She smiled and shrugged. "It's possible I just imagined it." A damp wind blew. Sophia shivered. It had been hot when she threw Owen out the window and now it was cold enough to snow. Soon enough everything would be covered in its equalizing white. Time passed.

Hank said, "Get in and start it. Did it happen when you were stopped at a light?"

Sophia got in but left the door open. "Maybe."

"Maybe?"

"I don't remember." She should just tell him she'd imagined it. Maybe it was the radio. She should send him home to his wife and son. She should go in and rub off the perfume and grow up and stop wearing too-tight jeans and trying to get attention from unavailable men. But it would be nice to feel desirable again. She'd had two dates since Owen was born, both of them before she threw him out the window. She couldn't exactly get herself tarted up for a night on the town anymore, not with people and their opinions.

Hank waved a hand at her. "Shut it off, now."

He had good hands. Solid, wide, nails filed down, a little bit of dirt around the edges to give him that rugged vibe she liked. It would be nice to feel desirable, even for just fifteen minutes.

27

Hank stood in the doorway of the dining room. It was raining a cold, heavy rain, and his face and hair were matted down. "What's all this about?" He shook water off his arms like he knew she was about to tell him something he wouldn't like.

Rose concentrated on placing the forks in the exact center of the triangular napkins. "We're having company."

Rose fetched Hank a towel from the bathroom, then straightened the napkins while he dried off. "I invited Sophia Leach for dinner," she said.

Hank draped his jacket over the nearest chair. "Why?"

Rose plucked the jacket off the chair, carried it to the bathroom, hung it over the shower. She couldn't look at him, couldn't be in the same room as his disapproval. When she came back into the living room, she kissed his rain-wet lips. "I'm sorry I didn't talk to you first. But you would have said no."

Hank untied his wet shoes and yanked off his damp socks. "Don't you think she knows you picked up custody paperwork?"

"You told her?"

"I didn't tell her anything. This is a small town, Rose. A tiny town. My money's on that someone told her."

Rose shrugged. She almost said that maybe it would be better if they talked about it, laid out their cards, told Sophia they wanted to adopt Owen and just see what she said. Maybe she'd be into the idea—she'd still get to see him, and Hank and Rose and Frederick were a ready-made Rockwellian family. But they couldn't discuss adoption unless Hank was on board with the idea and he wasn't. Not yet. Rose said, "It's all a moot point. We've decided not to adopt him, right?"

Hank stood, socks and shoes messily in his hands. "Right."

It would be another thing altogether if Sophia *wanted* to give them her son. If it were her idea. How could Hank say no to that? Rose debated taking out the gold-rimmed dishes they usually saved for Christmas but she decided against it— she needed Sophia to know they were financially stable but not stuffy. Rose decided on the everyday dishes, linen napkins the color of sand, and a small, low vase of pink and white roses. Rose thought of Vicky Leach's pink pitcher of milk and the haze of blue smoke.

"I'll go change," Hank said.

In the kitchen, Rose over-stirred the spaghetti sauce so that red flecks leapt out of the pot, onto the refrigerator, the back of the stove. She lowered the flame, dampened a paper towel and rubbed everything clean. She wanted Sophia Leach to be impressed by both the food and the cleanliness of the house.

For tonight's dinner, Rose didn't prepare something overly complicated that could have left room for failure. No rack of lamb or stuffed pork chops or lobster Alfredo. She would have had to call her mother to help with those, and

Cloris and Doug were visiting for the weekend. If she called her mother while they were there, she'd have to listen to Cloris wax poetic about the virtues of salad for dinner. Plus, she didn't want to tell them it was Sophia coming for dinner because already they'd told her not to get involved. Already, they'd said Rose was "fragile."

So, she'd tackled dinner on her own. Spaghetti and meatballs would be failure-proof and still impressive enough because she made the sauce and meatballs from scratch.

Hank called from upstairs, "Where's Frederick?"

"At my mother's. I didn't want Sophia to feel worse about not having Owen."

The doorbell rang and Rose rushed to answer it.

Sophia stood with her left hand holding up the hood of her windbreaker, her right hand holding a loaf of Italian bread. She smiled. "Is this okay? I hope you didn't make bread or anything."

Rose took the bread, leaned over and hugged the girl who hugged her back, one-armed. She'd made rolls but she could put them away. "This looks delicious."

Rose had spent the morning vacuuming and dusting. As she led Sophia into the living room, she could smell the floral carpet deodorizer, the lemon-scented wood polish, and the bleach she'd poured down the drain to get rid of the oniony smell. As she passed it, she lifted the hall window an inch to air the place out.

She'd needed a nap after all her efforts but when she'd tried to lie down with Frederick, he'd kicked and cried and she'd finally given up. Now, she felt exhaustion in every cell of her body.

Sophia inhaled. "Your house is so nice. I mean, the last time you didn't even know I was coming and it was still super-clean."

Rose did not say that the house was clean, in part, because people had been dropping over constantly since the baby catching. She imagined Sophia stepping over leftover pizza boxes and plates of cold macaroni and cheese to get into her living room. "Thanks for coming over," she said.

"It's not like I have a lot of places to go these days." Sophia wiggled out of her jacket. Drops of water puddled on the carpet. "I'm sorry," she said. She was wearing a dipped-low black t-shirt and tight jeans, clean blue and white sneakers, and no jewelry other than a pair of small silver hoop earrings. She could be the babysitter, or a niece. If Rose had started young enough, she could be her daughter.

They stood together in the living room for a moment, and the house was so quiet, Rose could hear the pasta water boiling in the kitchen, the abating rain dripping off the eves.

Sophia asked, "Where's your son?"

"Sleep over at grandma's."

Sophia smiled. "I guess we have that in common, then." They moved into the dining room and Rose offered Sophia a choice between soda and water. She picked water, then sat down at the head of the table. Rose didn't correct her. After a few minutes of talk about the unseasonably hot weather expected for the weekend, Hank came down in a sweatshirt and jeans. He poured himself a scotch. Sophia eyed it.

Hank raised his glass. "Would you care for one?"

Sophia glanced at Rose, then picked up her glass and sipped. "I'm fine with water, thanks."

"Sophia brought the bread," Rose said.

"FoodTown's finest." Hank tore off a large chunk and held it up to Sophia in a kind of salute. Rose didn't know if he meant Sophia or the bread.

They ate. They talked more about the weather (expected to turn cool again after the weekend), the leaves (pretty), the Christmas products already on display in Reny's (too soon to think about). Sophia cut her spaghetti and nibbled pieces of meatball, nodded in agreement about the weather and the leaves but when the talk turned to Christmas, she got watery-eyed.

"Do you want some more spaghetti?" Rose asked.

Sophia shook her head. "They say I might be able to get Owen back by Christmas."

Rose took a sip of water. "So soon?" She thought about the custody paperwork sitting in the bottom of her sock drawer.

"I hope so," Sophia said.

Hank smiled at Sophia and Rose smiled at both of them even though she wanted to scream.

Hank helped himself to another meatball. It missed his plate, rolled onto Rose's white linen tablecloth. "Sorry," he said, dabbing at it with his napkin, leaving a stain on both.

"Here," Sophia said, dipping her napkin in his water glass and rubbing it over the spot. "I do stuff like that all the time." She rubbed vigorously, head down, eyelashes long enough to brush her cheeks.

"It's okay," Rose said. She wondered if Hank would say something rude about the way Sophia had used his water glass to wet her napkin but when she looked at him, he was smiling. "You can leave it. I'm sure it'll come out in the laundry."

"Not if you let it set," Sophia said. She glanced up. "Right?"

Hank shrugged. "Damned if I know."

Rose stood, knocking her thigh against the table so the flowers rattled in their vase. So what if Sophia knew something about stains? It was probably because her mother made her living around hair dye and nail polish—but that wasn't all she needed to know. She needed to know about soothing a fussy baby, entertaining a toddler, child-proofing a house, keeping your kid safe at the playground. She needed to have a plan for holding down a job and having a social life and finding responsible babysitters. Most importantly, she needed to want her kid, which she'd already demonstrated to the world that she didn't. Rose gathered her plate and Sophia's. "Hank, why don't you grab the leftovers?"

Sophia stood. "Let me help."

And so, they all cleared the table of the spaghetti bowl, the dish of fresh-grated parmesan, the salt and pepper. In the kitchen, Rose handed Sophia the plates and mugs and Sophia and Hank arranged them for coffee and cake. Rose watched them from the kitchen, leaning toward each other, talking. The more comfortable Sophia got around them, the more open to the idea of adoption she'd be. Still, something about the familiarity between Hank and Sophia made Rose want to stand between them with very hot coffee.

Rose carried the chocolate layer cake to the table. "From scratch," she said. She'd burned the first one and thrown it in the woods so Hank wouldn't find it in the trash and tease her about it. This one was leaning slightly to the left and Rose hoped the frosting was thick enough that Hank and Sophia wouldn't notice.

"I made the coffee," Hank said, and his voice was light, teasing.

Sophia raised her mug and smiled. "Coffee's great."

Rose said, "It must be a lot for your mother to take care of Owen." She ignored the look of irritation Hank gave her and she tucked a small forkful of cake into her mouth.

Sophia chewed and swallowed. "She's managing. This is really good."

"She brings him to work?"

"Uh-huh. I always thought not using a box mix for cake was just a waste of time but this is totally delicious."

Hank said, "What difference does it make if she brings the baby to work, Rose?"

Rose said, "I would just worry about all those chemicals he must be inhaling every day—from the hair products, the nail stuff."

Sophia shrugged. "I turned out okay."

Rose set her fork across her plate. Hank stood. "Anyone want a little Amaretto in their coffee?" Hank asked.

Sophia leaned back in her chair. "I'll try some."

"She isn't old enough to drink," Rose said, a hand on Hank's arm.

"I don't think it's gonna make much difference at this point," Sophia said.

Hank laughed.

*****

They finished the meal with more coffee and Amaretto and the conversation drifted to work, and something funny the Graff kid said the other day, and why he was always so slow stocking produce. Hank leaned in and whispered that Jimmy Graff had a thing for Tessa in Produce. Sophia laughed and grabbed his arm, let go when she looked up and met Rose's eye.

Eventually Rose got up and cleared the dishes. She was starting the dishwasher when Sophia came into the kitchen and offered to help.

"All done." Rose said holding up her hands and spinning on her toe as if she were some kind of carefree soul. She laughed, and Sophia laughed, but Rose felt lies and half-truths strung between them like clothes on a line.

And then Sophia Leach was at the front door, thanking them for a nice meal. Hank reappeared at the doorway and they watched as Sophia waved on her way down the driveway. Rose and Hank waved back. Rose had one arm around Hank's back, one arm in the air, waving until Sophia's car was a speck of red light in the dark.

Finally, Hank turned to go in. "She seems like she's trying to get it together."

Rose leaned her forehead against Hank's back, put her arms around his middle. "Maybe."

Hank squeezed her hands in his, then pulled them away from his body. "I'm going to turn in."

"I'll be up in a minute." Rose listened as Hank ascended the stairs to their bedroom. She wrapped her arms around herself against the chill of late-evening fall air. Even though Rose knew she should leave it up to God and all that, she couldn't let go of the sense that there was too much injustice in the way things were working out for Sophia Leach.

28

She told him the baby felt hot, like a rock that had been in a campfire, and that she needed to be rid of him. Then she said he was slippery from his bath, and screaming, and that she took him to the window so he could get some air. She said she wanted to show him the stars, and that she'd had to lean way out. And then she was pacing and she tripped. He fell. She said it all happened so fast.

Hank put his arm around her thin shoulders, thinking he was being friendly, some might even call it paternal. But when she leaned into him, tucked her head against his chest and breathed in, he knew he'd gone too far. He shifted away, leaned against the car and crossed his arms, then uncrossed them. She told him about the doll's head but wouldn't show it to him. "You should call the police," he said. She'd called him over this time because her car was making that same funny noise again, she said.

"They won't care." She looked pathetic, standing across from him, shifting her weight from one sneaker to the other.

He said, "I remember the first time I held Frederick. I was sure I was going to drop him on his head." Now she leaned in—grateful, interested. Isn't this what Rose wanted, for them all to be friends? Hank was sure Rose wouldn't want him here alone with Sophia, letting her flirt with him. But Rose had picked up custody paperwork. Not that Hank believed in an eye for an eye. That was his mother-in-law's domain.

Sophia smiled. "But then you got good at it."

"Rose got the hang of it. I didn't do much. Still don't."

"Oh. come on. I bet you're a great dad."

Hank shrugged. Last year for Halloween, Rose had made Frederick a Tootsie Roll costume. She cut out the pieces, including the letters, stitched the whole thing together by hand. Hank had gotten home from work just as they'd come in from Trick-or-Treating. "It wasn't even seven o'clock and they were all done. I had bought a bag of mini candy bars I was going to glue all over my shirt so we'd match, kind of. I ended up eating them."

Sophia touched Hank's wrist just below where his jacket ended. His skin was cold, her hand, which had been in her pocket, was warm. "That really sucks," she said.

He'd told her about Halloween to make her feel less bad about her own parenting, but he liked that she could relate. Rose hadn't, when he told her it bothered him. "I thought they were going to wait for me," he said.

"And Rose didn't even call you to say they were going?"

The truth was that she might have. Hank couldn't say for sure. He'd been out front cleaning up the eggs some shit heads had thrown at the store windows and he thought he might have heard himself paged but he didn't answer. He said, "She said she didn't want to bother me." It wasn't true, but it felt true. Still, he felt shitty for saying it.

Sophia clicked her tongue. "Being a parent is so much harder than you think it's going to be, isn't it? I mean, you were working to put food on the table and then you miss out on all the fun."

Not all the fun, not always. Still, Hank leaned a little closer to Sophia and said, "I felt like an asshole not being the one to catch Owen." He wondered too late if this was the wrong thing to say. He didn't say anything about Rose losing the baby, although he wondered if he should.

Sophia gripped his arm. "I guess we're both assholes, huh?"

Hank laughed. "I guess."

She took a breath, stared at the ground, took another breath so deep her chest filled. "I really did trip." She flicked a glance at him. "But before that..." She ran a hand through her hair, tugged it into a ponytail at the base of her neck, let it go. "I wanted to be free of him. For just, like, one second."

Hank watched her watch the ground. Finally, he said, "Maybe we've all felt that, at one time or another." He didn't think this was exactly true, but it felt good to be able to say something comforting to someone. "Most people just don't act on it."

"I bet Rose has never felt that way." Sophia lifted her eyes to his, pleading.

"I can't say for sure what she's felt, but I know it's hard for her sometimes." He thought of the most recent miscarriage, and the way Rose cried into her pillow at night, and the way she wouldn't let him touch her even though the doctor had said it was okay.

"You really think so?"

When Sophia asked him in for a beer, he said no. He'd wondered about the car, and the perfume. And then, the way she'd been smiling at him. "Rose is probably waiting for me," he said.

Sophia nodded. "Got it."

"But if the car makes that noise again, you should definitely call me."

In the car on the way home, he felt virtuous, or nearly virtuous. Probably he should have told her to take the car into a mechanic if it started acting up. Between the car and the night she'd called him when she was puking up her guts, Hank figured he'd already crossed some line. But it was hard not to feel bad for Sophia Leach. She was barely twenty years old, still mostly just a kid herself. He was her boss, he was a good person, he was just helping her out.

29

It was Halloween night and, back before Owen, Sophia would have gone with her friends to egg some teacher's house or steal pumpkins from the neighborhood and smash them through the basketball hoop on the school playground. Her friends were probably out there tonight, still doing all that. Even if Sophia wasn't afraid of getting caught, she didn't feel much like causing destruction these days.

She drove across town, parked at the Post Office, walked to Rose and Hank's, and waited around the corner until they left with Frederick. She hadn't stopped thinking about the way Hank looked at her last night when he asked her stuff about the noise her car was making. Like he cared. Like he wanted to take care of her.

Vicky had taken her Trick-or-Treating only once that she remembered. She was ten, and she'd begged for weeks to get to go. In order to buy a costume, she'd returned bottles to the redemption center for a nickel apiece until she had enough to buy the mermaid costume from Rite Aid. Halloween night, Sophia slid into the plasticky bottom, did the Velcro on the sides, and secured the mask with the painted-blonde hair over her head, careful to get the eye holes lined up with her eyes.

At first, Vicky had pretended not to see her. Then she'd stubbed out her cigarette and stood. "Did you steal that?" She gestured to the glittery top, the fish-tale bottom, the slipping mask.

Sophia shook her head. She hadn't stolen anything, yet. For some reason, Vicky relented, put on her flip-flops, and handed Sophia a newly un-pillowed pillow case, white with little blue flowers and just a few yellow spots.

That night hadn't seemed so bad. She had her mother, and a costume, and a pillow case half-full of candy by the time Vicky said they were done. Her version of Halloween hadn't seemed lame until now, with Frederick in his home-made costume that looked like it could have been on a TV commercial for bananas. Soft brown felt formed most of his monkey-ness, with something stiff like a coat hanger making his tail just the right length so he wouldn't trip over it.

Rose held his banana-free hand and, in her other hand, she carried a plastic jack-o-lantern. From time to time, she leaned down and listened to something he said, repeated it to Hank, and they both laughed. Hank walked with one hand on Fredericks's back.

Sophia stayed far enough behind them so that she could ditch into a bush if she needed to. She probably looked suspicious, out here by herself. She'd put on one of those creepy old-man masks so she'd look like a Trick-or-Treater, but it stunk like wet rubber boots so she took it off and tucked it under her shirt.

Frederick pushed his banana into his mouth, smearing it all over his face and down the front of his costume. Rose put down the candy bucket and pulled out a packet of baby wipes from the diaper bag slung around her shoulder. She wiped his mouth, kissed him, laughed when Hank pulled out his camera and clicked off a few shots of them.

Between the moonlight and the porch lights, they glowed.

Even though she tried to blink it away, Sophia could imagine Owen right there in the thick of their little family. He'd be dressed as a miniature monkey, cradled in one of those bunting things against Rose's chest. No banana, but maybe some yellow socks to look banana-like.

Suddenly exhausted, Sophia sat on a rock at the edge of someone's lawn. She set her old-man head in her hands and looked down at him like he might offer her something. Plenty of mothers weren't perfect. Plenty of mothers were worse than she was, even. Plenty of kids were not Trick-or-Treating tonight and Owen was a baby and wouldn't even remember it. She'd made a mistake but she wasn't going to keep on making mistakes. She put the mask back on and then sat, taking rubbery breaths and listening to little voices asking "Trick-or-Treat?"

30

At seven-thirty on Halloween night, Sophia called to say she heard a noise outside and she was afraid. Hank had just come in with Rose and Frederick. Without even thanking him for schlepping along behind them, Rose had brought Frederick straight upstairs to the tub so that she could wash off the banana he'd mashed all over his face and hair.

Hank carried the phone into the kitchen and lowered his voice. "Where's your mother?"

Sophia laughed. "She dressed Owen as a lucky troll and took him to Bingo."

"It's probably just some Trick-or-Treaters," Hank said. "Did you give out candy?"

"I was too scared to open my door. Please, Hank. It sounds like they have rocks."

It turned out to be eggs—about a dozen as far as Hank could tell. Sophia's trailer didn't have a hose so he went out with buckets of water.

Sophia went behind him with a bath towel. "It could have been worse," she said.

He'd told Rose it was Jimmy Graff calling from the store and that he needed to go in to check on what was probably a prank. He felt like an ass for lying, but he couldn't tell Rose the truth without her offering to come. "Jimmy says all the carts are missing," he'd said.

Rose asked, "Why didn't he call Jay?" She was standing in the bathroom, Frederick wrapped in a towel and tucked against her shoulder, almost asleep.

"I'll be quick," he said, kissing them both on their foreheads. "Call my cell if you need anything."

As far as he could tell, it was pretty obvious he was lying, but Rose just told him to drive carefully.

"Thanks for helping me," Sophia said. She walked toward the kitchen. "My knight in shining armor." He was about to say he'd see her at work when she handed him a beer. If she'd asked, he would have said he didn't want one, that he needed to get going. But here it was, a cold beer in his hand. He popped the top.

She raised her beer to his. "Cheers," she said. "I'm sorry I made you come all the way over here for something I probably could have handled myself."

He'd glanced in the fridge when Sophia opened it and saw that she had seven eggs on the door. He opened the cabinet under the sink, pulled out the trashcan, and threw in the tab of his beer. No egg carton. Unless she'd been careful enough to buy decoy eggs and hide the carton, Sophia probably hadn't egged herself. He said, "We were done Trick-or-Treating anyway."

Sophia set down her beer and clapped her hands. "You got to go this year. Did you have a great time?"

All night, he'd felt unnecessary. For one, Rose held Frederick's hand and Hank couldn't hold his other hand because he was carrying a banana. Hank suggested ditching the banana but Frederick screamed when he tried to pry it out of his hands. And then, Rose seemed to know everyone they came across and Hank just stood there while she talked about how she made Frederick's costume. Felt, she said. Cut the pattern herself.

Now, standing too close to Sophia in her boot-sized living room, he said, "He got a lot of candy. Most of which Rose won't let him eat."

Sophia shook her head. "Did she give out candy? I would have expected carrot sticks."

Hank smiled. "Cupcakes. Homemade, of course." A pang because he knew he was playing along, making his wife seem lame when in fact he loved her cupcakes.

Rose had wanted Hank to stay home and hand out the cupcakes. He insisted on going Trick-or-Treating and they ended up leaving the cupcakes on a tray on the porch with a sign that said "Please take one." He told Sophia, "Back in Massachusetts you could never do that. The first kids who came by would take the whole batch and there'd be none for anyone else."

Sophia laughed. "What does that say about us Mainers? That we're nicer or just not as smart?"

Hank took a long sip of beer. He felt good.

Sophia said, "I really appreciate you running over here to help me. I don't have anyone else I can count on. Sometimes I really wish I had a brother or sister, you know?"

Hank shrugged. "I've kind of always liked being an only child."

"You weren't ever lonely?"

Hank thought of his mom towards the end, when he would sit beside her bed and hold her hand and wish to hell he could bolt out the door for an hour or possibly forever.

"Sometimes," he said. He swallowed. "Rose wanted to have another kid so Frederick doesn't grow up maladjusted."

Sophia laughed. "That must make you feel like shit." Sophia drank from her own beer. "You said 'wanted.' She changed her mind?"

There was hope in her voice. Maybe she thought Hank meant Rose had given up the idea of adopting Owen. Maybe, he should let her think that. He should not tell her about the miscarriages, the hysterectomy. He said, "She wants more kids. She just can't have any." He paused, drank, wished he could shut up. "There have been problems."

"Oh," Sophia said. "I'm sorry." She sounded sorry and so Hank looked up at her. She had nice eyes. She said, "I don't want to give up Owen. I made a mistake, and I'm going to spend the rest of my life making it up to him. I'm not giving him to Rose or anyone."

Hank exhaled and it felt like his entire body emptied out. "I don't blame you," he said.

Sophia flopped down on the couch, smiling. It was like they'd cleared the air, agreed on something. "Do you have to leave right away?"

He should have said yes and then done it. Instead, he shrugged.

She reached up, put her hand on his arm. "It's only eight-thirty. The older kids might be out later and I don't really want to be alone."

She said they could watch a movie. She named three and the third was one he'd been wanting to watch—a thriller about a kidnapped daughter, a ransom, an angry ex-con tapped for help. Rose had said it looked too violent. Hank called Rose and said he needed to stay to clean the eggs off the front windows at the store. He could leave halfway through the movie, as soon as he knew Sophia wasn't going to get harassed anymore.

He and Sophia sat on the couch, near each other but not touching. She said, "I followed you guys tonight."

Hank raised an eyebrow.

"For a little while." She shrugged. "I just wanted to see."

"What did you want to see?"

"You know. Normal." Her voice was thick, on the verge of tears.

Hank took a long drink from his beer, swallowed. "You think we're normal?"

"Compared to me." Sophia closed her eyes. "Rose is a really good mother."

Hank's stomach knotted. Rose *was* a good mother. Maybe Sophia was changing her mind about keeping Owen. Talking herself into something she didn't want. All he'd have to do was say she should think about what was best for Owen and she might agree, might hand him right over. Rose would be so happy. He could be the one to make his wife happier than she'd been in a long time. "Don't put yourself down," he said. "You just haven't had a lot of practice."

Sophia sighed and leaned back against the couch. "I hope you're right."

He wasn't sure if Sophia was capable of motherhood, but she seemed to want to try. Didn't that count for something?

At a slow part in the movie, Sophia said, "Do you think Owen will remember the feeling of flying?"

Hank hoped not. "He's just a baby."

"So, you think he'll be all right?"

"I think kids are resilient." He thought this might be true. What he knew for sure was how Owen had looked when he was caught in Rose's arms. But he didn't think Sophia wanted the truth.

Sophia leaned in and he knew what was going to happen. Hank closed his eyes, even though he never thought he'd be the kind of guy to cheat on his wife. Sophia kissed him and he kissed her back, feeling the slickness of her lip gloss, tasting the strawberry sweetness of it. He liked how she rolled her tongue over his like she was tasting something she'd never had before.

He could have let things go on. She had her hand between his legs and she was going for his zipper when he pulled back. "Thank you," he said.

Sophia took his empty beer can when he handed it to her. She nodded when he kissed her cheek.

In the car, his breath was all edges. He couldn't be the kind of father who saw his kid every-other weekend. If Rose divorced him, he'd never get Frederick on Christmas morning. The handoff for divorced fathers was always Christmas afternoon, when the kid was already full of gifts and disbelieving that Santa came to your house, too. Halloween, Thanksgiving, the Fourth of July. Ordinary school mornings. A loose tooth lost at dinner. Being a part-time father was not what he'd signed up for.

He started the car and backed out of the driveway. He was not a cheater. He wasn't. There were guys who cheated and guys who didn't and he'd always said he wouldn't have bothered to get married if he wanted to sleep around.

The lights were all off when he got home. He hoped Rose was asleep and would stay asleep. He was careful on the stairs, quiet when he took off his jeans and folded them on the upright chair next to his side of the bed.

Rose rolled to face him. In her arms was the blue, yellow, and green quilt she'd started making for Owen. The gray elephant grinned out from the center. "You finished the quilt," Hank said, feeling something like fear across his chest.

She looked down at it like she hadn't even remembered it was there. "Things okay at the store?"

His erection was long gone by now, but still he felt like she could tell just by looking at him. "Everything's fine," he said. He turned so that his back was toward her while he took off his socks. "Frederick didn't eat too much candy, did he?"

"I put it in the freezer."

"All of it?"

"Did you want some?"

"I don't need any." He climbed into bed, pulled the covers up to his chin. If he'd stayed home with his wife and son, he would not have kissed Sophia Leach. "When were you thinking of giving Owen the quilt?" He knew she was planning the quilt as a welcome-home gift for Owen, a happy-adoption present.

"Maybe Christmas." Rose rolled toward him. "Thanks for coming with us tonight. It was nice."

Hank wanted to kiss her but he thought of Sophia's sweet-smelling lip gloss and he wasn't sure he didn't still have some slicked on his face somewhere. He snaked his arm out from under the covers, fingered the edges of the applique elephant, the puffs and dips of the quilt itself. "Goodnight," he said. "I love you."

31

It was stupid. Idiotic. To put her job at risk. The job that wasn't easy to come by in the first place. For what? What did she think was going to happen? That Hank would throw himself at her, happy to have a completely screwed up fling? That he'd actually leave his sane and competent wife for her? That if Rose found out about them sleeping together, she'd have to see how lame it was of her to try to get Owen? Sophia was probably the last woman in Maine he'd sleep with given that she was the mother of the baby his wife wanted to adopt. God, she was so stupid sometimes.

Sophia wiped down the belt on her register with Windex. She'd seen Hank only once since Halloween, and he hadn't said much more than "good morning," "good afternoon," and "when you have a second, wipe down the front windows if you don't mind." Six days since Halloween. Not that she expected him to call. Not that she expected anything.

He'd walked by ten minutes ago and nodded at her. She called after him that her car seemed much better these days and he looked over his shoulder, smiled, and kept walking.

Jay Jackson, bigwig owner of FoodTown, was in the store today. Sophia straightened the candy out front of her register. Dusted the unsold Skittles and M&Ms, lined up the gum in even rows.

"Looks good," Jay said.

She hadn't seen him coming and Sophia jumped. "Didn't mean to scare you." He was all smiles, all I-had-braces teeth. Nice deep blue eyes, too.

Sophia smiled back. "You walk like a ninja."

Jay karate-chopped the air. "What can I say? People fear me."

"I bet." Besides her interview, during which Jay made it clear that the first time she screwed up even a little bit she'd be canned, this was the longest conversation they'd ever had. She'd been too scared during the interview to notice that he wasn't bad looking at all. Searching for some way to keep the conversation going, Sophia said, "It's been pretty busy in here today."

"Snowstorm coming. Makes people crazy."

Sophia widened her eyes. "I've totally noticed that. It's too early for snow, though."

"Life in Maine." Jay pretended to play the drums on the magazine rack. "Are you stuck here working late?"

Sophia nodded. "Hank asked me to stay. I guess a couple of the other girls called out."

"And you stepped right up to the plate, huh?"

"I guess." Now she wished she hadn't. She had a feeling he was going to ask her out and she wouldn't be able to go because here she was, working. Sophia reached up and fixed her ponytail, aware that, with her hands above her head, a fraction of her bare stomach could be seen. She noticed Jay noticing.

He said, "Too bad. I was going to see if you wanted to grab a bite. Me and some friends are heading over to the Chowder House later."

"That sounds like fun."

"Maybe next time." He did a little jazz step as he walked back into the front office.

He was too slick for Sophia's type, normally. But these days it wasn't like she had a ton of options. The guys in treatment were out. Flat-faced Ace, who she thought was kind of cute until she realized his expression never changed. New meds, they said. For his bipolar. Chuck in the leather jacket was okay other than the acne scars but it turned out he was a complete crack head. Who else did she meet these days? A few guy customers but most of them hardly even looked up from swiping their credit cards in a hurry to get the hell home.

She'd just finished ringing through a lady who was buying two gallons of milk and three half-gallons of ice cream ("In case the power goes out," she'd said, which made no sense at all) when Hank came and half sat on the end of her register.

"You shouldn't let Jay take you out to dinner," Hank said.

"Not that it's any of your business."

"He's just not a good guy, that's all."

Sophia would have liked to tell him to screw off. He'd had his chance and he'd gone all namby-pamby on her. She said, "Do you take this much interest in the personal lives of all your employees?"

"I'm just telling you what I think."

When Hank asked her to stay late this afternoon, she'd taken it as a compliment but now she was just annoyed.

Jay Jackson was no more than thirty-five and he owned FoodTown, which meant he probably had some money. Plus, he was good-looking. And single. "You don't get to decide my personal life, Hank."

"He's known to be a ladies' man."

"'Ladies' man'? What is this, nineteen fifty?"

Hank hopped off her register. "I'm going out front to shovel," he said. "Page me if my wife calls."

It snowed all afternoon and hardly anyone else came in the store. At five, Hank came by with a ham and cheese sandwich. He handed it to her. "A peace offering."

"Did you make this yourself?" Sophia said it teasing in a sweet way. She didn't want them hating each other.

Hank smiled. "I even cut it right down the center." Sophia pretended to admire the two halves of her sandwich. "You're a master," she said.

At six, Hank said the store was closing early. "The roads are bad," he said. "How about if I drive you home?"

"I can make it," she said. "I have to work at seven tomorrow."

"You have a shit box of a car and I have to work at seven tomorrow, too. I can pick you up on the way in."

He had to know what was going to happen, that's the way Sophia figured it. Halloween night he'd said no, and then he spent the next six days regretting it. The snow storm was the excuse he was waiting for.

She didn't feel guilty when she asked him in for a beer, or when she kissed him before she even handed him the bottle, or when he didn't pull away and she led him to the bedroom. The only time she felt guilty was when they were done and she went to the bathroom and she heard him on the phone, in a low voice, and she knew he must be talking to Rose.

She brushed her teeth extra-long to give him time and when she went out, she expected him to be dressed, ready to leave. Instead, he was still naked, still half-beneath her sheets. "I told Rose I'm sleeping on the pullout at work," he said.

"And she believed you?"

"It's supposed to be a late-fall blizzard, according to the weatherman. And it's not even Thanksgiving. I hate Maine."

"Someone might have seen you drive in here but not out."

Hank shrugged. "Thank God for trees and long driveways."

True, the neighbors couldn't see his car where it was parked up beside hers unless they came all the way down the driveway. But they might. Just going for a walk, they'd say. Checking to see how you're making out in the storm. If Hank wasn't going to worry, why should she?

Sophia climbed back into bed and hooked her body next to Hank's. For a while, they were quiet. Then she traced the edge of his face with her fingers. Soft, like he was a master piece. "Owen's going to be okay, don't you think?"

He rolled toward her so that they were fully skin on skin. "Yes," he said. And then, after a pause, "I don't know."

32

Rose thought she heard water running in the background, like someone filling a coffee pot or taking a shower.

Hank said, "I'm not going to make it home for dinner. It's crazy here with the storm coming."

The phone was full of static and Rose didn't remember the FoodTown phone ever having interference. "Did someone call out?"

Hank laughed. "Practically everyone has called out."

Practically everyone. That could mean, *Sophia's here.* Rose shifted the phone slightly away from her ear. Before they had Frederick, Hank would rush home from work and, even before he shed his coat, he'd be kissing her in the hollow of her collarbone. Sometimes they would leave dinner cooling on the table while they rolled into each other on the rug. She had barely let him touch her since the hysterectomy.

"Drive carefully," she said. "The roads are starting to slush up." As soon as she said it, she knew he'd call back within the hour and say he'd decided to sleep on the couch in his office, for safety's sake. He'd stayed at work before, but only a couple of times. Once during the ice storm and once when the power went out and FoodTown's main generator failed. But this time, the roads weren't that bad and Rose felt the gut-twist of knowing. Rose took a breath, "I miss you," she said.

"I love you, too," Hank said, automatic.

She could call back, see if he was really at the store. But if he was, he might answer and she'd have to say she forgot that she needed him to bring home milk, eggs, oatmeal. He would be able to tell from the pitch of her voice that she was lying. And if he wasn't there, it would mean he was some-where else. Rose could have mustered the courage to ask him outright if he was with another woman—she could have even named Sophia—but what would she do if he answered with the truth? She'd have to be angry, and then desperately sad. She'd say he betrayed her, and that they could work it out, maybe, in time. But what if he didn't want to work it out? He might say she betrayed him by picking up the custody paperwork. She'd be the single mother of a two-year-old. She would probably not get custody of Owen. She would lose whatever was still good about her marriage.

While she watched Frederick feed himself chicken nug-gets, Rose drank tea so hot it scorched the back of her throat. She'd started Frederick off with cooked carrots but he threw them on the floor and so she'd given in and defrosted the nuggets.

Rose tried to remember the last time she'd reached for Hank. When was the last time she'd even held his hand? The night of their anniversary dinner, when she'd been newly pregnant and full of hope?

When they were dating, she'd wanted him so much and so often that she regularly lied to her mother and said she was too sick to go to Mass just so she could have another hour or two wrapped up with Hank. And then, when they were trying to get pregnant, she made a big effort with silk nighties and impromptu sex—straddling his lap while he watched NASCAR, joining him in the shower on a weekday morning. But after Frederick was born, she felt so exhausted that even brushing her hair was an effort. When they were trying for the second baby, Rose rubbed the small of Hank's back when she thought the timing was optimal. And then after the hysterectomy, she'd been wounded in more than one way. Lots of women had hysterectomies and their marriages didn't end. Couples disagreed about one kid or a couple of kids and they stayed together. Rose knew she had to get over Owen Leach. Get over the fact of catching him, of Sophia throwing him, of wanting him in place of the baby she had lost. She had to, but she couldn't.

Frederick threw a chicken nugget and it landed in her tea. "That's not nice," she said.

He stuck out his tongue, revealing half-chewed chicken.

She fished the chicken out of her tea, drank what was left in the cup.

He threw another nugget and it hit her on the side of her head.

"I guess you've had enough." Rose got up, lifted Frederick from his high chair, and carried him into the living room.

He kicked his legs and wailed. "No!"

"If you're throwing your dinner, you aren't eating it." She put him on the couch. He slid off like a dying seal and sprawled on the floor, wailing.

Rose left him there, went into the kitchen and called her mother. She could handle bad days. She wasn't going to throw him out a window.

Camilla said, "Is that Frederick crying?"

"He's having a meltdown."

"Maybe he's teething."

"He's not."

"Did you check the back teeth?"

Rose took a breath, held it until her lungs ached, let it out nice and slow. "I'll get the Orajel." In the bathroom, she found the little tube, squirted some on her finger. When she got near Frederick, he squirmed away. She reached for him and he ducked. She reached again and dropped the phone and when she bent to pick it up, he threaded his hands into her hair and pulled. "Stop it!"

From the phone on the floor, her mother's voice came—half concern, half rebuke, "Do you need some help there, Rosie?"

"I'm fine," Rose said, finally retrieving the phone. She left Frederick kicking the couch and went onto the back deck. "We're fine."

"I can be there in ten minutes," Camilla said.

Rose watched a patch of clouds track across the moon. "Am I still making the pies for Thanksgiving?" If Hank left her, she'd have to face Thanksgiving without him. He'd get Frederick for half the holidays, weekends, school vacations. Rose felt the prick of tears. He wasn't going to leave. She shouldn't have picked up those stupid custody papers without talking to him.

Through the screen door, she could hear Frederick crying while in her ear her mother chattered on about who was making what. Cloris was doing sweet potatoes, which weren't traditional for them but Camilla thought the kids would like them, at least. Rose forced herself to go back into the house. She was not allowed to run away. "Definitely," she said. She sat on the edge of the couch, thinking that Frederick might fling himself apologetically into her lap. Instead, he grabbed his stuffed monkey and pretended not to see her.

It was possible the running water she'd heard when Hank called was him getting himself a glass of water. Rose wanted to ask her mother if she'd ever suspected her father of having an affair but that wasn't the kind of conversation they could have. Probably, Camilla would have pretended it wasn't happening, and Rose couldn't blame her.

Rose didn't want to be alone. She didn't want to eat dinners of chicken nuggets and crackers and tea. She didn't want to never set the dining room table. She didn't want to not bother making the bed, or to make a pot of coffee and throw half of it away. She didn't want to face every-other-weekend without anyone to watch movies with or go to the park with or talk about the new washing machine they needed or what they could do about the weeds growing up along the walkway. She definitely didn't want to start dating again.

Camilla said, "Do you think anyone still wants salad?"

"Hank likes salad. I can do the dressing."

"I'll do the dressing, sweetheart. You've got so much going on already."

"I don't really." She had Frederick, and part-time sewing at Margo's, and not much else. The fanfare from the baby-catching had already quieted down. The paperwork for getting custody of Owen was still folded in her sock drawer.

"You have a whole household to manage," Camilla said. "Let me do this one thing for you."

Rose leaned against the wall and watched Fredrick cradle his stuffie while he kicked the couch. "I love you, Mom."

33

Hank was supervising Jimmy and the new kid hanging the giant cardboard turkey over the deli counter when someone came up behind him and clamped his shoulder.

Hank turned, ready for some big-boss crap from Jay. Instead, he found himself looking into the grinning face of his former Loaf and Lemon coworker, Jeff Dalton.

Hank felt his bowels knot up but he smiled and said, "Hey, man. What the hell are you doing way up north?"

They shook hands and Jeff made a show of pushing his Rolex up his wrist. Hank pointed at the watch. He said, "Are you trying to run away to Canada because you emptied out the corporate accounts?"

"Ha. I wish." They slapped each other on the back. "Bought this with my last bonus. Nice, huh?" Jeff glanced up at the water-stained ceiling tiles. "I'm guessing you don't get a hell of lot of bonuses around here."

Hank shook his head. "The slower pace makes up for it, though." A lie, but one he'd believed in when he'd agreed to move to Maine. Jeff had grown a layer of fat since the last time Hank had seen him, but all it did was make him look satisfied. Hank said, "How the hell are you? How'd you get out of the stores the week before Thanksgiving?"

"Using my corporate pull. Things are great. But you're the one we're all wanting to hear about. How's life in the small city?"

Jimmy and the new kid made their way down from their ladders and were standing around with their hands in their pockets. Hank wanted them to stand up straight and look alive, for God's sake. Not that the kids in Massachusetts were much better. "You guys are all set," Hank said.

They stared at him. Hank looked at the wall clock so he wouldn't have to flash Jeff his Timex. It wasn't like they were strapped for cash but he couldn't just go drop several grand on a watch. Jimmy and the new kid shuffled their feet. "Bring the ladders out back, then take your fifteens."

"Together?"

"Yeah, fine."

The boys shrugged, folded up the ladders, and bumped them out through the swinging doors.

Sophia was on register three. He could see the top of her ponytail.

"Kids, huh?" Jeff said, still grinning. "They're the same no matter how far north we go. Except up here they sleep with their sisters, right?" He laughed, nudged Hank's shoulder.

Hank wanted to play along with Jeff's idea of rural Maine, but some of the stock kids were listening as they put up boxes of cereal. "Nah," Hank said. "None of that, as far as I know."

Jeff laughed again. "You're turning into a real Main-ah." Hank noticed hand smudges on the deli case. Dammit. Why was he always having to tell these kids how to do their job? He angled his body toward the pumpkin display and hoped Jeff wouldn't notice the handprints on the glass. But he probably would. Not to mention the cracks in the floor tiles, the dust he could just make out on the overhead florescent.

He needed Sophia to stay on her register. Not come down here pretending she had some beans to restock and then just happen by, smile at Hank and Jeff. Jeff would know something, or everything. Probably Jeff would slap him on the back, maybe even out-loud congratulate him on bagging the bagger. And then Hank would feel shittier than he already felt.

Hank said, "How come you're up this way? You're not stopping in to check our prices, are you?"

"Hell, no. Tiff and I just bought a condo at Sunday River. Got a hell of a deal. We're passing papers tomorrow, then she wants to measure for furniture. We figured we'd take you guys out to dinner tonight."

Hank felt a fish-flop of anticipation. A dinner with people Hank knew, and more or less liked. They could talk about the old store, the people they knew in common, the pranks they used to pull on each other.

Sophia sashayed down the aisle with a can of Spam in her hands. "Guy decided he didn't feel like clogging up his arteries tonight, I guess." She smiled at both of them. "Hey."

Hank nodded but kept his eyes on Jeff. Jeff had his eyes on Sophia. When she was out of hearing range—barely—he said, "Not bad."

"She's just a kid," Hank said.

"Not that much of a kid."

Hank shrugged.

Jeff nudged his shoulder. "You're married, not dead. You can look."

"Not my type," Hank said.

Jeff threw his hands in the air. "Picky, huh? Anyway, Sunday River's already started making snow, can you believe it? Pretty soon, fresh powder." Jeff rubbed his hands together. "I can't wait, man. Maybe you and Rose can come up for a few days. Call her about dinner. You know how women need time to get ready."

Hank needed to get his heart rate under control. He walked over to the rice, straightened the pilaf, then the Uncle Ben's. Hank used to ski with Jeff and his wife, back before they got married. Rose never liked what she called Jeff's arrogance, and so they'd never gone as a foursome. Hank said, "Sounds great." He meant about the skiing, even though he knew they'd never go. But as soon as he said it, he realized he'd just agreed to dinner.

"Hey, speaking of your wife, I thought there would be a big banner out front, announcing "Grocery Store of the World-Famous Baby-Catcher." Or something like that."

Hank smiled even though he felt the gut-jab of Jeff's bullshit offer to ski. This visit wasn't really about him, or the good old days. "News travels, I guess."

"It does. And big news like that—how could you expect to keep it secret? Heard you were the guy standing by with his hands in his pockets." Jeff laughed and Hank laughed along because what the hell else was he supposed to do?

Were they all talking about him in Massachusetts? Is that why Jeff wanted to take them to dinner? To rub it in? Swallowing down the last inch of his pride, Hank asked, "How did you hear?"

"Tiffany told me. My guess is Rose told her."

Was Rose really telling people Hank hadn't done anything but just stand there while she caught the baby? He said,

"I didn't know they were still in touch." From out back, he heard Jimmy and the new kid whoop for what he assumed was no good reason. A text message, a hot pepper in someone's olive loaf sandwich, a popped pimple.

Jeff laughed. "I'm sure we don't know half the shit our wives do, right? It's better that way." He dug into his back pocket and pulled out his phone. "Got a few family pics to show you. Took the kids to Disney in August. Hot as hell but they loved it. You been yet?"

"Maybe in a few years." Hank took out his wallet. He only had an old picture—Frederick just a couple of months old and Rose gazing down at him. He'd never realized how saintly she looked in that picture until right now. He handed it to Jeff.

"Cute. What is he now, three?"

"Almost."

Jeff nodded. "So, lay it on me, man. You really like it up here in sticks-ville?"

How could he say no? Admit he'd been conned into moving up here—promised some kind of family-land utopia that had never really materialized, despite the addition of Frederick? "It has its perks."

"Like what?"

"No traffic."

"Yeah, okay, I'll give you that." Jeff slung his arm around Hank's shoulders. "Hey, whatever, man. I'm not here to harass you. We just miss your sorry ass down in the great Tax-a-chusetts."

Meaningless. "I miss you guys, too."

"There's always a job with your name on it of you decide to migrate south."

No doubt an offer as empty as Tiff 's pretty little head. He thumped Jeff on the back. "Thanks, buddy, I'll keep it in mind."

*****

The restaurant they decided on for dinner was the same one they'd been on their way to when Rose caught Owen. Hank had suggested a place closer to Sunday River but Jeff said Tiffany had her heart set on someplace "sweet and local." Hank definitely wasn't going to take them to the puke-yellow-and-electric-blue-checked diner. Or the piz-za-slash-hardware store. So, Moose & Co. was really the only option.

Rose had not been thrilled. She did not like Jeff, and Hank imagined she'd rather have tacos in the car than dinner with the Daltons. To her credit, she didn't refuse outright. She'd called her mother to watch Frederick, brushed her hair, put on a sliver of lipstick and a clean black t-shirt. She didn't ask Hank if she looked okay. He might have raised an eyebrow, told her she had great legs and suggested a skirt instead of jeans. It was probably just as well that he hadn't.

Jeff speared a hunk of steak and popped it into his mouth. "I told Hank there's a job waiting for him back home whenever he's ready to blow this popsicle stand."

Hank took a long drink of Dewars and tried to look neutral. If Jeff was offering the job a second time, maybe he meant it.

Rose produced a close-lipped smile. She sipped her water, took her time swallowing. "We really like it here."

Jeff laughed. "Do you?"

The more Hank thought about the job offer, the more perfect it seemed. They weren't trying to conceive anymore. There was more opportunity in Massachusetts. The housing market was good. They could get Frederick into Catholic school. Plus, out of sight and out of mind for Owen. And Sophia.

Tiffany used her glittery square-tipped fingernails to pat Jeff's arm. "Be nice, honey. I think it's sweet up here."

"I know you do, baby." Jeff leaned down and kissed her hand.

Tiffany rolled her eyes and retrieved her hand. She sipped her wine, leaned into Rose. Hank saw Rose stiffen. Tiffany said, "So, this was the place you were headed to when you caught the baby?"

On the way here, she'd asked Rose to point out the apartment building, and then she'd made Hank pull over so she could have her picture taken in front of it. He knew Rose would say, later, that it was a tacky and unfeeling thing to do. As if Hank could have done anything to stop Tiffany.

Hank drained his glass of scotch and signaled the waiter. Rose nodded at Tiffany's question. *Yes, this was the place.* She didn't elaborate.

"So, were you, like, all dressed up?" Tiffany asked.

Rose murmured something, then picked up the dessert menu and pretended to be absorbed in the decision between bread pudding or blueberry pie a la mode. Under the table, Hank gave her knee a squeeze. When Tiffany and Jeff leaned in for a kiss, Rose rolled her eyes. Hank grinned.

Jeff pried his lips off his wife and lifted his glass. "I bet I can get you back in top management, no problem." Scooped from the same pile as the bullshit offer to ski. But, still.

Hank shrugged. "Put it in writing and we'll see."

Rose spooned some of her roasted potatoes onto Hank's plate. "Have you guys been looking for a condo for a long time?"

Jeff said, "You'd make a hell of a lot more money if you moved back."

Rose cut her broccoli until it looked like something she could feed Frederick. "And he'd work more hours."

Hank ate his extra potatoes.

Jeff leaned across the table like they were all best friends. Like it hadn't been nine fucking years Hank had been living in Maine and this was the first time Jeff had bothered to "stop by." Jeff said, "You can't really like working in that dinky place."

Hank took his time chewing. If he defended the shitty little store that was his gainful employment, he'd come off as a redneck sellout. If he didn't, he'd give Jeff license to gloat. To go home and tell his bowling buddies Hank was wallowing in his mud boots.

Rose took Hank's hand and ran her thumb over his. "Hank and I have been talking about buying a little campground."

Hank had to swallow to avoid choking. They'd talked about the campground thing once, years ago. He hadn't thought about it for more than ten minutes after he realized the sellers weren't willing to negotiate. "It's a great place," he said now. "A real money-maker." Why not let Jeff think he needed to sweeten the deal if he really wanted Hank back on his team? Under the table, he let his hand travel into Rose's lap. She swatted him away but smiled.

Tiffany squealed. "A campground sounds so fun!"

Jeff raised his glass. "Good for you, buddy. I've always been a believer in the entrepreneurial spirit."

"You never know what's going to happen," Hank said.

*****

When they got home and Jeff and Tiffany finally kissed and hugged their way out the door, Rose said, "We could take out a loan for that campground."

Hank felt all the night's levity rush out of him like a vacuum hose come loose. "I thought you mentioned the campground to help me negotiate a higher salary."

Her eyes grew bright and watery and Hank looked away, studied a fleck of something on the sleeve of his sweater. She said, "You really want to go?"

She'd lost a baby and he'd slept with Sophia Leach. He should give his wife whatever she wanted. He said, "I'm a Mass-hole who doesn't belong here."

Rose took a breath. "I don't want to move back."

"What if it's a good offer?" Hank picked a miniscule piece of steak off his sweater, flicked it onto the floor. Avoided looking at Rose. "It might make sense to go."

Rose ran her fingers through her hair. "My mother is here."

"She'd move back with us."

"She's settled here."

"She can stay, then. It's only a couple of hours for you to drive up and visit her." He hadn't meant for it to come out like he didn't care that his mother-in-law had uprooted her life to be near her daughter and grandson. "I'm sorry," he said. He moved close enough that he could smell Rose's flowery lotion.

Rose said, "It doesn't seem fair to just up and leave her in Maine without any family."

"We could build a place with an in-law apartment."

Rose closed the gap between them, leaned her head against Hank's chest. "I want to raise Frederick in Maine. You know that."

"It might be really good if we went."

Rose tipped her head up and looked at him for a long moment. "I'll think about it," she said finally.

He bent and kissed her.

34

Sophia's trailer was shotgun-style—two bedrooms down the far end, a bathroom, the kitchen just where the door left you off, and a living room big enough for a couch, TV, and a TV tray wedged in beside the couch and wall.

She kept it really clean—even scrubbed the dirt that collected between the windows and screens, the crumbs in the corners of the kitchen counters and floor, the dust on the lamps in the living room and bedroom. And she'd done her best to decorate it with the green flowered curtains from her old apartment, a small painting of a vase full of daisies she'd found at the Goodwill, and, on the TV table, a lacy tablecloth that had once been a runner on Vicky's bedroom bureau. Since she'd started seeing Hank, she took all her candles—mostly strawberry-scented votives—and arranged them on a sandwich plate in the center of her coffee table.

Sophia was elbow-deep in once-powdered mashed potatoes so when he knocked, she hollered for Hank to come in. "I could have been one of those psychos leaving beheaded babies on the lawn," he said, locking the door behind him.

She kissed the air. "Sweet of you to worry."

Hank went over to the thermostat and turned it down. "I can't even breathe in here."

She shrugged. "Heat's included in my rent." She scooped the potatoes into a big bowl she'd borrowed from her mother.

"Smells good in here."

"I don't know about you but I know I'm going to have a shitty Thanksgiving. So, we're having a pre-Thanksgiving just-for-two today."

"You cooked a turkey in that little oven?"

With her elbow, she nudged the open Joy of Cooking she'd borrowed from Barbara, one of her fellow cashiers who had to be eighty-five and was slower than a one-legged dog when it came to ringing people through, but was sweet as could be. "A turkey breast. Mashed potatoes, pumpkin pie, green beans." The green beans were previously frozen but she'd added slivered almonds so that was something. "And," she reached into the cabinet and turned around like one of those girls, "Your favorite drink."

Hank blinked. "You can't afford that."

She'd taken the money for the Dewars from her register but was it really stealing if you used the money to buy something from the store? Something that probably had a fifty percent markup, at least. FoodTown, even though it suffered with scrawny apples and brownish lettuce, had a pretty decent liquor aisle. One paid-for-from-the-register bottle wasn't going to make a big dent in their profits. Getting caught was a risk, but she'd watched other girls stuff tens and twenties in their pockets and none of them had gotten so much as a warning. True, the other girls weren't trying to prove what good mothers they were, but Sophia figured she could cry and deny, if need be.

Sophia said, "My mother already told me we aren't watching the parade because she wants to watch some weepy

Hallmark movie. Are you looking forward to your family thing?"

Hank took the bottle. "Sophia..."

"And then, to make things worse, my mother gave Owen his first haircut yesterday. She didn't even ask me. I got to her house and it was done. And, she didn't even buy a turkey. Says it's too much work. We're having chicken. Which you can eat any old day."

Hank was still staring at the bottle.

"You keep looking at that bottle and you're going to make me jealous." Sophia cut right into the center of the turkey breast to check for pink. It looked white enough to her. She pulled down two of her unchipped plates.

"I thought you were short of cash."

"Not anymore I'm not."

"We aren't paying you all that much."

"Do you remember Frederick's first haircut?"

"Not really."

Sophia figured Rose probably kept the clipped-off hair in an envelope. "I need to get Owen back. I feel like I'm missing too much of his life."

"I'm sure you will."

"You are?"

"Sophia, can you please just explain to me how you had enough money to buy a fifty-dollar bottle of scotch?"

She shrugged. Maybe she shouldn't have chosen the White Label—he might have been less suspicious if she'd picked something cheaper. "I was trying to make this a celebration for us." She took down a glass and poured him a solid drink. "Here. Relax."

Hank didn't sit. He paced the space between the bath-room and kitchen counter—back and forth, three steps in either direction. "Did you steal this, Sophia? I need to know if you did."

She didn't want to tell him. She blocked his path, put her hands on his chest. "It's not something you need to worry about."

Hank took her hands and squeezed them, a little harder than gentle. "You'll get fired if you get caught."

"Don't act like I'm the first person in history who's ever slipped cash out of the register."

Hank picked up his drink, then set it back on the counter. "I went to bat for you. I said you'd be a good employee. I told Jay we could trust you."

"No one knows I took anything, Hank." She wished she hadn't admitted it.

"What else have you taken?"

"Let's just sit down and eat."

"Is this part of that personality disorder they say you've got?" He stopped in front of the TV, his face as pale as the underside of Owen's feet, his mouth angrier than she'd ever seen it.

She threw a potholder but it landed on the table. "Fuck you," she said.

"Sophia, you can't steal from my store."

The oven dinged and they both stood there for a second, staring at each other. Finally, she crossed the carpet between them, leaned in, and ran her tongue along Hank's lower lip. "I'll stop, okay? Let's not let this ruin dinner."

Hank didn't move. "What if I gave you some money?"

"You already give me money."

"I could give you more. Enough so that maybe you won't have to work."

"You don't want me there?" Sophia felt tears thicken the back of her throat. "I can't be the only person—"

"You could spend more time with Owen if you didn't have to work."

Sophia left him standing there, went into the kitchen and filled the plates even though her stomach was shaking. "You know I'm not allowed to see him unsupervised." She put the plates down, sat, stared at the pile of food she'd been so happy about five minutes ago.

"You aren't allowed to steal, either."

Sophia scooped up a mouthful of potatoes. Screw him if he didn't want to eat. "Why are you being so mean? I can't believe you've never taken anything that wasn't yours."

Hank rubbed his eyes. "I took a little rubber ball from Kmart when I was seven. My mother made me return it to the manager. Confess what I'd done. Then she grounded me and for three weeks that summer I had to help her clean the house instead of going outside to play with my friends."

"That's harsh."

"I never did it again." Finally, he sat at the table, cut into his turkey.

Sophia watched him eat. "It's good, right?"

"I can give you as much money as you'd make working. Why don't you just let me do that?"

Rose wasn't even that great of a cook. That time they had Sophia over for dinner, the spaghetti sauce wasn't half as good as Ragu. Hank said she had a few things she made and she liked to put on a show for being all domestic but she hardly ever tried new recipes. Sophia had added garlic and fresh chives to the potatoes. "You've got enough money that your wife won't notice a couple hundred bucks a week gone missing?"

"Let me worry about my wife."

It's not like she loved working at FoodTown but she also wasn't stupid enough to believe the promises men made. "The potatoes are the best part, huh?"

"It all tastes great."

"The social worker said I should have some kind of a job It'll help me get Owen back."

"I'm sure you'll find something."

"I don't know. People in small towns have long memories."

Hank put down his fork. "Maybe once you get custody of Owen you could move somewhere. Start over."

Sophia laughed. "Sounds like you're really trying to get rid of me."

"Not true."

But there was something in the way he said it that made Sophia think it was dead-on true. For the rest of the meal, he ate quickly and silently. She lobbed a few other questions at him, chattered about Owen and cranberry sauce, then finally gave up like this was just any other bad date.

When Hank was done with his turkey, he said he'd pass on dessert, both in and out of the bedroom. "Put it in the fridge and we'll have it next time, okay?"

Probably he'd have homemade pie tomorrow, anyway. Sophia stood on her stoop and watched Hank leave.

Pretty soon Christmas would be here. The trailer across the road had a plastic Santa propped up next to a rusted-out pickup. Sophia figured she should start to think about hanging some lights or getting a tree. Most people around here started decorating right after Halloween and already it was almost Thanksgiving.

She definitely wanted to make Owen's first Christmas special. He was getting big enough that he might be able to unwrap presents if she didn't use too much tape. He seemed really into birds right now. The last time she was with him, he flapped his arms every time a crow went by. It gave Sophia the creeps but maybe she'd try to find a bird toy anyway. A wind-up penguin or something.

She had no intention of quitting her FoodTown job but extra money from Hank would be nice. If she could convince him she wouldn't steal anymore, he might be willing to give her enough money to buy lights, a real tree, and a bunch of gifts to pile under that tree.

35

Cloris's house pulsed with noise. Hank could feel it in his bones the minute the door was flung open and Cloris's husband Doug stood there with his horsey smile, leaning forward to hug Hank despite the suitcase in each arm, the duffle bag yoked around his neck.

The kitchen was where the women were, but it was also where the scotch and soda was. Tucked high in the cupboard above the refrigerator because Doug worried that one of the "munchkins" would get at it. Hank waited a beat, guessing that Dim-Doug would figure out that he needed a drink after a three-hour car ride through three states with his wife, two-year-old, and mother-in-law. But Doug just went on asking Hank about the best-selling brand of ham in the deli.

"Sara Lee," Hank said over his shoulder. Why should he care if that was true or not?

The conversation stopped as soon as Hank was through the swinging door. Cloris looked up from mashing the potatoes and stared at him. She was pink-cheeked and shinier than usual, her lank hair plastered to her forehead. Hank rubbed at his face, wondering if he had a smear of Frederick's baby food on him somehow. "What?"

Cloris went back to mashing with more force than Hank thought was necessary. Five minutes they were in the house—had they already been talking about his unwillingness to adopt Owen? He'd specifically told Rose he didn't want to get into it with her family. As it was, Camilla had started in on him in the car: "What's going to happen to that baby if you don't help him? And after all Rose has been through..."

She'd said it sweetly and let her thoughts linger, like she was just musing about what good people they were. But he knew better than to trust her—Camilla was all about whatever Rose wanted. Whatever either of her girls wanted, for that matter. In the car, Hank had cranked the radio to the weather and ignored them.

"Help him," that's what Rose and Camilla kept coming back to. Like Owen would be alone on the streets holding up one of those cardboard signs if they didn't adopt him. Who was to say Sophia wasn't going to get it together and become a decent mother?

Hank wasn't stupid enough to start defending her. He was pretty sure Rose already had her suspicions about him and Sophia. She'd sniffed his jacket the first night after he got home from Sophia's. Sniffed it and then gave him a look and then asked if his back was bothering him from sleeping on the break room couch at work. She told him he should go for a massage, left the laptop open to the webpage and everything.

In the three weeks since that first night, Hank had gone to Sophia's trailer five more times, usually during his lunch hour. Only once had he used the working late excuse again. Since moving to Maine, he'd only worked late a handful of times before Sophia and it couldn't turn into a semi-regular thing without Rose getting suspicious. But someone might have told Rose about his extended lunches (always after two because that's when Sophia got back from therapy), his car turning down Sophia's driveway, his particularly cheerful mood. He was prepared to defend himself on all counts if Rose asked but she hadn't asked yet. He thought Rose might be trying to get him to give in about Owen by making him feel guilty. It might have worked, except that he thought Sophia could get her shit together and be a decent mom. Despite the fact that she stole from the register. He didn't want to think about that right now.

Ignoring the hateful look from his sister-in-law, Hank took down the bottle of scotch and a juice glass. Was the affair what they were talking about now? He hoped not. Maybe Rose wouldn't find out about him and Sophia. He'd have to figure out how to end it soon. How to get things back on track with his wife. The stealing should have been the end of it. But Sophia apologized and Hank was an asshole.

He decided to skip the soda and have scotch on the rocks. Two ice cubes. The burn in the back of his throat. If Rose knew he'd slept with Sophia, wouldn't she have said something about it by now? Unless she was going to use it against him later. Unless she hated him too much to bother. He never should have started sleeping with Sophia Leach. He took his drink and bowed his way out of the kitchen. Rose kept on whisking the gravy, her back to him, her eyes on the stove. Cloris kept mashing and glaring. Camilla looked like she'd been crying while she folded cloth napkins into triangles.

*****

Cloris's fat-assed husband carved the turkey like he knew how. Hank was on his fourth scotch, sipping now, trying to slow down the numbness around his lips. Although he liked it. It made him think of the way Sophia bit his lips, her little teeth nip nipping until he thought he'd go crazy. He liked thinking about her with his mother-in-law sitting to his left, his asshole brother-in-law grinning at him from down the table. One man at each end. Anchors away! Let them wonder about the look on his face—pure bliss, he bet.

Maybe they were patting themselves on the back, thinking how great it was that Hank was such a family man. How he'd fit right into the DiSanto family. And then he thought of their most recent lost baby and he swallowed more scotch. Maybe they'd ask him to do the blessing. He'd been with Rose nearly ten years and they'd never once asked him to do the blessing. First it was the old man, hauling himself half out of his wheelchair to say how grateful he was for his wonderful family. And then the honor—such that it was—fell to good ol' Doug. Because he'd been around longer, maybe. You'd think they'd swap off, though. Take turns. It was that they never thought Hank was good enough for Rose. They always figured she'd settled because it was time. She'd wanted to start a family and he was nearby and available. He wasn't making that up—Cloris took him aside after the wedding and told him as much. Told him he should do everything he could to hang on to such a prize.

Doug raised a glass of red I-showed-you-the label- earlier-to-impress-you wine and waited until mostly everyone quieted down. Frederick kicked steadily at the leg of the table. Rose put her hand on his leg, leaned in told him to stop it, please.

Doug went on, thanking God for their family, their health, and most of all for the good fortune of Rose catching Owen Leach. A miracle, Doug said. Cloris—bless her malnourished heart—rolled her eyes. Hank was glad his mouth was dulled by the liquor. Otherwise, he might have said it was possible it was all a blessing in disguise. A Trojan horse. He pictured Sophia Leach coming out of the wooden horse's stomach and this made him nearly laugh out loud.

"Amen," Doug said. And they all echoed him. Amen, amen, amen.

Doug and Cloris had money, not that you'd know it to look at them. Cloris in her flowered dress that might have come from a wedding in the eighties. Doug with his faded jeans and a potbelly peeking out from under his fake-silk shirt. A cheepo gold necklace around his tree-trunk neck. Hank had never gone in for jewelry, except for his wedding ring which he figured he had no choice about. The kids were dressed nice, though—the girl in a lacy dress with a bow around her middle, the boy in a button-down shirt and a little tie, both of them with napkins tucked under their chins so they didn't ruin their finery.

The money Cloris and Doug spent was on nutcrackers. Dougie kept what must have been a thousand of the creepy, big-teethed things in the den and living room, all on shelves Doug and Cloris had specially built. What kind of a man collects fucking ball-crackers?

"How's work these days?"

"Swell," Hank said. "Couldn't be better." Rose looked up and he was sure her eyes were full of tears this close to being shed. Make him feel like a real asshole.

"Let's not talk about work," Camilla said.

God bless his mother-in-law. Not too many men would say that but Hank and Camilla had always gotten along, more or less. Hank thought it was because she'd pretty much given up on the idea of Rose ever getting married, until Hank came along. Of course, she wouldn't have too many nice things to say if she knew he was sleeping with the newly hired Sophia Leach. Or that he had no intention of adopting her kid. Break out the nutcrackers.

Camilla scooped some potatoes onto Cloris's plate. "You need to eat."

Cloris waved her hand over her plate. "I don't want potatoes, Ma."

"I'll eat them." Doug slid his plate under the spoon and waited for Camilla to unload the potatoes.

. The idiot would be burying his skinny wife soon if he didn't get her into some kind of rehab.

If Hank had the kind of money Doug made working for the IRS, he'd have the good sense to join a gym. Hank put in his running miles, sit-ups, pushups. Death-stoppers, that's how he saw his workouts. He was no male model but he was a hell of a lot more fit than Dougie. Plus, he knew when to call it quits with the potatoes and pie.

Hank took a piece of turkey when the platter came his way, then helped his nephew load his plate with three pieces. The kid was skinny now but he didn't stand a chance—in twenty years he'd probably be as fat as his father. When Frederick was old enough, Hank was planning to take him out running. They'd start off slow, a half mile, three quarters. But eventually it'd get so they'd be running half-marathons together. Although they'd never go in for those tiny shorts some guys wore, their balls practically flapping in the wind.

For being so skinny and pinched-looking all the time, Cloris was a good cook. Just not a good eater. Hank watched as she cut her turkey into miniscule pieces and then forked one into her mouth, chewed about a hundred times before she swallowed, then wiped her lips. Hank would bet dollars to donuts she'd spit the turkey in that napkin. Up to her old tricks. No one except Hank was watching Cloris, although maybe they should have been. She must have felt him looking at her because she looked up from pushing food around her plate. Hank waved.

"How is it?" He shouted down the table.

Cloris shrugged. Rose narrowed her eyes at him.

Doug and Cloris sent their rug-rat kids to private school. That's why they sat so nice and polite at the table, knowing which fork to use and all that bullshit. Third grade, fourth grade, whatever. Neither one of them was near high school age. What useful things could you learn in third grade that you couldn't learn in regular public school? Probably they'd both go off to Harvard or some shit.

Hank leaned in to Frederick. "Mom tells me you've been singing your ABC's. You wanna show us how it goes?"

Rose, without looking away from whatever conversation she was deep into with Cloris, said, "Not while he's trying to eat, Hank."

"He hasn't even taken a bite."

"Give him some turkey." Rose came around the table, cut up the turkey on Frederick's plate even though Hank had already cut it. She handed Frederick a piece which he took and threw on the floor. Hank smiled.

Hank's mother had money, once. But by the time Hank had met Rose it had been eaten up by the nursing home.

Early onset Alzheimer's, they said. She's safer here, they said. At three grand a month it better be fucking Fort Knox with crystal chandeliers. All the money went away, every last wrinkled dollar bill. Hank started at the grocery store at sixteen, worked three to nine three afternoons a week and all day Saturdays. He kept the house by letting people think his made-up step-father still lived there. Otherwise, they would have sent him to go live with his aunt in Sacramento. Not that it would have been so bad being around the warm weather, but then there would have been no one to see his mother on Sundays.

He let Doug refill his scotch and thought about how the nurses used to dress his mother up nice, especially on the holidays. Probably because she still had nice skin, hair that wasn't thinning at the crown, nails that weren't brittle as eggshells. They'd put her in whatever new sweater he'd bought her, dress slacks, loafers he'd bought at JC Penny. They'd set them up in a special room where there were usually meetings, just the two of them. Away from the stink of urine and prune juice and stewed tomatoes. They'd even let him light candles as long as he was careful. He'd spread out the Honey Baked ham he bought from the store up on Route One, the rolls and apple pie from the bakery. He didn't bother with the salad or vegetables and she never said anything about it. She just ate like a lady, asking him questions about work and if he'd talked to his father lately. He used to think she wasn't as bad off as they made her out to be because she had pretty good questions. But then he realized they were the same ones, over and over, and that it didn't matter what he answered. "Dad's on the moon, Ma," he said once when he was in a rotten mood. "He flapped his arms and flew there."

She tucked her ham into her cheek. "Oh, good for him," she said.

He brought Rose to have Thanksgiving with him and his mother the first year they were together. Rose was polite, maybe a little nervous, and she talked too much about the snow they might get and how good the ham tasted. But he'd loved how gallantly she tried to keep the conversation going. When his mother asked where Hank's father had gone off to, Hank and Rose shared a look. Rose smiled. "I think he went to the store for the vanilla ice cream to go with the pie," she said. His mother nodded and, in the next moment, forgot all about her long-dead husband.

When they were leaving his mother kissed his cheek and told him Rose seemed like a nice girl. Her lipstick smelled like wax. That was the last Thanksgiving his mother was alive. She died in March that year and Hank always had the feeling that she'd been hanging on until he met someone.

Hank shuffled his turkey around on his plate, ate a bite of roll, drank a little more. To Doug he said, "What's the most shitfaced you've ever been?"

Doug laughed. "My buddy had a bachelor party. This was back, I don't know, ten years ago——"

Cloris raised a skinny hand. "Not in front of the kids, Douglas."

"Come on Cloris. Lighten up. They won't even know what I'm talking about."

"They'll know."

"I'll spell out the bad words."

And like that Hank felt flying metal against his cheek. "Did your wife just throw her fork?"

"I think so. Yes." Doug bent to retrieve the fork. He picked it up, wiped it on his napkin, and carried it back to Cloris. He kissed the top of her head.

Hank would have to be careful if he got up and did the toast now. He'd probably tell them to go fuck themselves. But Doug had already given the toast, hadn't he? They were past that now, everyone eating, talking across the table, some of them letting off bits of food mid-word. Doug said something about heroes among us and Hank could see right away where this was going. He took a drink, set his glass down, leaned back and closed his eyes. Rose the hero. Rose the baby-catcher. Miracle, miracle, blah blah blah. He heard Cloris say, "You believe pretty much everything Rose does is saintly, if not miraculous." And then, the next thing he knew, one of the kids was whacking his knee.

"Jesus, kid—" and when he opened his eyes, they were all staring at him. The whole friggin' family, waiting for him to say something. He must have dozed off for a second there. He raised his glass. Smiled. They were still waiting on him. "What did I miss?"

Rose stared down at her still-foodless plate. At least he hadn't been asleep that long. Camilla said, "We were just saying how we hope you're coming around to see how wonderful it would be to have Owen as part of your family."

Cloris said, "We weren't all saying that."

In front of Frederick? They were talking about this in front of the kid now? He was at that age where he was starting to repeat things. And the other kids, too. They'd probably start an Adopt-Owen fund-raiser at their private school. Was this part of a trick? Hank's mouth felt slack, loose around the jawline. He opened and closed it, just to make sure it worked.

Maybe he was on his fifth scotch now? His sixth? Finally, he said, "Sophia doesn't want to give up her kid." He was looking at the honey-brown liquid in his glass, carefully avoiding the eyes of his son, especially.

Beside him, Camilla said, "You have our blessing, that's all."

"I don't even know why we're still talking about this." His voice wasn't slurred, was it? His tongue felt thick but he'd spoken slowly, carefully. He didn't want them all saying he was drunk.

Doug said, "If the kid's mother wants him, why not get a baby from China or something?"

Hank could have kissed him. He puckered his lips and air-kissed. "The voice of reason!"

Camilla frowned. "Don't you believe in miracles?"

Cloris shook her head. "A miracle is a big deal, Ma. Maybe it was luck, but I don't know about anything else."

Camilla said, "I'd just like to see everyone happy." Cloris and Doug and the kids that weren't Hank's were all leaning in, talking over each other, practically killing themselves with enthusiasm on one side or the other. Thank God for Dim-Doug and his skeleton bride. Who ever thought he'd be saying that?

Only Frederick was ignoring the whole thing, kicking, kicking the leg of the table. Hank was proud of the kid for being a little rebel, just doing his own thing. Ignoring all the bullshit, not even looking up, even though everyone around him was talking. He was just kicking, kicking, kicking.

Probably imagining kicking them all into outer space. Smart kid.

Hank stood, even though he had to look down at his legs to be sure they were still there. There they were—two legs in black dress pants when that prick Doug got away with wearing jeans. He picked up his drink, held it with both hands, and walked with precision into the living room where he fell onto the sofa and waited for Rose to eventually bring him a slice of apple pie.

36

Her mother stood hunched over the sink, her fingers scraping at the bits of dried-on residue on the turkey platter. Rose slipped beside her, nudged her with her hip. "You must be exhausted, Ma. Let me take over."

Camilla looked up and Rose was surprised by the shadowy lines around her mouth and eyes. Rose said, "I'm sorry Hank was such an ass."

Cloris, loaded down with a stack of plates taller than her head, backed into the kitchen. "You can say that again. Did anyone start the coffee yet?"

"I've got it." Rose took down the coffee maker from above the sink. "Doug wasn't exactly helpful."

Cloris said, "Your husband was drunk before anyone even mentioned Owen."

Camilla waved a hand through the air like she did when they were kids to get them to stop bickering. "Girls, please."

While she stood and ran water over the plates in the sink, Cloris said, "You're always on her side."

Camilla shook her head. "I'm not on anyone's side."

"You moved away to be literally at her side."

"It was Ma's idea. I didn't make her do anything."

"I like having a little land," Camilla said.

Cloris rinsed the forks and knives and flung them into the dishwasher. "There's land in Massachusetts."

And then she was gone, calling after her kids, telling them to go outside and play until dessert was ready.

Rose put her head on her mother's shoulder. Camilla, always small, was smaller now and Rose had to bend her knees to reach her. But the feeling of being nestled was worth the ache in her back. "Why does she always have to give me a hard time?"

"You girls are lucky to have each other."

"I know."

Camilla brushed strands of hair off Rose's forehead. She had to reach up to do it and Rose wondered if her mother would someday just shrink away. Camilla said, "How are you feeling, honey?"

"I'm okay, Ma." Rose caught her mother's hand and held it. "Just tired." It wasn't true, but talking about her sadness wouldn't make it any better. If she admitted how, at night, she could feel the baby she had named Lilliana Rose pressed against her chest, it would only make her mother worry more than she already did.

From the kitchen window, Rose watched Doug in the backyard with the kids. As Frederick climbed up the front of the jungle gym, Rose felt her breath catch in her chest. He wasn't that steady on his feet. She could almost see his head cleaved open, blood tangling with his blond curls. But then Doug was behind him, a hand on Frederick's bottom, and Rose let her breath go.

Who was watching Owen?

Camilla went back to the sink, rubbed at a stuck edge of grease on the platter, then looked at Rose again. "Maybe you shouldn't try to adopt that baby if Hank doesn't want to."

Camilla's words felt like a thousand needle pricks in Rose's throat. "I thought you agreed with me. Who knows what will happen to him if we don't? His mother, his grandmother——"

"I know, honey. But you shouldn't jeopardize your marriage."

"Hank will come around." If she believed that enough, maybe it would be true.

Camilla frowned. "But what if he doesn't? And what about the baby's mother? Maybe she's really trying. Maybe it won't be so easy to get her to give him up."

"Easy isn't the point, Ma. What kind of mother throws her baby out a window? Does it matter if she's trying? What does that mean——'trying'——what will happen to Owen if she fails and I'm not there to catch him?" Rose's throat closed with tears. Why couldn't anyone understand that saving Owen Leach was not something she could just walk away from? That she was owed something for losing her Lilliana Rose? She gulped air. "I'm doing the right thing."

Camilla dried her hands and put an arm around Rose's waist. "I know you are."

Rose leaned into the warmth of her mother. Maybe she'd be okay on her own. What good was Hank, anyway? Passed out on Cloris and Doug's leather couch, the football game blasting on TV. Rose's father had never changed a diaper, never made a meal, never ran the vacuum. But he was a good man. He went to work, came home for dinner at six, joined his family for church on Sundays, looked over his daughters' report cards and told them they were smart as whips. She said, "If you'd wanted to adopt a baby, Dad would have gone along with you."

Camilla let go of Rose, leaving a gap of cold air between them. "Your father and I would have talked about it, honey. I don't know what we would have decided." Camilla went to the refrigerator and took out the apple pies. "These look good, Rosie."

"No, they don't." She'd made them last night, hastily overworking the dough and not taking enough time with the edges.

Camilla kissed her cheek. "You tried, honey. That's what matters."

Rose thought of her father, calling to her mother from the living room for a soda. And her mother, setting aside the pizza dough she'd been kneading in order to carry him a can of ginger ale and a glass of ice. "I can't just give in to whatever Hank wants."

Camilla said, "A good marriage is a blessing from God, too."

Rose remembered her mother leaning down for a kiss, her father asking her to sit a minute with him while he watched the race.

Rose cut a slice of refrigerator-cold pie and slid it onto a napkin.

Camilla touched her hand. "Don't you want that heated up?"

Rose shook her head. Camilla cut herself a slice of pie, then slid the rest of the pies into the oven. Together they stood at the counter and forked bites into their mouths while they waited for everyone else's pie to heat through. After several bites, Camilla said, "You'll do the right thing, honey."

37

Hank told Sophia about this psychic Rose went to see but he swore he didn't know what Psychic Lucy said, only that Rose didn't seem thrilled by the whole thing. Which could be really good news, as far as Sophia could see.

"I'll bet she told her to get off my back."

"Maybe she told her about us," Hank said.

"We weren't even together back then. Besides, you'd be sleeping in the garage by now if that was the case."

Hank might not believe in psychic power but Sophia one hundred percent did. She'd seen them on TV and some of them were really amazing. Although she'd also seen the Dateline episode where they outed a bunch of phony psychics. Sophia trusted her instincts to know whether or not Lucy was legit.

She was surprised to get an appointment the day after Thanksgiving but it worked out fine, seeing she had to be in Portland for Group until three.

Lucy wasn't dressed in red, with long crimson nails. She didn't have a turban around her head. No cards, no crystal ball. Just a cat on the table in front of her and a pile of meaty little treats stacked like a pyramid. Probably she was so good she didn't need to play dress-up.

"You're early," Lucy said, moving the cat to the floor.

"Shouldn't you have known I would be?" Sophia sat down. Lucy had a puff of blond hair that looked like it could be a wig, and a line of blush thick enough to skip over. Maybe she was playing dress-up. The room itself was not much more than a done-up living room. Sophia could see the cat-magnet covered refrigerator from where she sat. It seemed like Lucy wasn't trying too hard to set up the whole experience but maybe she didn't need to bother. Sophia said, "So, you're the kind of psychic who talks to dead people, right?"

Lucy smiled. "I often see and hear people who have passed."

Sophia smiled back—her Merry Pines smile but brighter. "My friend Rose was the one who recommended you. She was here a few days ago."

"Isn't that nice."

"Maybe a few weeks. It's hard to keep track with the holidays." If Lucy was psychic, she could probably read minds and she'd know easily enough that Rose and Sophia weren't really friends. "Anyway, she said you told her some really amazing stuff. I thought we could start there."

Lucy tugged at the ends of her hair and powder puffed into the air. "You want me to tell you what I told your friend?"

Sophia nodded. "She was too upset to tell me herself."

Lucy tapped her index finger on the table and Sophia half-expected a rabbit or a fire. "Was it your baby she caught?"

Sophia grinned. "I knew you knew."

Lucy smiled back so hard her lipstick cracked. "I try," she said. She reached across the table and took Sophia's hands.

Sophia was grateful her hands weren't wet or fuzzy from the cat. "Let's see if we can make a connection for you."

Sophia willed herself to keep her hands in Lucy's. Somewhere in the distance, a cat purred. She said, "How long will that take?"

"Just a few minutes but I need you to relax."

A cat stood in the kitchen sink and Sophia watched it nuzzle against the faucet. "Do you see me with my son?" It was possible that in the future she'd have another son. "I need to know if I get to keep Owen."

"I feel like you aren't relaxing," Lucy said.

"Why don't you just tell me what you told Rose, then?"

"I can't do that."

"It's not like there's some law against it or anything. Some protected information thing. Right?" Sophia let go of Lucy's hands and wiped her palms on her jeans.

"It's bad karma."

"No, it isn't."

Lucy rummaged around on the shelf behind her. "Let me give you my card, in case she lost it."

"The thing is that she wants to get custody of my baby." Sophia laughed, trying to make the whole thing seem like no big deal.

Lucy held out a business card and when Sophia didn't take it, she set it on the table.

"I'm not giving him up," Sophia said.

Lucy touched the ends of her hair and nodded. "I don't blame you."

"I just hope you didn't make her think she had a chance."

"I only tell people what I hear or see from the other side. What they do with that information is up to them."

"Right. Got it." Sophia stood. Another cat darted out from under the table.

"You have my card," Lucy said.

*****

Sophia brought Owen to the nail salon and set him in the corner they'd cleared for him and his things. It was a small space behind a hairy pink chair and Sophia worried that it would be easy for Vicky to forget he was even there. Except for his crying. Sophia thought he'd have grown out of it by now, but even though he could nearly sit up by himself, he still cried for reasons Sophia couldn't figure out.

"I don't get what he wants," Sophia said.

Vicky shrugged. "Babies cry."

"But all the time?" What if he was running a fever or had some kind of other sickness and they just ignored him? Sophia tucked his blanket around his feet, then held his big toes. "Are these your piggies?" He smiled. Her heart flipped over.

Sophia kissed his cheek, stood, looked in the mirror, fluffed her bangs, leaned in closer and picked at a zit on the side of her nose. She thought of Rose's skin, smooth like Owen's bottom. She should call and ask her what she used but it was probably some cream in a jar that cost a fortune. In magazines, Sophia had seen those lotions that supposedly fixed your face and she'd wondered who on earth had that kind of money. People like Rose Rankin. People who bought Oshkosh for their kids while Sophia dug around at Goodwill to find the shirts with the least stains. Except for the few times she'd managed to steal nice outfits from Kmart, but even then, they weren't that nice—a little sailor-suit shirt that Owen spit peas down the front the very first time she put him in it, a railroad conductor hat she couldn't resist but Owen wouldn't keep on his head, a little pair of yellow rain boots that were ridiculous but she had to have them. The boots he hadn't minded but she'd lost one at the mall.

She leaned in closer to the mirror and picked a speck of something off her teeth. She had a good smile—nicer than Rose's. And more sincere. Rose smiled like she knew she was better than you. Little did she know that her perfect husbandly-husband had come all over Sophia's breasts just two nights ago. The look on his face—like he appreciated it so much. That's how Sophia knew what he wasn't getting at home.

Vicky looked up from the woman with cherry-cola hair whose nails she filed into daggers. "Any work gossip we need to know about?"

Sophia thought about mentioning her visit to psychic Lucy but seeing she'd found out nothing more useful than the importance of blending in your blush, she decided to skip it. Red-head smiled, showing a gap in her front teeth. She was a regular for getting her nails done but Sophia couldn't think of her name. She lived a couple of towns over in one of the nice houses with a deck out back and bushes that looked like upside-down soup bowls.

"That bleached-blond cashier I told you about went out on three dates with Jay Jackson and then mysteriously quit. I heard from one of the other girls that he took her to Pizza Hut and then expected her to sleep with him anyway." It was probably only a matter of time before Vicky heard a rumor from one of her customers that Sophia was sleeping with Hank. Since

Halloween, he'd been coming over a few times a week, at lunch or after work, parking his car in her driveway like they didn't give a damn what anyone thought. If anyone asked, they were planning to say he was helping her fix the heat or whatever. There were plenty of things that could go wrong in a crappy little rental trailer. Sophia figured outright telling her mother would lead to Vicky blasting her about giving it away free to a guy who could at least help with the rent. Which he was helping her pay, but that was none of Vicky's business either.

Vicky said, "A job with drama but low pay. I don't know why you can't tell Rose Rankin that the baby she saved needs money to keep him in diapers." Vicky laughed, Red-head laughed along with her. "I can't support you and your kid for the rest of my life."

She made it sound like helping to pay for Sophia's measly rent for the past three months was forcing her into starvation. "I'm doing the best I can."

To the red-head, Vicky said, "Two days a week is all she manages to work."

Even though she was down to half-day sessions, Sophia still had Group five days a week, and that meant she couldn't really work more hours. Hank said FoodTown needed the most help on the weekends, anyway, at least until the summer when the tourists got here.

Vicky said, "I watch her kid—day and night—and work here and give her money and she goes to Portland every morning to sit around and talk about how she feels."

Red-head laughed spittle at that.

"It's not like I love 'Tell me how that makes you feel' ten times a day," Sophia said. She went over to the shelf of polish. When she was a kid and her mother went out for a smoke, she used to unscrew the tops, lean her nose right up in close, and sniff. She liked the sharpness of the scent, the chemical rush to her brain, the knowledge that it was unacceptable and strange, even though it had never been expressly forbidden. She wanted to do it now, to feel that chemical rush. To escape her life for five seconds.

Instead, she thought about Hank. She liked the way he looked at her when she was undressing. She liked the way he took his time with her, the way he kissed the inside of her elbows, the way he told her she was beautiful. Not that he was the only guy to ever feed her a line like that but he seemed to mean it more than anyone else ever had.

The last time they were together, Sophia asked Hank why he and Rose didn't have a dog. She'd always imagined Perfect Families to have at least one dog.

Hank had shrugged. "Rose didn't grow up with pets. She says it's hard to keep the house clean around pet hair."

Sophia said, "But what about you? Don't you think boys should have dogs?"

Hank shrugged again. "Sometimes it's easier to just not argue."

And so, Sophia had inserted two dogs into the fantasy of what her and Hank's life would be like.

Vicky was still talking. "These social workers claim I get enough money to take care of the kid but I'm telling you, it isn't near enough."

There she went again. If Sophia wasn't going to help out with money, she'd put him in foster care, she said. She liked to say she didn't see how she had any other choice. And then Sophia might be able to visit him, or she might not. As it was, Sophia had already missed him rolling over for the first time. Vicky told her about it, said he looked like a beer bottle washing up on shore. Vicky said it was a shame she'd missed it, and Sophia felt a stab of regret under her ribcage.

Red-head made a tsking noise as Vicky slid her nails under the hand dryer.

Sophia said, "I'll be able to help you out soon, Ma."

"Promises."

Red-head had a mass of corkscrew curls and Sophia thought about the time her mother decided her hair was too flat and needed a perm. She was eleven. Vicky dug a boxed perm out of the medicine closet, made Sophia put on a ratty sweatshirt, sat her down in front of Dr. Phil. The show was about racism and the whole time Vicky rolled Sophia's hair and pinned the curlers to her head, Vicky murmured under her breath about the way people get away with things, just because. She never said it outright but Sophia had the feeling she was talking about Black people and she had the sickening unease that she often felt around her mother. The way she smoked her endless cigarettes. The way she cursed at people in line at the grocery store who had twelve items in a ten-or-less line. The way she always asked for the "family discount" at the diner where they sometimes ate breakfast, even though Sophia's uncle hadn't been the owner there for as long as Sophia could remember.

Vicky finished rolling the curls and then poured liquid that smelled like vinegar and cat pee all over Sophia's head. The phone rang. Vicky told her to hold still. Sophia waited. Her scalp itched and burned. Dr. Phil looked all furrow-browed while talking between two white guys. Finally, she heard her mother hang up the phone and when she didn't come right out, Sophia went into the kitchen to find her. Vicky took one look at her and said "Why didn't you come get me sooner?"

Sophia cried while her mother unrolled curler after curler and the hair just fell off, big clumps of it. "Crying isn't going to help," Vicky said. Sophia's hair was piled all over the floor when the phone rang again and Vicky went to answer it. So, Sophia got up, swept the hair into a dustpan and dumped it into a grocery bag. Her hair, limp and too dark but still it had been hers, and better than being bald. This bagged hair she kept under her pillow until her mother found it and threw it out, calling her a pig for holding onto it. What was left of Sophia's hair Vicky buzzed into a boy cut and told her to act confident and the other kids would think it was a trend. Sophia knew better than to believe that so she stole a floppy hat with a pink flower from Reny's and she wore it, minus the flower, every day until her hair grew out past her ears.

That was before Vicky went to beauty school, and maybe it was the reason she went. She'd never said so but she wasn't one to give Sophia credit for anything.

Sophia picked out Ocean's Away polish and squeezed behind the hairy pink chair. She thought Hank might think the color was sexy in an off-beat way. Something his wife would never wear. Owen was asleep. Sophia sat down on the floor beside him and put her head next to his. She whispered, "We'll get big dogs, don't you think? A Shepard and a Husky, maybe. One of them we can name Slayer. Or maybe that's too mean. We'll think of something to make them sound tough but loveable." Owen's eyelashes fluttered and she thought maybe he was dreaming of running with the dogs. Sophia sat up, uncapped the polish after a good shake, and then painted her nails with a steady, sure hand.

38

Rose dreamt of a sky full of gray hummingbirds, the flap of their wings like rain.

She woke determined. In the kitchen, she pulled out the griddle and centered it over two burners. She measured out the pancake mix, the water, the egg. Hank came downstairs in a pair of gym shorts and his Boston College sweatshirt. Rose smiled like the women in ads for breakfast cereal. Like morning was the best time of day. Like anything was possible. "I'm making pancakes," she said.

"Frederick's still sleeping?"

Rose set the baby monitor next to Hank's place at the table. "You can let me know if you hear him." Frederick was getting too big for his crib. Twice Rose had found him about to climb out of it. She was about to say something about them needing to go shopping for a big boy bed but she stopped herself. Not now. She had to make pancakes with real maple syrup heated up the way Hank liked it. And then, she intended to show him he was wanted. What Hank needed was to feel not pushed aside. Then she might be able to talk him into adopting Owen.

Hank poured himself a coffee and sat down with the Sunday paper. He sniffed the butter-heavy air. "What's all this about?"

"I just wanted to do something nice for you." On the baby monitor, Frederick began to whine. Rose got a plate from the cabinet and slid two pancakes on it. "Start with these," she said, kissing Hank's unshaven cheek. He picked up his fork and started right in without even glancing up.

She paused and listened. Maybe Frederick was just talking to himself. Maybe she could leave him, just for a few more minutes. She made two more circles on the griddle.

"Aren't you going to get him?"

"He's fine." Rose flipped the pancakes. They were still a little underdone and batter spurted onto the stove. Rose felt a shakiness in her legs. If she was going to do it, she'd have to do it soon. She turned off the griddle.

Hank was halfway through his second pancake when Rose knelt on the tile floor. She felt the cold through her nightgown, down deep into her knees but she forced herself to stay there. Hank looked down. "What are you doing?"

She put a hand on his knee, inched closer to him. Without looking up, even though she could feel him looking down at her, Rose reached her hands into her husband's lap. It took her a moment of fumbling to locate the flap in his shorts. She heard Hank swallow. Hoping her hands weren't cold or sticky, she maneuvered his penis out into the open, scooched herself closer, and took him in her mouth. She heard his fork clatter against the plate. She heard the quickening of his breath. His hands tugged at her hair. She refused to think about Sophia Leach.

On the baby monitor, Frederick whimpered again. Rose ignored him. She worked her mouth until Hank got hard and then she got her hands involved. She was trying to remember the specifics of how he liked it done. Hank moaned. Frederick started to cry full on. Rose tried to stay focused but she wondered if she could go check on him, maybe get him a bottle and then come right back. Hank was saying yes now, and she could feel the quiver in his whole body. When this was over, he would be so much more willing to talk. Frederick wailed. Rose glanced at the baby monitor. Hank's hands stilled, then pushed her head away. Softly at first, then with more force.

"Go," he said.

Rose shook her head. Hank pushed more firmly until she had no choice but to let him go. He tucked himself back into his pants. "I can't with him screaming, anyway."

Rose stood, went to the sink, stuck her mouth directly under the faucet, spit into the drain. Hank went back to eating his pancakes. Rose rinsed again, then drank a glass of water. Frederick cried harder. Rose switched off the baby monitor, took another drink of water, then went upstairs to fetch her son.

39

After she got fired, Sophia took the job cleaning toilets in the dumpiest motel in three towns. They had a reputation for hourly rates, bedbugs, and moldy shag carpeting. She had never been in the place before, opting on several occasions for the backseat of a car over the Can't Beat Retreat. The outside alone had scared her away from a check-in. And when she went for her job interview, she'd almost turned right around and beat it the hell out of there. But she was out of choices.

It was a single-story grayish-tan building with six brown doors on either side of a bigger, more central door differentiated by a black plastic "Office" sign. Outside each door sat a concrete slab and a single once-white plastic chair. The front lawn of the Can't Beat was a dip-down mud hole with a few face-high tufts of grass. Nestled in among the dirt and greenery was an array of plastic cups, food wrappers, cigarette butts, and who knew what else. Sophia spotted a pink t-shirt hanging off a random tree branch.

Sophia worked "on call" which made Vicky mad because she couldn't just drop Owen off willy-nilly. Plus, they paid her fifty cents less than minimum wage, saying she'd make it up in tips. But the kind of people who stayed at the Can't Beat were not the kind of people who left tips. What choice did she have but to go along with it? Jay Jackson had fired her the Friday before last, saying that her drawer had been short and that FoodTown had policies. Hank swore he hadn't turned her in but she doubted it. She'd gone out looking for jobs right away but every place within an hour drive besides the Can't Beat had said no thanks, even when they had a red Help Wanted sign slapped up against the window.

On her first day at the Can't Beat she found a used condom stuck to the toilet seat in room 3. She used a paper towel to peel it off and made a mental note to bring rubber gloves next time. She poured Clorox in the bowl, scrubbed it with the yellow-brown toilet brush, and then moved on to the rim, the sink, the moldy shower.

Fuck Hank. He had to have been the one who told Jay. It wasn't the first time she'd taken a twenty from her register and she for sure didn't believe it was just a coincidence that Jay decided to check her cashout that day. Hank must have told him to keep an eye on her. Fine, she shouldn't have been stealing. Stealing was crappy and selfish and it wasn't like she was stealing food for her kid or anything. It was a habit and she felt entitled and she heard all about it in Group and told Hank what fat Bev and the others said and how she knew she had to stop and how that wouldn't be a problem. She wasn't compulsive or anything. He just nodded like "Good for you." Sophia swiped at long strands of hair half in the drain, used her fingernail through a paper towel to scrape the soap scum off the shower walls. By the time she started on the floor (on her hands and knees with an already dirty sponge) she thought probably this place had never been cleaner.

The brown and orange shag carpeting felt damp when she knelt on it to check under the bed. Bad idea. There was something under there. Maybe a jacket? Maybe a pair of shoes. Possibly something furry and dead. She stood up, buried her mouth in her shirt and tried for a couple of deep breaths. Probably no one but her had looked under the bed in a decade. Whatever was there could stay there.

She stripped the sheets off the double bed and rolled them into a ball. There was a thick black sock in between the fitted and flat but Sophia rolled it right in, pretending she hadn't noticed. No way was she touching it, plucking it up with her fingers, the way she did when she found one of Hank's in between her baby-pink sheets. How was it possible he went home with one sock in the dead of Maine winter? Did Rose wonder about the sock or was she so busy being Super-Rose she just figured it was a casualty of the dryer?

Sophia scrubbed at something sticky on the rickety little table next to the bed. She hoped this job was temporary. Her plan was to work here long enough to show Hank that she didn't need his conditional help. Maybe then he'd see her as more than a casual thing and he'd get up the nerve to leave Rose and she and Hank could buy a little house somewhere way up in the woods. Somewhere within driving distance of a grocery store so Hank could get work. Someplace with enough land so Sophia could put in a vegetable garden. Maybe even some flowers. Tulips were her favorite. Hank would probably tell her she didn't have to work but she wouldn't mind finding something in retail if they were near a CVS or something. They'd get Owen back and they'd have Frederick every other weekend and maybe for whole summers. On Hank's days off they'd take the boys fishing down at the lake.

She ran the carpet sweeper over the shaggy carpet, careful to get the edges as best as she could. She'd have liked to open a window to air the place out. For all her cleaning, it still smelled like mold and sweat covered by a perfumey layer of chemical. But the Can't Beat manager, a pimply blond kid who couldn't have been any older than Sophia, told her they weren't about to "heat all outdoors." So, she left the place closed up and locked behind her, hoping that the next customer would be happy enough with her effort.

So far, Hank had given her five hundred and fifty dollars and the promise for more. She could have spent it on a new dress to wear to tonight's Christmas party at the VFW. The hall itself was nothing special—no VFW she'd ever seen was anything more than utilitarian. Big open room with scuffed hardwood floors, outdated kitchen near the door that led to the back parking lot, black laminate bar kitty-corner by the front door. Just because the room was nothing special didn't mean she had to blend in. Sophia had her eye on a tight hot-pink number she'd seen at the consignment shop. Hank and Rose would be there, and Sophia would have loved to see the look on Rose's face when she saw how good Sophia looked. But it was hard to know when Hank might change his mind, tell her the gravy train had left the station or some other not-so-nice way of saying game over. She had to save.

The VFW Christmas party was a good chance to show off her mothering skills, Sophia figured. Vicky had agreed to bring Owen because there was a bar. But there was also Marjorie's husband Fred who dressed up as Santa, and the Parker community band playing Christmas music, and there was a Yankee swap for the kids. Owen was too little to participate in the give-a-gift-swap-a-gift tradition, but Sophia had bought a coloring book and some crayons so she could hold him, select a present from the pile, and help him unwrap it. Most everyone in town who had a kid would be at the party. Sophia would look motherly, competent. They would say she'd changed. They would say she deserved another chance.

The get-together would be awkward now that she was sleeping with Hank but it wouldn't be the first time she'd been in the same room with the wife of the guy she was screwing around with. In high school, she'd slept with the dad of one of her classmates. The girl was pimply with dish-water hair and she wasn't bright enough to figure out that Sophia wasn't sleeping over her house because she enjoyed watching *The Breakfast Club* fifty times over. While Heather Howard mooned over Judd Nelson, Sophia was in the rec room with Mr. Howard mooning over her. And, in the morning when Mrs. Howard served French toast while still in her nursing scrubs from the night shift, Sophia ate like she was starving.

Rose must have her suspicions. Hank kept parking his car right out in Sophia's driveway and, even though you couldn't see it from the road, lots of people might have seen him drive in. Plus, the nosy post-office people would have seen his car every time they delivered the mail. Hank said he'd told Rose she was having trouble with her heat. Sophia was pretty sure any wife with eyes would see right through that alibi. Maybe Rose didn't care. Or, maybe she thought she'd get Owen in exchange for Hank. She was wrong there.

40

Rose almost called Margo and said she wasn't coming to work today. There'd been a faint snow all morning, with clouds that threatened worse, and Rose was afraid she'd get stuck at Margo's. She had to leave Margo's by four because they had the VFW Christmas party tonight and it took her forever to get Frederick dressed.

To Margo she said, "I bought Frederick a new sweater for tonight. Red and green with an elf on it. It's really cute. Hopefully, he won't spill chocolate milk on it before I get him out the door."

Margo plucked at a loose thread on the dress she was hemming, caught the thread between her shears, and clipped it off. "Did I hear Sophia Leach is going to be there, too?"

Rose sat down with the dress she was hemming upside-down on her lap. She'd pinned it in place two days ago, when Ginny had been at Margo's to try it on. Smiling, telling Rose and Margo about the dance she and Alan were attending on New Year's Eve. Rose folded and pinned and told Ginny to hold still and she thought about how she and Hank used to go dancing on New Year's, usually at some swanky Boston hotel where they could get a room for the night, drink too much champagne, sleep in past noon the next day. Two days ago, Rose had said, "Things change" and Margo had raised her eyebrows at her. Ginny had just kept on chatting.

Now, Rose said, "And her mother, I guess."

Margo bit off a thread, tied it with her thumb and index finger. "Don't you think it'll be a little awkward?"

Rose pretended not to know what Margo was getting at. She'd heard bits of conversation that trailed off when she walked around the corner at the grocery store. The last time she went to the post office, Melody had given her a long, searching look along with her book of stamps. Rose wasn't stupid. There was something going on between Hank and Sophia. But he'd fired her, hadn't he? So, maybe whatever it was had ended. Rose said, "I'm hoping she's starting to see us as an extended family. We're practically old enough to be parents." She laughed.

Margo laughed along with her. When she stopped, she said, "Is Hank feeling paternal, too?"

Rose's stomach flopped. "I hope so," she said. An acknowledgment would make it more true and she couldn't stand that.

Margo said, "Well, maybe that explains it." A pause, a half-smile. "I thought I saw his car at Sophia's yesterday."

Wind rattled the trailer's windows. Rose hoped there wouldn't be impassable snow. Hank hadn't made any secret of being at Sophia's—to help with her heater, he said. Rose had been telling herself that the more Sophia liked them, the more likely she'd be to give them custody of Owen. She'd been telling herself there was nothing to worry about. Rose said, "She's been having some kind of problem with the heat in her trailer. And then he was going to help her put plastic on the windows."

"You're okay with him being there without you?"

Rose kept her voice deliberately neutral. "He's just helping her out."

"Shouldn't that be something she calls the landlord for?"

Before she left the house this morning, Rose wrapped a plastic keyboard for her Yankee swap item. All the presents went into a pile, but she hoped Owen would get the keyboard or that Sophia would swap whatever he picked for it. Rose imagined his chubby fingers exploring the keys, the look of surprise when the first note sounded, and then his understanding that he could cause the music. Rose said, "I think the landlord lives in Massachusetts or something."

Margo dipped her head and started back in on the hem. The dress would fall just above the woman's ankles, a slight flare at the bottom. Maybe they were going to a concert at the Merrill. Once everything was settled with Owen, maybe she and Hank could get back to doing things like that. Get a babysitter a couple of Saturday nights a month. Maybe Margo would even do it. She adored Frederick. She'd been thrilled when Rose had found out she was pregnant with Lilliana, devastated when she died.

Margo said, "The landlord must have a guy he can call."

Rose, annoyed now, said, "I don't see the harm if Hank going over there makes Sophia like us more." She did see the harm, but she didn't want to.

Margo set aside the dress she was hemming. It was deeply cut in the bust and silver sequined and Rose thought it was something Hank would like to see on her. Margo leaned over and took Rose's hand. "What if it's only Hank Sophia really likes?"

Rose yanked her hand away. "Can we just talk about something else?"

Margo rubbed an index finger over her eyebrows. "Rose, you know I don't like gossip but people have been talking about Hank and Sophia. I don't want them to make a fool of you."

Rose felt desperate and unmoored. "Since when do you listen to what people say? Since when do you believe gossip?"

"I'm just worried about you." Margo stood, let the dress slide to the floor.

She put her hands on Rose's shoulders but Rose shrugged her off. "I don't want your worry. Or your pity. Hank wouldn't risk everything to sleep with some half-witted baby-thrower." Rose stood, kicked the dress away from her feet. Where was her coat? Had she left it in the car?

"I'm sorry, Rose. I just wasn't sure you knew. But if you feel like there's nothing going on..."

"That's exactly how I feel. Because there is nothing going on. You small town people with your small-town minds find the drama in the littlest things." She was furious, panicked, and certain. She knew Hank had been lying about all the things wrong in Sophia's trailer. She'd known it since the night of the snowstorm but she hadn't wanted to know it. Now, what she wanted was simultaneously to run to Hank and to run away without him.

"I just don't want you to be embarrassed," Margo said. "People are starting to say things and I feel terrible—"

Rose said, "I'll call you tomorrow, okay?" Without intending to, Rose slammed the door behind her, hard enough that the plastic snowman on Margo's door rattled himself crooked.

*****

Rose stopped off at the house and then drove to Vicky's with an infant-sized lemon-yellow snowsuit with red racing stripes down the sides. She could have driven over to Sophia's trailer and seen for herself what was going on. She could have waited at home with a glass of wine and plans for a civil discussion. But she didn't want images of her husband and Sophia seared into her brain. And she didn't want civil discussion. She didn't want to hear about mistakes and I'm sorry and I never meant for any of this to happen.

Rose stood with Vicky's screen door propped against her foot and waited for her to hand over Owen. Her blood ran like fire through her veins. She was sure she was flushed, sure Vicky could see it, but Vicky only tapped her foot and said it was kind of damp-feeling out.

"You sure you want to take them out in this?" Vicky asked.

Suddenly she cared? Rose didn't have a clear plan other than that she'd take the two boys and go somewhere to think. She'd call Hank when they were settled, tell him she knew about the affair, tell him she didn't want to hear excuses. She'd give him an ultimatum: leave Sophia now or lose Rose and Frederick. She wouldn't say anything about Owen right away. After he chose her, she'd tell him. She'd say she wanted them to run away together.

"He'll look like a banana," Vicky said, pointing to the snowsuit. She curled her lips around a skinny cigarette and inhaled. "Sophia didn't say anything to me about sledding plans for the kid."

Rose shrugged like it didn't matter to her either way. At home, she'd collected Frederick from her mother, packed a bag with sippy cups, bottles, toys, two changes of clothes for each boy, and the elephant quilt she'd made for Owen. She'd told her mother she'd see her tomorrow. Camilla had asked about the party at the VFW and Rose said Hank didn't really want to go, that they'd changed their plans.

Now, to Vicky, she said, "I'm taking Frederick anyway. Why not let me give you a little break? Plus, I think he'll have fun."

Vicky's mouth pooched around her cigarette. "If you say so." She waved Rose in. "Give me five minutes—he's sleeping."

Rose stood in the entryway. She kept her gaze divided between her car—which she'd kept running with Frederick in it—and the hallway down which Vicky had gone. A clock in the shape of a fat cat ticked loudly. The worst-case scenario would be Vicky coming to her senses and calling Sophia, then finding out she didn't know anything about sledding.

Rose had mentioned the big hill where they made snow and had huge plasticky tubes and a tow line to get you back up the hill. Which was ridiculous because no way would you ever take an infant there. But maybe Sophia wouldn't even care. Maybe Sophia would say it was fine anyway. Because maybe she didn't know any better or maybe because she was distracted by whatever was going on with Hank.

In seven minutes, Vicky came back to the door and handed Owen out to Rose. The weight of him in Rose's arms was like something she won. She leaned down and kissed his head and Vicky looked at her like she might say something. But she just pulled her cigarette from her mouth and kissed him on the forehead, nearly banging her head into Rose and leaving a faint smear of lipstick she didn't bother wiping. "Have a good day, pumpkin."

What kind of a woman just handed off an infant without even asking if Rose had formula, a bottle, a car seat? Rose had all those things, of course. She was prepared.

She was going to make the decision easy for Sophia. Once Sophia knew Owen was somewhere safe with Rose, she'd see how much easier her life would be without him. She'd get back to her pre-pregnancy dreams, whatever those might have been. She'd grow up, get married, start a family when she was really ready.

Somewhere in the recesses of her brain, Rose knew it wouldn't be that easy. But she couldn't let herself think about the fact that Sophia seemed to actually love Owen. For whatever that was worth.

While she drove, Rose called a farmhouse in Vermont she and Hank rented once when they were first married. The place turned out to be available for the winter. Rose imagined building snow families in the front yard, cooking local squash into purees, baking gingerbread men, and taking the boys into town to share the cookies with the neighbors. "Perfect!" She said, and she could have sworn both boys smiled.

She'd call Hank when they got there, tell him he could make his choice now.

From Vicky's, Rose drove through the outskirts of Parker, past the antique stores with their swaths of green garland, rocking horses with red bows, silver tea sets arranged just so. She drove past the church and the plastic nativity and she said a quick prayer for herself and the boys and sweet Lilliana Rose, looking down on them from heaven. She drove past the road that would take her down to Sophia's and there she sped up a little and held her breath. If Hank was going home now—right now—he'd see them for sure. But his car wasn't in sight and Rose let out her breath.

Both boys were strapped into their car seats in the back. Rose looked in her rearview mirror and waved to them. Frederick was asleep but Owen's eyes flicked over to her waving hand and she thought he smiled again.

In town, Rose drove past the hardware store, the pharmacy, the hairdresser's where Vicky worked, the Chinese food restaurant, the pizza shop. All of the windows were swagged in evergreen garland or sprayed at the edges with fake snow. All of them promising a Merry Christmas. "We'll make our own merry," Rose said out loud. She turned the radio until she found "Holly, Jolly Christmas." She sang along.

First stop, the bank. Second, the gas station on the other side of town. They'd stop for lunch in a few hours, maybe at a McDonald's so Frederick could get out and play. Depending on how many times they needed to stop, she may have to get a hotel somewhere for the night. But that would be okay. She pictured Frederick on his stomach on the big hotel bed watching cartoons while she gave Owen his bath in the hotel tub. She'd allow Frederick to eat pizza from room service for dinner and she'd have a candy bar while she fed Owen his bottle.

In a few hours, she was going to call Sophia and tell her she'd taken the boys out sledding but the car had broken down. Maybe that's what she'd tell Hank, too, at first. She was going to say it was late, and the boys were both asleep, so she'd keep them for the night. Sophia was the kind of mother who would say yes without giving it much thought.

At the bank's drive-through window, the dusty-haired teller frowned at her computer. "I'm sorry, Mrs. Rankin," she said, leaning too close to her microphone. "The account's been overdrawn."

"That's not possible," Rose said, rummaging through her bag for a cookie for Frederick, who was awake now and asking for a snack. Owen started to cry. "Okay, guys. Okay," Rose said, smiling at them, then at the teller.

The teller said, "I can print you out a statement. It looks like there have been some recent withdrawals."

Rose, holding the cookie, stared at the teller. She lowered the radio. "Are you sure?"

"Yes, ma'am."

Rose felt the pull of understanding she didn't want. Her lips stuck to her teeth as she tried to smile. "I'll have to check with my husband," Rose said. Normal, normal.

"Have a good day," the teller said.

Rose drove off with the cookie clutched in her hand, Frederick crying now in tandem with Owen.

Hank might have transferred money to their IRA. But he would have told her. That was the kind of thing they talked about. And why would he take out so much that he'd leave their account overdrawn? They didn't keep that much in there, but always there was a cushion. Rose knew the overdrawn account meant Hank had been hasty, not thinking, his mind elsewhere. Had something happened with the car she didn't know about? Maybe he'd needed to buy something for the house—hadn't he said something about the gutters? He'd had his eye on a snow blower but they'd decided they couldn't afford it—hadn't they? Maybe he'd been putting money aside for Christmas. Would he buy her something special to get them back to the way things used to be? Or maybe something great for Frederick—they'd looked at the Toys-R-Us catalogue last week and Hank had lingered over the mini-Jeep.

Rose felt her stomach pinch with the certainty she was trying to justify the unjustifiable. Was he buying Sophia jewelry? Toys for Owen? Elaborate flower arrangements? Dinners, vacations, clothes? Or worse, was he planning some kind of future with her? Putting the money into a different account that she knew nothing about? The thought made Rose shaky. Had Sophia Leach really managed to take every-thing from her? First, she killed Lilliana Rose, and now she was taking Hank, taking their money, probably planning a future for her and Hank and Owen and Frederick. At this Rose sobbed. She could not have Frederick. How could Hank be stupid enough to think Rose wouldn't find out? Maybe he didn't care anymore. Was he actually planning to leave her for Sophia?

Rose pulled the car into a parking spot in front of the Methodist Church. Frederick, in the backseat, said "Cookie!" She handed him the dampish cookie, wet from her sweaty palm, and wiped her hand on her pants. While he stuffed it in his mouth, she rested her head against the seat. Owen had cried himself back to sleep. She felt like someone had turned her inside-out.

She couldn't access the IRA without Hank's signature. She'd already deposited her most recent paycheck from Margo. Where did that money go? How far could she get without money? Rose knew there were only a couple hun-dred dollars left before she maxed out the credit card. That would get her a night, maybe two, in a hotel. And then what?

Her mother was living off slim savings. She couldn't ask to borrow money from her.

Rose could turn around right now. Bring Owen home. Tell Vicky it was too cold or too icy. Or she could take the boys sledding. And then what? Go home and pretend like nothing had happened? One son and an unfaithful husband. Would that ever be enough?

She knew it wouldn't. She put the car in drive, pressed on the gas, and told the boys they were going to have an adventure. She cranked the radio back up and belted out "Joy to the World."

41

Just before Sophia's shift ended at the Can't Beat, Vicky called to say Rose wasn't back with Owen yet and she needed to leave for the VFW's pre-party Bingo. "I was planning to take the kid with me but you're going to have to get your ass over here and wait for them."

Sophia was still thinking about the gummy underside of the bathroom doorknob she'd just encountered and she was slow to understand what her mother was saying. Sledding? That was nice. "Where did they go?"

"Somewhere. I wasn't listening. She said you knew all about it."

Rose hadn't said anything to her. Maybe the call didn't come through on her phone. Cell reception was spotty at the Can't Beat. "Whatever. I'll be home soon." Sophia tucked her phone between her ear and shoulder and washed her hands in the dingy "Employees Only" bathroom sink.

"She said she talked to you yesterday."

"I haven't talked to Rose in ages." Her face in the wavery mirror was greased with sweat. Sophia shook water off her hands, then patted her face. The cool felt good.

Vicky said, "I don't know what the hell she was talking about then. Just get home."

"Right."

The conversation left Sophia wondering. Shouldn't Rose be home getting ready for tonight? It was just like her to suddenly be hot to take the boys sledding—show Sophia that a real mother can do it all. And she'd brought Owen a snowsuit, which was probably one Frederick had outgrown. Still, it meant she knew Sophia didn't own one which was insulting.

Instead of going home to shower and change like she'd planned, Sophia drove straight to Hank and Rose's. Neither car was in the driveway. Hank was probably still at work. *There's nothing wrong,* she told herself. But it was strange—Rose showing up to take Owen sledding and telling Vicky she'd called Sophia and told her about it. Shouldn't she be ironing Frederick's overalls?

Sophia backed out of the driveway. The place Rose worked, Margo's Sewing, was just across town. It couldn't hurt to go there, see if maybe Rose had said where she planned to take the kids sledding. It couldn't be anyplace very big or intense. Owen was too little. Wasn't he? Sophia could meet them there and maybe they'd all get in a few runs together and then she could say she was tired and Owen was cold and she could take him home.

Rose's car wasn't in the driveway at Margo's, not that Sophia had really expected it to be. She knocked on the trailer's door, righted the crooked snowman while she waited.

Margo, her gray-blond hair piled on top of her head in a messy bun, her mascara smudged off one eye, opened the door. "Has something happened?"

Sophia and Margo knew each other in the way people who'd lived in the same town all their lives know each other.

In passing, a friend of a friend. An ad in the paper, the police blotter.

Sophia felt fear grip her between the shoulder blades.

She said, "Why do you think something's happened?"

Margo sucked in a breath so that her sweatshirt lilac receded and bloomed. "Rose was upset when she left here. And then you show up and I just thought...I don't know what I thought."

Sophia felt a roller-coaster loop of anxiety through her body. She said, "She picked up Owen and told my mother she was taking the boys sledding."

Margo's smile was pasted-on. "That sounds nice."

"What aren't you telling me?" Sophia took a step closer.

Margo opened the door to let her in. "Is Hank with you?"

"Why would Hank be with me?" Sophia walked into the trailer which wasn't much bigger than her own but was nicer. Coffee-brown curtains framed a sliding glass door that led out onto a huge back deck, white unstained carpet went everywhere except the kitchen which looked like it had a real tile floor and maybe granite on the countertop. Whatever it was, it was black and gleaming and so clean Sophia could have used it for a mirror. She felt Margo's nerves like a fly over sugar. She said, "What's going on?"

Margo leaned against her countertop and her palms reflected against themselves. She said, "Everyone in town knows about you and Hank."

Sophia wasn't surprised but now she was really jittery. "Including Rose?"

Margo nodded.

"So, she's mad."

Margo said, "She wouldn't do anything to hurt those boys."

"But maybe she's trying to scare me." Sophia walked outside and pulled her cell phone out of her pocket. She forced herself to very calmly dial FoodTown. She asked for Hank.

"He's in a meeting." The girl, probably Amber at the service desk, sounded like she couldn't have cared less if she tried.

"Please. Tell him it's his wife and that there's been an emergency." Sophia thought that by now they should know Rose's voice but she doubted anyone paid enough attention to care.

Hank came on the phone sounding breathless and scared. "Honey?"

"It's me." Silence. "Sophia."

"They said it was my wife. Did you tell them you were my wife?"

"Have you heard from Rose this afternoon, Hank?"

"I'm at work."

"Margo said she knows about us."

More silence. "How do you know Margo?"

Sophia said, "I think Rose took Owen."

"Why would she take Owen? Maybe your mother asked her to take him for a few hours." A pause, the sound of voices in the background. "I was in a meeting."

He sounded defensive and Sophia felt the sudden loosening of being set aside. "She came to my mother's three hours ago and said she was taking Owen and Frederick sledding. She hasn't come back, Hank."

"Maybe they're having a good time."

"She told my mother I knew all about it, which I didn't. And you guys are supposed to be going to the VFW party tonight. Why isn't she home making handmade ribbons for the Yankee swap gift?"

"Is it possible she mentioned it and you forgot? I think she wrapped the gift last night."

Sophia closed her eyes and leaned her head against the cold exterior of Margo's trailer. "Just do me a favor, Hank? Try to think where Rose might have gone if she was going to run away."

"She wouldn't run away." And then, "I have no idea."

He wasn't even trying. "Please, Hank. Owen is my son. I know I haven't been the world's best mother..."

A shifting sound, like Hank moved the phone from one ear to the other or, possibly, against his chest to say something to someone in the room with him. Into the phone, he said, "I swear to God, Sophia, I'd tell you if I knew."

Whatever Sophia had done in the past, all the horrible things, she was sorry for them. Every one of them. "Please," she said. "Doesn't her mother live in town?"

"She could have stopped by there, but I really don't think—"

"Maybe we should call the police. It's a missing person's case, right?" If Rose knew about Sophia and Hank, then she knew she wasn't going to get Owen.

Hank said, "It's too soon to call the police. They could just be sledding. Maybe she took them for hot chocolate." His calm made Sophia want to scream until his eardrums exploded.

"I'm going to call the police unless you have a better idea of how to find them." Sophia let herself back inside Margo's trailer. Margo was in the kitchen, dunking a tea bag in and out of a reindeer mug, complete with antler-handle.

Sophia paced the hall. Paintings of mountains and lakes lined the hallway and Sophia wanted to close her eyes and transport herself to any one of those perfect, pristine places. Instead she was here, like a caged dog. Needing something but unable to do anything. She couldn't call the police because wouldn't they have to report a missing Owen to child protective services? It would not be points in her favor even though, technically, this was Vicky's fault. If they decided Vicky wasn't competent, Owen would be shuffled into foster care and then who knows how or if or when Sophia would get to see him. But maybe she should call anyway. It was worth the police thinking she was an idiot mother as long as Owen was safe. Rose wouldn't hurt him, though. Would she?

Finally, Hank said, "Let me call Camilla and see if they're there."

Sophia pressed her head against the wall and closed her eyes. "If we call and Rose is there, she could take off again."

"You're making too much of this, Sophia."

"I'm going over there with or without you." She hung up and then counted to one hundred, then two hundred before he called back.

It took Hank less than fifteen minutes to get out of work and show up at Margo's. In that time, Margo said twice that Rose was a good person and that Sophia and Hank could have used some discretion, at least.

Sophia met Hank in the driveway. "Thank you," she said. Rose's mom lived a few streets over from Hank and Rose, in the nice part of Parker. It would take ten minutes from Margo's. Hank switched on the radio, then turned it off. He opened his window a half inch. "Are you cold?" He asked.

Sophia shook her head. She wished he'd step on it a little. When they finally pulled up to Rose's mother's green and white new-build, Sophia opened her door before Hank had a chance to come to a full stop.

"Rose's car isn't here," Hank said.

"I see that." Sophia felt like she could break apart, scatter into a thousand pieces. She ran up the walkway and knocked on the door. If Owen wasn't here, he could be anywhere and she might never get him back. She probably didn't deserve to be his mother because she'd lost him out a window and she definitely didn't deserve to have him because she was a generally crappy person who stole stuff and slept with married men. And maybe the only reason he was alive was because of Rose Rankin. But she wanted to be his mother and that counted for something. If she got him back this time, she would do everything she was supposed to do to make his life as near to perfect as she could manage. She prayed to whatever god might be listening.

It took a minute but a woman who looked like an older version of Rose answered the door, looking past Sophia. "Hank?"

Sophia hadn't realized he'd come up beside her but she was grateful. She put her hand on his arm and squeezed.

"Hi, Ma." Hank leaned in and kissed her. "This is Sophia Leach."

Camilla gave Hank a searching look, then led them both inside. She listened while Hank explained about the sledding, and the fact that Rose hadn't returned, or called, and wasn't answering her cell.

Camilla made the sign of the cross over her body. "Something must have happened. An accident. Have you called the police?"

Hank looked at Sophia. "I didn't want to do that, Ma. If Rose has Owen—"

Camilla whacked Hank's arm. "They could be lying bloody in a ditch somewhere. What are you doing? Why are you wasting time?"

Sophia said, "We would have heard if there had been an accident. There hasn't been an accident." She wanted that to be true. She hadn't thought about an accident. How could she not have thought of that? Normal mothers always worried about accidents. What was wrong with her?

Camilla stood and paced her white-on-white kitchen. "The roads might have been icy."

Sophia shook her head. "The roads are dry. All the way over, there was no ice."

Camilla narrowed her eyes. "You don't know what's happened."

"I just want to find my son."

"And I just want to find my daughter. Safe and sound."

"So, let's look for them," Hank said. "Let's calm down and make a plan and we'll find them."

42

Where else could she go? Cloris and Doug's house was the only place that made sense. They would never let her forget that she'd come to them for help, but there was no one else she could turn to. She'd let her Massachusetts friendships lapse and this was way too personal to take to someone she was only on Christmas-card terms with. She couldn't call her mother because that was the first place Hank would look and Camilla would judge her, say she should have kept a better eye on her husband. Margo didn't have room for them.

Rose gripped the steering wheel and told herself it would be worth it. Cloris and Doug could give her enough money to get on the road. And it's not like they were big fans of Hank—they definitely wouldn't call him.

Rose drove around with the boys for a while because she didn't want to get to the house too far in advance of Doug. Because she knew Cloris would have to ask Doug about the money, and she'd say she couldn't call him at work and bother him. Rose hoped the kids might still be at after school activities when she got there—Darla at karate, Drew at basketball—so they wouldn't be around to overhear. Groveling to her sister and brother-in-law was bad enough. And, Cloris and Doug would tell the kids anyway because money decisions "affected the whole family." Still, Rose didn't want to see their wide eyes, their sweetly nodding heads.

Rose drove to a park where she and Cloris used to play when they were little. But then she drove away, even though Frederick shouted "Swing! Swing!" She couldn't take the chance Cloris would be there running laps or something.

She decided on McDonald's because she knew Cloris would sooner die than take the kids to any place where you paid before you ate. Frederick made straight for the indoor playroom and Rose let him, figuring she'd get him to eat something later. Owen started to cry as soon as she stopped the car and once they got inside, she took him out of his carrier and cradled him. He hiccupped a sigh. A teenage girl with her hand in the pocket of her boyfriend's jeans walked by. "He's adorable," she said.

Rose smiled. "He really is."

Rose fed Owen a bottle and kept half an eye out for Doug in case he came in for a milkshake before he went home for kale salad and carrots. Who could blame him if he did? She'd have to confess she was on her way to their house. She'd offer him some fries. Maybe it would be easier to ask Doug for money without Cloris frowning and doling out her opinion about how she'd never much cared for Hank to begin with.

It was six when Rose got to the house. She sat in the car for a minute, looking at the battery-operated candle in every single window of the two-story colonial, the enormous wreath covered in glittered fruit on the front door. The huge spruce in the yard twinkled with perfectly placed white lights. Cloris and Doug hired a crew to decorate their house. As did everyone else in this town. Tasteful. Perfect. Quaint. Not the understated quiet of Parker, which at this time of year with deer found crunching through the yard and snow sliding off the roof. This was a more antiseptic quiet, with just the faintest purr of car engines escaping over the highway's sound barrier.

Had Rose not convinced Hank to move to Maine, this likely would have been their life, too. The house they'd sold had been in a town like the one Cloris and Doug lived in. But Rose had come to like Parker's tacky plastic Santas and haphazard lights and watered-down hot chocolate at the skating hut by the lake. Her throat closed with tears. That was the life she wanted—with a son she gave birth to, a son she saved, and a husband.

Cloris answered the door with the phone in her hand. While Rose waited for Cloris to say her goodbyes, she unzipped Frederick's jacket, un-tucked Owen from his blankets. They smelled like French fries and Rose wished she'd opened the windows in the car to air them out.

Cloris said, "This is a surprise." She didn't smile but she kissed Rose on the cheek and wrinkled her nose slightly. "You smell like grease." She touched Owen's foot. "Are you babysitting?"

"This is Owen." Rose smiled, even though what she wanted was to burst into tears, lie down on Cloris's wine-colored rug, and bury her head in her arms. "We took a little road trip." A commercial for Lucky Charms played somewhere in the house. Rose said, "I need a favor."

Cloris nodded as if she'd seen this coming for years. "I was just setting the table."

"We already ate."

Cloris took their jackets and hung them over the railing. Not in the closet. Clearly, she wasn't expecting them to stay long. She said, "Doug's just having a drink. Can I get you a cocktail?"

Rose shook her head.

Darla and Drew tripped down the stairs, a whirl of shouts and laughter and "Auntie's here!" and then they were gone, into the kitchen, the refrigerator door opening.

"We're having dinner in five minutes!" Cloris called after them. "Go wash your hands!"

Frederick had toddled over to the large potted tree in the corner of Cloris's dining room and was scooping dirt onto the floor. Rose grabbed his hand. "Stop it." He made the about-to-cry face and Rose dropped his arm. "Please, Frederick." And then, because she felt like they were all inches away from a meltdown anyway, Rose blurted, "I'm leaving Hank and I need to borrow some money."

Cloris re-scooped soil into the plant pot. "You took Owen."

Rose shook her head. "I'm babysitting."

"So, if I call his mother..." She swished her hands together to get the dirt off, then held them aloft, as if they were radioactive instead of simply not clean.

"Just help me, Cloris. Please." Rose's stomach clenched.

Cloris raised an eyebrow. "I guess we'd better get Doug."

In the den, Rose distracted Frederick with three balls from the pool table. He knocked them around on the floor, chased after them, giggled when they smacked together.

Rose sat beside Doug and looked at the TV. He was watching the news. Hank was probably watching the news, too. Unless he was out looking for her. She said, "Hank cleaned out our accounts." Her voice wavered. She felt clammy. Cloris returned from the bathroom, wiping her hands on a lily-white hand towel.

Doug sipped his drink, then spread his arms wide on the back of the couch and turned his head in her direction. "That asshole." He did not lower the volume on the TV. His nutcracker collection leered at them.

"I need to go somewhere and start over. I went to the bank and the money was gone."

Doug shrugged, smiled. "Maybe he just moved it. I do that sometimes to keep my darling wife from buying out the shoe store."

Rose thought suddenly of how easily "Doug" could become "Dog."

Cloris swatted her tree-branch hand at his leg but missed by a good three inches.

Rose didn't care about Cloris and her excessive spending, which it probably wasn't. Doug was cheap. "The money is gone," she said. "Or at least inaccessible to me."

Doug took another sip. "We can help you out, Rosie. That's what family does." Doug and Cloris exchanged a look. Cloris held her hand against her mouth—just like she did when they were kids and she didn't want Rose to know that she was telling Mary Andrews that she liked the red-headed boy—and whispered something to Doug. Doug nodded. To Rose, he asked, "What's the situation with Owen?"

"He's better off with me," she said. "There's no way that's not true." Rose hated his smug smile but she was too needy to tell him to shove it. She would take the money and start over with two kids and an extended family she could invent when strangers asked her about them.

"You could go to prison for kidnapping."

"Are you going to help me or not?" She would find a way to convince Sophia that this was all for the best. She would not go to prison. They would work this out.

Doug fixed her with a stern stare. She wanted to pull his eyes out. He said, "Of course we'll help you. We're just worried about you."

"Thank you," she said.

She and Cloris left Doug alone so he could catch the weather. In the dining room, Rose filled the water glasses. The last time they were here was Thanksgiving, when she still imagined that happiness was a possibility. She thought of psychic Lucy telling her to be careful, telling her that Nonny had a warning for her. Maybe she should have listened. Paid more attention. She could have at least been putting money into a separate account.

The clatter of a salad dish against a dinner plate roused her and Rose realized she was still standing in place, holding a water pitcher in one hand and an empty glass in the other. It amazed her that Cloris used her good china for everyday meals, even with two small kids.

"You'll stay the night," Cloris said. "We can figure out the rest in the morning. Have you called Mom?"

Rose put the water pitcher on the sideboard and folded a red cloth napkin into a triangle. She tucked it beside a white and gold plate. Her hands shook. "I don't want anyone to know where I am."

"Don't you think Hank's going to worry?"

"Maybe. I don't know."

"He'll go looking for you at Mom's."

Rose didn't know what Hank would do when he discovered she was missing. Would he go straight to Sophia so they could commiserate? She would have talked to Vicky by now—she'd know Rose had Owen. He'd call Camilla, eventually. And Margo. Those were the only two places she'd be, normally. Would he come looking for her? Would he ask her to forgive him?

Cloris served a dinner of from-scratch minestrone soup and whole wheat rolls. Rose didn't feel like talking or eating but she appreciated the chatter around her—Doug and the kids talking about school and homework, Cloris asking Frederick if he knew the words to "Row, row, row your boat." Then there were dishes, and helping Cloris's kids with math questions, and getting Frederick into his pajamas.

And then, five hours after she arrived at Cloris's, Rose was changing Owen on the guestroom bed when she heard a car pull into the driveway. Her body iced over. It had to be Hank. Who else would show up at eleven o'clock at night? He'd have seen her car by now. He'd be relieved at first and then what? Furious, righteous, terrified. She couldn't just stand around waiting to find out.

Rose rushed through wiping and carried Owen downstairs. Cloris and Doug were in the living room, glasses of white wine set aside. Cloris stood at the window. "It's Hank."

Rose said, "You called him."

Cloris gave her a look that meant she was crazy. "I would never do that, Rose."

"You called Ma, then. And Ma called Hank."

"She called here. She was worried sick about you."

"Why didn't you at least warn me?"

Cloris picked up her wine and drank. "I didn't think she'd tell Hank. But, how many places could you go without money? He would have figured it out eventually."

"I would have been gone in the morning," she said. And then the doorbell rang, and Doug got up and answered it. There was the sound of not only Hank's voice but Sophia's. Rose wanted to run but she couldn't decide which way to go. Why hadn't she insisted Doug give her the money tonight so she could get on the road?

Rose grabbed Cloris's hand and squeezed. "You're hurting me," Cloris said.

"You have to help me," Rose said. "You have to distract them. Keep them busy." She could still get out, get away. She just needed ten minutes to get to her car and get a head start. Hank and Sophia were still at the front door, talking to Doug. Negotiating. Asking. Everything was still very nice, very calm. Casual, even. Rose darted into the kitchen and considered the back door. She had Owen in her arms, but Frederick was upstairs on a cot in Drew's room. She would not leave without Frederick.

Cloris followed. "What are you going to do? Sneak out the back?"

"They can't take my kids. Go get Frederick and meet me outside."

"Owen isn't your kid, Rose. They'll call the police."

"I don't care." Her body vibrated with adrenaline and she knew that if she didn't keep moving, she'd collapse.

Cloris said, "I can't go to jail as an accomplice for you." Rose spun around, "All the years I've covered for you, and you can't do this one thing for me? All the years I swore to Mom I saw you eat your lunch. All the times I didn't tell her I saw you feed your dinner to the dog. The times I said I didn't think you looked too skinny when she was ready to ship you off to the hospital, Cloris, and you begged me not to let her do that to you."

Cloris twisted her bird-hands together. "But none of that affected anyone but me."

"That's not true. We were all scared to death you were going to die. And if you had, mom would have blamed me." From the hall, Hank's voice was louder, insistent. He called Rose's name, over and over like a desperate plea. He sounded worried. He sounded scared. She'd only heard his voice thinned out like this once before, the night he called to tell her his mother had died.

Rose wanted him to do or say something irrevocable. Wanted him to give her more of a reason to go.

Sophia was crying, gulping and pleading like she was just an ordinary mother to whom something terrible had happened. Rose wanted to scream at her, shake her, tell her she had no idea what it felt like to lose a baby, tell her all of this was her fault. And then Hank was in the kitchen and Sophia was behind him. Her hair was wild, her face greasy, her eyes panicked. Rose turned to run out the back door, but then she thought again of Frederick asleep upstairs. She lunged for the stairs, but Hank was suddenly in front of her, blocking her. Rose pushed at him with one hand, held Owen tight with the other.

"You're going to hurt him," Sophia said.

"It's a little late for you to worry about that," Rose said, not looking at her. "Move," she said to Hank. "Get out of my way."

"You can't take them," Sophia said. At the same time, Hank said, "Rose, please."

To Hank, Rose said, "How could you bring her here?"

Hank's breath was fast, panting, nearly animal. "You can't go."

Sophia grabbed Owen around his waist and pulled, but Rose held the baby tighter even though he'd started to cry. She said, "You've been having an affair."

"That doesn't mean you can steal my baby." Sophia pushed and slapped Rose's arm. She dug her nails in and screamed, but Rose held fast. She didn't care if Sophia's nails burned like fire. She would not let Owen go.

"Get away," Rose said. "Before I call the police." She knew it made no sense to threaten with the police, but she didn't know what else to say. She needed them to go away. From upstairs, Frederick began to wail. Rose needed to get Frederick and get out of here.

Cloris appeared at the bottom of the stairs. "Let me get him. He's going to wake the other kids."

Hank followed Cloris up the stairs. "I'll get him," he said. "He's my son." But then he stumbled as if he'd been pushed from behind. He stopped, rubbed a hand across his chest. "I don't feel well," he said.

Sophia turned toward him and, in that pocket of free space, Rose rushed up the stairs to the guest room. Cloris was leaning down to tuck the sheet around Frederick. She wasn't getting him ready. She wasn't helping Rose gather him so they could go.

Frederick slept on his back, his head lolled to the side. For the briefest moment of sheer terror, Rose thought he was dead. He'd just been crying but maybe it wasn't him, maybe it was Drew. "Frederick!" She shouted and he jerked awake, started to cry again. Owen joined in.

"Stop," Cloris said. "It's all right. It's okay."

Rose heard Hank's thudding footfall on the stairs, Sophia telling him he should sit down, that he didn't look well. Frantically, Rose turned to Cloris. "Help me get him up and dressed."

Cloris shook her head. "You can't do this."

And then Sophia was in front of her, pushing her, and Hank was on his knees moaning and Rose thought the whole thing was an act to distract her. "You aren't a good mother," Rose said. Sophia had her cornered between the bureau and the wall. White-lacquered wood iced Rose's back where her shirt rode up. Hank crawled forward. Sophia tugged at the baby again. "No," Rose said. "No. You're going to hurt him. Stop it stop it stop it."

"Give her the baby," Hank gasped. His face had gone grayish-green. He was still on all fours, like a dog, like he was play-acting a dog.

"Go to hell," Rose said. He looked like he was going to throw up and she imagined the mess that would leave on Cloris's pristine white carpet. She kicked at Sophia's shins. "You already made me lose one baby. You will not take this one from me." She caught a glimpse of herself in the mirror and saw a mad woman—spittle and frantic hair and a face like a tornado.

Sophia stopped, caught her breath, let Rose's kicks land. "What are you talking about?"

Hank half-stood, stumbled into the wall, slumped against it, and slid down like a cracked egg, thrown. Sophia stepped toward him as Rose inched closer to the door. And then, Sophia knelt beside him, and Rose thought they were embracing. *How sweet*, she thought. *How fucking sweet.*

But then, Cloris shouted to dial nine-one-one. Still, it took Rose another minute to understand the embrace was not an embrace, but that Sophia was giving Hank chest compressions and breathing into his mouth. Even then her brain couldn't work out what was happening. Why was she doing that? Weren't they taking things a little too far? Rose stood against the wall, clutching Owen to her chest. Cloris comforted Frederick and Drew while Doug went to check on Darla. Sophia breathed and compressed and Hank stayed very still.

The wail of the ambulance seemed to make everything speed up. Sophia kept working at Hank like she knew what she was doing. Did she know what she was doing? She must have learned CPR when she worked in the nursing home. Probably it was a requirement. Rose wanted to crawl into bed with Frederick, and then suddenly she had. She wedged Owen in between them, looped her arm and half her body around both of her boys. "It's going to be okay," she said.

Frederick slid out of bed and crawled toward Hank. "Daddy, Daddy, Daddy." It was the sweetest thing Rose had ever seen and she could not stop herself from crying.

Sophia paused in her compressions long enough to look at Frederick, then at Rose who was laying on the bed even though now she knew she should be doing something more. Doug scooped Frederick into his arms and bounced him around the room and Frederick laughed and then cried. "He's okay," Rose said, not knowing if she meant Frederick or Hank. The paramedics fluttered into the room and everything became more urgent, more chaotic.

As they wheeled him out—when had they put him on the stretcher? Had she closed her eyes?—Rose saw his terrible stillness. She felt the tug of tenderness for the man who held her hand when the doctor told them there would be no more babies. The man who had cried with joy when Frederick was born, had wept when she screamed at the blood that had been Lilliana Rose. "I'll be at the hospital when you wake up," she said.

During the chaos, Sophia stood in front of her again, tugging at Owen. Rose had no more strength. She couldn't hold on. She let him go.

43

The tattoo place was in a strip mall, next to a sandwich shop. Sophia wondered if you could be in there, eating your turkey club, and hear the whiz of a needle marking someone next door.

"I want a name," she said to the guy at the counter. "Owen." The guy was small, not big and beefy like Sophia thought a tattoo artist should be. He looked more like an acrobat, one of those guys in the circus who gets shot out of a cannon. Not that Sophia had ever seen anything like that, but she'd heard about it from a guy she went out with once, and she could picture this guy in an orange and red striped body suit, hurtling through the sky. He only had one tattoo that Sophia could see, a line of paw prints starting at his wrist and going up to his elbow.

He showed her pictures of the different styles of lettering and said things like Roman and Gothic. He said, "You could make the O a heart or something if you wanted to."

Sophia could see that he was trying and she didn't want to disappoint him but she shook her head. She ended up picking a script, so that it looked like she'd written Owen's name across her thigh in her best handwriting. The guy talked her into letting the N trail off into a vine. She hoped she wouldn't regret it later.

Way back, when Hank had asked her how much money she needed to get by, Sophia named a figure twice as high as she thought she could use for rent and other bills. Because you never knew when a guy like Hank would pull the plug, say he couldn't do it anymore because his wife found out or his car broke down or his kid wanted to go to Disney. But he didn't even argue the amount when she said it. He just went to his wallet and gave her the cash. She'd felt guilty about it but it turned out she was right because look what happened—a heart attack followed by a stroke followed by a letter from Rose telling Sophia that Hank would live but he didn't want to see her. Sophia believed both things.

She remembered the feel of Hank's ribs crunching under her hands, the stillness of his lips as she breathed into his mouth. The heat in the room, the pain in her own chest. When the paramedics arrived and took over, the girl with the blond ponytail smiled at Sophia and told her she'd done a good job.

The needle pinched going in. "You said this wouldn't hurt."

The tattoo guy—he said his name was Davy—said "Just a sec." And he kept at it, his head down, his hand steady.

Sophia hissed through her teeth. This hurt more than childbirth, or at least what she remembered from childbirth. Back then, she'd had whatever drugs they'd offered her and somewhere during the night they'd handed her Owen and said he was hers.

When she looked down at her thigh, Davy was closing the loop of the O.

"We can't stop now," he said. He smiled up at her, briefly, like a co-conspirator.

She smiled. "Nope."

He started in on the W. Sophia sucked in a breath. "This a boyfriend?"

She shook her head. Was he flirting with her? He was shorter than she was by an inch, maybe. And thinner, although she could see the muscles below his short-sleeved t-shirt. Usually she went for bigger guys, like Hank. Guys who dwarfed her, made her feel safe, or at least contained. She licked her lips. "It's my son."

"You don't look old enough to have a son." The W had a loop at the top, connecting it to the middle of the O. Sophia had chosen a dark blue ink and she watched as her skin bled around it.

"How long will this take to heal?"

"Couple days. How old's your son?"

How could he not have heard about Owen? Maybe he just wasn't connecting the dots, and Sophia for sure wasn't about to connect them for him. Or maybe he wasn't a news guy. "He's a baby," she said.

Davy started on the e, linking it to the w by a thin ribbon. He said, "I love babies."

"Me too." She almost wanted him to ask why she was getting the tattoo. Her own baby's name, wasn't that unusual? Maybe it was something you did if your baby had cancer, or had already died from something terrible. SIDS. Leukemia. A house fire you couldn't rescue him from. Sophia felt the tears start down her face.

"It's okay," Davy said. "We're almost done."

She would make something up if he asked because the truth was none of his business. But she would never pretend that Owen had died. Or that he had some terrible disease. She didn't want him to be gone.

She also wouldn't tell Davy how afraid she'd been when she thought Owen had been kidnapped by Rose Rankin. How sure she was that she was getting exactly what she deserved, and how badly she didn't want that to be true. What was so messed up was that Owen would have been fine. He would have grown up with a brother and probably a dog and three hot meals a day and sheets that were washed every Monday and dried outside in the bright sunshine. Rose would not ever tell him that he'd once had a mother who threw him out a window and he'd be able to grow up believing that he was always wanted. There was a part of her that thought she'd done the wrong thing by rescuing him.

Sophia closed her eyes and tried to see if she could tell by the feel that he was making the N. His left hand had settled on the inside of her thigh. She felt him slide it higher. She opened her eyes. Davy's right hand was still steady, making the hump on the N. "Maybe we shouldn't do the vine," she said.

He looked up at her, a kicked-dog look in his eyes. "No vine?"

"I just don't want to ruin it. What you've done looks so pretty."

Davy smiled. "You could always add it later."

Sophia watched as he finished, a small curlicue at the end of the N. She imagined a long trailing vine leaking off the letter, leaves nudging down into the crook of her knee. She thought that Davy would be the kind of guy who would circle each leaf with his tongue. Not conservative like Hank. If she was ever alone again with him so that she could show him, she was sure Hank wouldn't like the tattoo.

Sophia thanked Davy, paid for the tattoo, and wrote her number on the scrap of paper Davy slid in her direction.

Someday, she would sit with Owen on her lap and teach him the letters of his name.

44

The black fuzz at the nape of Sophia's neck choked him. He was rubbing her bare shoulders while they watched a movie about stolen cars and then he leaned in and kissed her neck. Somehow, he inhaled the threads of her hair. He coughed but he couldn't clear it, couldn't catch his breath.

"Keep coughing." It was Rose's voice. Rose was at Sophia's trailer? Hank felt a stuttering panic followed by self-loathing. Why was he there? He had a wife, a son, a home of his own. He willed himself to keep his eyes closed. Maybe he was dreaming. When he opened his eyes, Rose stood next to him and he was lying down. There was gray daylight through a large window, a small TV with a game show playing, a sink with a pink basin.

Hank said, "What's going on?" But his mouth didn't make the words. His lips pulled one way and then the other, his tongue felt like someone was holding it in place. He tried again: "What's happening?"

Rose took his hand. Hank could see her holding it but he couldn't feel it and when he tried to squeeze her fingers, nothing happened. Was he dead? Was this hell?

Rose said, "Hey, sleepyhead. Nice to see you."

She looked content, but Hank could not figure out why that would be true. He remembered the baby, and going after him, and Rose holding him like she would sooner die than give him up. Hank closed his eyes. Not because he wanted to rest but because he wanted it all to go away.

He could hear Rose move away from his bed. He heard her say "He was awake a minute ago." And then a murmured answer from someone who must have been standing farther away.

They'd had an argument. She'd found out about Sophia. But they weren't in Sophia's trailer when that happened. He'd had pain in his chest, across his arms. Hank had an image of Rose holding the baby—Owen—and Sophia crying. They'd been someplace very white.

Rose scraped a chair over to his bedside. Hank slit his eyes open.

"I'm sorry," she said. "I didn't mean to wake you."

Had he been asleep? Hank gazed out the window but his room was high up and all he could see was sky. Pale gray—the kind of sky that could be mid-January threatening snow, March with icy rain, October after the sun went down. The few branches he could see were bare but that only eliminated summer. He couldn't hear wind or traffic, only the bump and squeak of noises in the hall. Was he in a hospital or a nursing home? Once, after his mother had died, he and Rose had promised each other that they'd never resort to nursing home care. That they'd take care of one another at home, no matter what. But he wouldn't have blamed Rose if she hadn't held up her end of the bargain.

A blur of pink came into the room. "Hi there, Mr. Rankin. Let's get you washed up."

He and Jeff Dalton used to joke about how much they'd love having pretty nurses give them sponge baths. Hank closed his eyes and tried to convince himself to feel pleasure instead of humiliation. "Sit tight," she said. "I just need to get another set of hands to turn you."

Hank's breath felt full and wet. He coughed but it felt inadequate, loose but trapped in his chest. He felt like he was sitting in a pool up to his nose, and someone was pulling on his feet to make him slide under.

"We can suction him if we need to," the nurse said. Back now beside his bed with an even younger nurse with her. This one blond. Jeff would say he must have had brain damage to not enjoy all the attention just a little. Maybe there was brain damage. Hank tried to scroll through his mind. He knew the alphabet. He could read the clock. It was three-thirty. Must be afternoon. Hank could feel a puddle of drool running down his chin but he could not move his tongue to catch it.

The nurses finished cleaning him and they left Hank on his side, facing Rose through a metal railing. She put her hand against the metal but did not touch him. "The doctors say you'll come through this."

She did not say "eventually" or "probably" but he heard it anyway.

He would have liked to explain to Rose that he was planning to put the money back in their accounts once things got settled with Sophia. She'd needed heating fuel for the trailer but she was going to pay him back now that she was working again. He'd gotten her fired and he felt like he owed it to her to help her out a little. He liked that she needed him. But he wanted to stay married. He hadn't ever not wanted to be married to Rose. There was too much to say and he couldn't say any of it. Hank closed his eyes.

"Rest now," Rose said.

He didn't see that he had much choice.

45

The doctor with the long face and horse teeth told her that Hank wouldn't die. That, in time, he'd likely regain use of his left side. "Most of it, anyway."

"And his speech?"

The doctor consulted his clipboard. "Hard to say."

Rose fed Hank some cream of wheat, wiping his lower lip with the spoon. He survived the heart attack but then, after the bypass surgery, he'd had a massive stroke. Not that unusual, the doctors said. They talked to her, around her, above her—she felt surrounded by voices.

Her mother, kissing her at the door before Rose left for the hospital, said, "It's a miracle that you still have him at all."

"This is not my idea of a miracle," Rose said.

Her mother made the sign of the cross. "Be grateful he's alive, Rosie."

If Hank had gotten help sooner, the heart attack might not have been as severe. The stroke could have been avoided. The doctors didn't blame her. Or, they didn't say outright that it was her fault. She asked, "How long before I can take him home?" She thought that a wheelchair is like a stroller, and nothing like a stroller. She imagined tucking Hank into bed and nestling Frederick on one side of him, Owen on the other. Sophia might still change her mind.

The doctor said, "Two weeks, give or take. If that's what you decide."

That gave Rose enough time to replace the stairs leading into the house with a ramp, to convert the dining room into their bedroom, and to get a hospital bed rented and delivered. She had left Sophia five voicemails in four days, at first polite and thanking her, then asking after Owen, then saying she'd like to see him, then pleading that it would be good for Hank to see him even though Rose knew that last bit made no sense at all.

The doctor said, "You know you could place him."

"In a nursing home?" She imagined Sophia in a nurse's uniform, her fingers seeking a pulse on his wrist. She blinked it away.

He nodded. "A rehab facility. The choice is entirely yours but you should know it won't be easy to care for him at home."

Rose laughed even though she felt like screaming. "Nothing is ever easy."

When the doctor left, Rose wiped Hank's mouth with his cloth bib. He wrinkled his forehead and moved his lips.

"Do you want more to eat?"

He tipped his head, ear to shoulder, ear to shoulder. "No? You're full?" People would say she was a saint, the way she stayed with her husband and took care of him, even after he was unfaithful to her, and with that tramp baby- thrower, no less. Rose imagined herself telling Melody at the Post Office that it was simply the right thing to do.

Surely, everyone in town would encourage Sophia to let them have Owen. Even now, when Rose clearly had her hands full.

Hank looked steadily at her.

"Okay, honey. I'm not sure what it is. I'm not sure what you need." Rose sat on the bed and took Hank's limp hand in hers. And she talked, because in these past few days she'd become accustomed to talking to fill in the deeply unsettling silence all around Hank. She said, "Frederick's been having a great time at my mother's. She called me yesterday, put him on the phone and he told me about the yellow flowers he found poking up through the snow in her yard. Crocuses, my mother said they were. They went inside to get a camera and Frederick asked her if he could get a blanket for them. Isn't that sweet?" She didn't tell him that she'd followed Sophia to the mall, watched her wheel Owen into the toy store and pick out a plush giraffe almost as big as him. She saw them laugh, ducked when Sophia glanced around as if sensing Rose's presence. She didn't tell him how her arms ached to hold Owen, how she thought maybe maybe maybe. How only the shame of Hank's needs held her in place behind a rack of red sequined dresses that seemed to laugh at her.

A knock on the doorframe and Rose looked up to see Father Rob. She felt a pinch of fear, apprehension. "He doesn't need Last Rights," she said.

Father Rob nodded, kissed her cheek, touched Hank's hand. "You look well," he said to Hank. He smiled at Rose. "How are you holding up?"

"Fine," she said. Exhausted, lonely.

"The ladies at the church have started a prayer circle."

"That's wonderful," Rose said. Wasn't it too late to pray?

Father Rob, still holding Hank's hand, said, "What a miracle it is that he survived both the heart attack and stroke. Your husband is a strong man."

Rose blinked. "I thought you said miracles were hard to come by."

Father Rob tipped his head, considered. "Hank's living proof of how resilient the body and spirit can be."

"But that's not a miracle."

"Isn't it?"

When he left, Rose turned the conversation over in her head. Luck or miracle? Fate or coincidence? Sophia was allowed unsupervised visitation these days. Most of the time, she took Owen to a park or the lake, as if she was afraid to be completely alone with him. Rose could do it. She could take care of Frederick and Owen and Hank. It would be as if she had three sons instead of two. A multiplying of the loaves. The loves. At this, she felt a humming laughter in her stomach and pressed her hands against the swell of it.

Rose and Hank watched Wheel of Fortune followed by Jeopardy. When it was over, she told him that she'd called Sophia again, just to see how Owen was doing. "She didn't answer," Rose said. "I thought she'd want to know how well you were doing."

Hank flinched. "Does something hurt?" Rose asked.

With great effort, and with a sound like a mouthful of golf balls, he said, "'s okay."

Rose didn't know if he meant it was okay that she'd called Sophia or if he was just commenting on the weather. Either way, it was nice to see him make an effort. She inched her chair closer to the bed and watched out the window as day faded into night.

46

The day was cold for April but clear and bright as ice. Sophia bundled Owen into his stroller with three blankets tucked around him. Winter had lingered longer than usual, even for Maine. "Whoop!" She said, carefully bumping the stroller over the remaining icy patches on the shady path. Owen laughed.

She was "making progress." This was her third unsupervised visit. In an hour, she would take him home to her mother, kiss him goodbye, and tell him that pretty soon he'd stay with her all the time, day and night. She would ignore the tiny flutter of fear that came with that promise.

At the lake, she unstrapped him from the stroller, tucked the blankets all around him, and settled him on her lap on the bench facing the water. He leaned his weight against her and she held him against her chest and pointed to the sparkle of sun against thinly frozen water. Soon, the remaining ice would melt, the lake would open, and winter would be forgotten.

"It's nice, right?"

Owen made a noise she took to be agreement.

"It'll be summer before you know it, and when it gets warm, this will all be open water. There will be ducks and loons and fish and little boys and girls swimming."

He was so much heavier now than he was a few months ago. Solid. Real. Impossible to throw. She wouldn't throw him. She untucked his hands from the blanket and kissed his pudgy knuckles. "Ever, ever," she said.

Parker was a small town, and someday he would hear about his short flight from her arms to Rose's. He would come home from preschool or middle school and ask her about it and Sophia would tell him that she tripped over a rug and that he slid out of her hands and that it was lucky that a woman named Rose had been in the right place at the right time. No matter what they said in therapy, Sophia didn't see how anything about her feelings would do anyone any good.

Sophia kissed the top of his hatted head, then felt his cheeks to make sure he wasn't getting too cold. He laughed. She kissed him again. "You seem okay," she said.

Acknowledgments

This book took me eight years to write. I started it in my first semester of my MFA program and, had it not been for my teachers, mentors, a community of other writers, and my supportive family, I probably would have given up after the first draft.

Thank you to everyone who championed me along the way. Most especially, Aaron Hamburger, who was my first mentor at Stonecoast and whose encouragement and insight kept me going not only then, but through many lonely writing sessions since. Thanks also to Sarah Braunstein, Liz Hand, Elizabeth Searle, and Suzanne Strempek-Shea for believing in both this book and in me.

One of the smartest decisions I ever made was to enroll in the MFA program at Stonecoast. The mentors, my fellow classmates, the administration, and the entire Stonecoast community both pre-and-post graduation have been some of the most insightful and encouraging people I have ever known.

Thanks to Monica Wood for generously reading an early draft of this novel.

To Melanie Brooks and Elisha Emerson, who read more than one draft of this book, and many, many drafts of other, often terrible, writing. For their friendship, their excellent feedback, their unwavering belief that bad sentences beget good sentences, I am eternally grateful.

To everyone at Apprentice House Press who has believed in this book. I knew I'd someday find a home for it and I'm so grateful it's with this lovely group of smart, open-minded, open-hearted people.

To my Mom, who copyedited this book and who would have retyped the whole thing for me if I'd needed her to.

And finally, to my husband, Steve, who has never not thought this book would make its way into the world. And who once, coming up from anesthesia, told a nurse to get my autograph because I'd one day be a famous writer. It's a true gift to have someone who believes you are more than you think possible.

About the Author

Jen Dupree is a librarian, freelance editor, and former book-store owner. She has an MFA in Creative Writing from the University of Southern Maine's Stonecoast program. Her work has appeared in *Front Porch Review*, *The Masters Review*, *On the Rusk* and other places. She is the winner of the Writer's Digest Fiction Contest for 2017, and both a winner and a finalist for Maine Literary Awards. She lives in Maine with her husband and Portuguese Water Dog, (Pink) Floyd. Find her at www.jenniferdupree.com.

Apprentice House Press
Loyola University Maryland

Apprentice House is the country's only campus-based, student-staffed book publishing company. Directed by professors and industry professionals, it is a nonprofit activity of the Communication Department at Loyola University Maryland.

Using state-of-the-art technology and an experiential learning model of education, Apprentice House publishes books in untraditional ways. This dual responsibility as publishers and educators creates an unprecedented collaborative environment among faculty and students, while teaching tomorrow's editors, designers, and marketers.

Outside of class, progress on book projects is carried forth by the AH Book Publishing Club, a co-curricular campus organization supported by Loyola University Maryland's Office of Student Activities.

Eclectic and provocative, Apprentice House titles intend to entertain as well as spark dialogue on a variety of topics. Financial contributions to sustain the press's work are welcomed. Contributions are tax deductible to the fullest extent allowed by the IRS.

To learn more about Apprentice House books or to obtain submission guidelines, please visit www.apprenticehouse.com.

Apprentice House
Communication Department
Loyola University Maryland
4501 N. Charles Street
Baltimore, MD 21210
410-617-5265
info@apprenticehouse.com
www.apprenticehouse.com